She creates characters of great depth, who are easy to
relate to and sometimes downright entertaining."
—*Romantic Times BOOKreviews* on *Still Lake*

"Before I read…[a] Stuart book I make sure my day
is free…once I start, she has me hooked."
—#1 *New York Times* bestselling author Debbie Macomber

TINA LEONARD

DISCARD

"It is a fun, fast-moving story
with just enough seriousness to make it
a delightfully heartwarming romance."
—*Romantic Times BOOKreviews* on *Catching Calhoun*

"The cast of marvelous characters,
each with their own secrets and problems,
snappy dialogue and some dangerous action,
keeps you involved from page one. Delightful,
well-written story from author Tina Leonard."
—*Rendezvous* on *Never Say Never*

DISCARD

MARION LENNOX

"Marion Lennox pens a truly magnificent tale.
The romance is pure magic and the
characters are vibrant and alive."
—*Romantic Times BOOKreviews* on *A Royal Proposition*

"Marion Lennox's second Castle at Dolphin Bay story
resonates with deep emotions, relieved by flashes of wit."
—*Romantic Times BOOKreviews*

ABOUT THE AUTHORS

Anne Stuart loves Japanese rock and roll, wearable art, Spike, her two kids, Clairefontaine paper, her springer spaniel Rosie, her delicious husband of thirty-two years, fellow writers, her three cats, telling stories and living in Vermont. She's not too crazy about politics and diets and a winter that never ends, but then, life's always a trade-off. Visit her at www.anne-stuart.com.

Tina Leonard is a bestselling author of more than forty projects, as well as a popular thirteen-book series for Harlequin American Romance. Her books have made the Waldenbooks, *Ingram* and Nielsen BookScan bestseller lists. Tina has been blessed with a fertile imagination and quick typing skills, excellent editors and a family who loves her career. Born on a military base, she lived in many states before eventually marrying the boy who did her crayon printing for her in the first grade. Tina believes happy endings are a wonderful part of a good life. You can visit her at www.tinaleonard.com.

Marion Lennox was born on an Australian dairy farm. She moved on—mostly because the cows weren't interested in her stories! In her nonwriting life Marion cares—haphazardly—for her husband, kids, dogs, cats, chickens and anyone else who lines up at her dinner table. She fights her rampant garden (she's losing) and her house dust (she's lost!). She also travels, which she finds seriously addictive. As a teenager Marion was told she'd never get anywhere reading romance. Now romance is the basis of her stories, and her stories allow her to travel. If ever there was one advertisement for following your dream, she'd be it! You can contact Marion at www.marionlennox.com.

ANNE STUART
TINA LEONARD
MARION LENNOX

Christmas Getaway

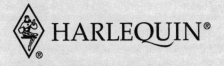

HARLEQUIN®

TORONTO • NEW YORK • LONDON
AMSTERDAM • PARIS • SYDNEY • HAMBURG
STOCKHOLM • ATHENS • TOKYO • MILAN • MADRID
PRAGUE • WARSAW • BUDAPEST • AUCKLAND

ISBN-13: 978-0-373-83729-8
ISBN-10:   0-373-83729-1

CHRISTMAS GETAWAY

CONTENTS

CLAUS AND EFFECT

Anne Stuart

For my fabulous partners in crime,
Marion Lennox and Tina Leonard.
Merry Christmas!

CHAPTER ONE

JAMES FITZPATRICK, known to his co-workers as Fitz, his mother as Jimmy-boy, his stepfather as That Kid, and most of the women he met as a heartless bastard, slid through the shadows, blending in silently. It was a cold night in Boston—the wind was blowing, but at least the snow had stopped for the time being. Two weeks before Christmas and the snow on the ground was wet and slushy. He was wearing black Converse All Stars, because they were fast and light and blended in with the night. They were also made of canvas and soaked with wet, dirty snow.

His feet were the least of his problems. The patrol car was cruising past the alleyway, the bright beam of light scouring every corner, but he was skinny enough to duck back, flattening himself against the brick wall, holding his breath. He didn't want to have to shoot another cop, but he wouldn't hesitate if he had to. Right now there wasn't room for sentiment. He was out to survive, at all costs.

The police cruiser kept moving, but he didn't allow himself to relax, even for a moment. Two blocks over, the Downtown Crossing district was jammed with shoppers, and there was always the possibility he could blend in with them. But the police were everywhere, searching for him, and he couldn't count on luck.

He slid out of the shadows, cursing as the pain lanced him. The bullet had gone straight through him, ruining the expensive leather jacket his ex-girlfriend had given him, which was probably a good thing. He was tempted to dump it, but he was bleeding like a pig. The cops didn't know they'd winged him, but it would be easy enough to follow the blood trail.

He bent down and scooped up a handful of the dirty snow, packing it against his side where the bullet had grazed him, letting out a low, profane litany of curses under his breath. The rapidly melting slush should slow the bleeding down, just enough so that they'd lose his trail. In the meantime he had to find a way to get the hell out of there and find the woman he'd targeted.

He could hear the noise of the crowd two blocks over, the incessant ringing of the bells from the sidewalk Santas. If he didn't figure out how to get out of Boston fast, he was going to end up dead. Boston cops had a habit of shooting to kill when one of their own was shot, and Detective Grady Barber was dead. The man who killed him had to pay.

He turned the corner, keeping close to the sides of the building. Macy's and Farnham's were up ahead, along with the various big discount stores that had taken over the rest of the stately old department stores his mother had loved. He could see the lights up ahead, the crowds milling. He couldn't hide in the shadows forever. She'd be in there somewhere, but with the hole in his side he couldn't wait forever for her to emerge.

He glanced down at his side. He was wearing a black T-shirt, and any blood would be hard to spot. He could stay in the shadows and wait for them to find him, shoot him.

Or he could move.

And James Fitzpatrick moved.

"THAT IS THE MOST hideous dress I have ever seen in my life," Jackie said, never one to mince words.

Dr. Eloise Pollard ignored her, staring at her reflection in the three angled mirrors. "You're right," she said. "Nothing I can do about it. It belonged to Richard's mother and he's insisting it would break her heart if I didn't wear it. I'm just lucky that Farnham's is willing to do the alterations on it."

Jackie shook her head. "I wouldn't call that luck. It serves you right for waiting 'til the last minute to choose a wedding dress. If I know the old bat she's just trying to make you look ridiculous so Richard will change his mind. Even with professional alterations you're going to look like something out of *Gone With the Wind*."

Ellie closed her eyes for a moment, hoping when she opened them the reflection would be better. It wasn't. She looked like a giant wedding cake, festooned with garlands of lace. Exactly the wrong look for her strong, big-boned body. "It's just for one day, and it means a lot to Richard. And isn't that what matters?"

"Absolutely not. If you go into a marriage trying to please your fathead of a husband you're doomed from the start," Jackie said, leaning back against the dressing-room wall.

"He's not a fathead."

"I would have thought an Aussie would have more common sense," Jackie went on, undeterred. "You're all supposed to be practical and down-to-earth. Richard has a stick up his ass. He'll probably want you to stop practicing medicine and stay home to raise his fatheaded children."

"Hey, they'll be my fatheaded children, too," Ellie protested. "And I can keep my practice and be a mother at the same time. It'll just require a little juggling."

"I don't see Richard as a juggler." Jackie pushed away

from the wall. "I need a cigarette. Take off that godforsaken dress and come with me."

"I don't enable," Ellie said absently. "And the dress isn't that bad, is it?"

"It is."

"I'm getting married in a week—I don't think there's anything I can do about it." She tugged at one ruffle, trying to smooth down the frilliness. She should have known better. Women who were six feet tall didn't look good in girly-girl ruffles, particularly if they were possessed of a traditional hourglass figure. She should have told Richard no, should have chosen something plain, something that would disguise her voluptuous curves like her lab coat.

"I'm going for a cigarette," Jackie said again. "I'll meet you outside when you come to your senses."

"Don't hold your breath," Ellie muttered. There were times in her life when she didn't have much of a choice, and this was one of them. She wanted to marry Richard—he was the perfect man for her. Tall enough, elegant, old-Boston money that had at first dazzled her. She'd had no one left in Australia when she came to Boston for her residency, and no reason to go back. Richard came equipped with a new family—his gorgon of a mother, his three overbred sisters, who looked at her as if she were a rabid dog, and three totally cowed brothers-in-law. All Richard's sisters had flat-out refused to wear The Dress, and she should have realized why.

She sighed. Worse things had happened in this life. She reached behind to unzip the dress, only to encounter an endless row of silk-covered buttons that she couldn't even begin to unfasten without dislocating her shoulder.

"Bloody hell," she muttered. Jackie had fastened the damned thing for her, and now her friend was off polluting her lungs and the less-than-pristine air of downtown Boston, while Ellie was trapped inside this spun-sugar creation, waiting for the tailor who would alter it for her.

To top it all off, an alarm suddenly blared through the sound system, drowning out the manic cheer of "Holly Jolly Christmas."

"We've been ordered to evacuate the building by the Boston Police Department. Please make your way to the nearest exit in an orderly fashion. There is no need to panic. Leave your packages behind—you'll be allowed in to collect them as soon as we're given the all-clear."

Ellie yanked harder on the dress, but the buttons held. The siren kept blaring, so loud that it was giving her an instant headache. A moment later one of the staff knocked on the door. "We need to leave the building, Dr. Pollard," she said. "Please come now."

Ellie could just hear her over the noise of the alarm. She shoved her feet into her turquoise Crocs, grabbed her purse and headed for the door.

The woman had already gone, along with the location of the overcoat Ellie had given her, and the crowds were heading for the escalators like a herd of cattle heading for the slaughterhouse. She had no choice but to join them, holding her pouffy skirts close to her body and mentally cursing. At least Jackie was already outside.

The escalators weren't working, and they had to walk down them. Ellie nearly went flying when she hit the uneven last few steps, but there were enough people packed around her to keep her from falling. In the distance she could see the glass-fronted doorways leading out to Washington Street, and snowflakes had begun to drift down once more.

"Happy bloody Christmas," she muttered, letting herself be

swept along by the crowd, spilling out onto the slushy Boston streets with what seemed like thousands of other shoppers.

There was no way she could find Jackie in all that confusion. The police were herding people away from the building, and they were armed to the teeth, an unnerving sight. She could hear people muttering—terrorists in Farnham's department store? A mad bomber?

People were starting to panic, and she felt herself being pushed and pulled by the crowd, shoved away from the building as the police entered it at a run, their guns drawn.

"Crap," she said, unnerved, as she was shoved against another body.

A body in red. She found herself eye-to-eye with one of the sidewalk Santas. His face was covered with the fake silk beard and wig—only his eyes were visible. They weren't reassuring. He had cold, bleak eyes, with long dark lashes, and the snow fell on them, melting instantly.

"Excuse me, Santa," she said breathlessly, trying to move away from him.

His white-gloved hand came down on her arm so hard she let out a squeak of pain. "Where's your car?" he demanded, his voice rough, dangerous.

"My car?" she echoed. "Are you out of your mind…?" Her voice trailed off as she felt the metal jab against her rib cage.

"Do you know what that is?" Santa said.

"I expect it's a gun," she said in a calm voice.

"You're right. Now where's your damned car?"

"I took the T," she said.

"No, you didn't. You have car keys hanging off your purse. Now where the hell is your car? Don't make me hurt you."

His fingers were digging hard into her forearm. She was

going to be bruised for her wedding, she thought, feeling a little giddy. "The parking lot on Winter Street."

"Take me there."

"Listen, you just take the keys," she said, reaching for her purse to fumble with them. "It's a blue Toyota, license plate EKU-893. I won't tell anyone…."

"Start walking," he said. The pressure on her arm didn't lessen. "Now."

It wasn't like he gave her any choice. His hand was clamped on her arm, he was holding her close enough so that no one could see the gun pressed up against her ribs. She was going to die, she thought. She'd run up against a serial killer with a bride fetish and she was going to die.

But not any sooner than she had to. She started walking, in step with him, away from the crowds, into the shadows of the city. Normally the side streets would be almost as crowded, but everyone was heading in the opposite direction, going to see what the fuss was at Farnham's. They didn't even give the unlikely combination of Santa and a bride a second glance.

"Are you the one they're looking for?" she asked in a low voice.

"Who? What?"

"The police. They evacuated the store and someone said they were looking for a terrorist."

His laugh was totally without humor. "They're not looking for a terrorist," he said. "They're looking for a cop killer."

"And that would be you?" She didn't know why she asked, she really didn't want to know the answer.

"That would be me," he said. They'd reached the parking lot, but there was no attendant. Unfortunately her Toyota was in plain sight—if it had been buried behind other cars, he would have had no choice but to leave it. And her, hopefully.

He didn't even ask if it was her car—he just hauled her over to it as he yanked the key ring from her purse strap. "Don't make any noise," he said, shoving her into the front seat. The skirts of her dress billowed around her, and he pushed them in after her before slamming the door.

She yanked at the hem, but some of it was still caught in the door, and she started to open it when he slid in beside her, behind the steering wheel, tossing a brown sack into the backseat. "Don't do that," he said. "I don't want to have to hurt you."

"Look, you've got my car. What do you need me for?"

Santa looked at her from behind the masses of false hair, his eyes cold and hard. "Comic relief," he said, and started the car.

A moment later they were out of the parking lot, just missing the attendant, who'd emerged to demand payment. And they were off, heading through the crowded, slushy streets of Boston, past the Christmas decorations and the bright, festive lights and the sounds of carols and "Joy to the World" floating on the cold night air.

They were off. And she was going to die. Two weeks before Christmas. In her wedding dress. Killed by a crazed Santa Claus.

In for a penny, in for a pound. She leaned forward, switched on the radio, and Christmas music poured out, filling the car.

Santa cursed, shutting it off. "I'm not in the mood," he snarled.

"Are you going to kill me?" Her voice was steady.

"Not if you don't annoy me. I'll drop you off somewhere outside the city—you can find your way home."

"Aren't you afraid I'll tell the police?"

He shot a glance at her from under the heavy white wig. "Good point. You're right, I should kill you." He sounded so offhand about it her stomach churned.

"Oh, don't feel you need to," she said politely. "I'd be happy to keep it quiet for a few days. I'm going to have to in-form my insurance company after a while, but you're more than welcome to keep the car for now."

She couldn't see his mouth, and she didn't want to, but for some reason she had the sense that he was smiling. "And I'm supposed to trust you?"

"I'm a bride. Who could be more trustworthy?"

"Saint Nick," he said wryly. "And that's a butt-ugly wedding dress."

"I beg your pardon?"

"You heard me. That's a butt-ugly wedding dress. Your boyfriend blind?"

"It's his mother's."

"Oh, honey, you're marrying the wrong man."

Her initial panic was fading, replaced by real annoyance. "I'll have you know this is a very expensive, very pretty dress," she said, fluffing out the billowy skirts. "And I…" She stopped. The dress was stained, large splotches of red against the side and the skirt. The side he'd held her. "Have you been stabbed?" she demanded, the rest of her fear vanishing.

"What's it to you?"

"Answer me. Have you been hurt?"

"Shot," he said. "Just a graze. It's been bleeding like a son of a bitch, but I'll live."

"You need to have it looked at."

"Gunshots get reported, bride. I can't afford that."

"Then let me look at it. I'm a doctor."

His look was derisive. "Oh, yeah? How many gunshot wounds have you taken care of?"

"Enough. I did a rotation in the E.R. How bad is it?"

"I'll survive," he said.

"Will I?"

If she could see him clearly she would have guessed he was

rolling his eyes. "If you shut up and stop asking me stupid questions, yes."

Ellie leaned back in the seat, belatedly fastening her seat belt. From what little she could see of his face, his color was good and his voice was strong and annoyed. She could see the darker patch of blood staining the cheap red velvet of the Santa suit; it wasn't bad and it wasn't spreading. Of course he could be bleeding internally, as well, but for now he sounded relatively strong and in charge.

They were already out in the suburbs, heading north. "Did you steal that outfit?" she asked, keeping her hands folded in her lap.

"No, my elves made it for me," he said, annoyed. "What do you think?"

"Did you kill the man who was wearing it?"

"The man who was wearing it is now enjoying a hundred dollars. Any other questions?"

"Did you really kill a policeman?"

He kept his eyes straight ahead. "Honey, you don't want to know."

She fingered the bloodstain on her fluffy white dress. "No," she said. "Maybe I don't. I'm Eloise Pollard, by the way. My friends call me Ellie."

"And I'm not one of them. Just be quiet and let me think, Dr. Pollard. There's too much noise in my head."

Great. She'd been kidnapped by a schizophrenic. Next he'd be telling her that his dog ordered him to shoot a cop.

She glanced at her door. If he slowed down enough, maybe for a Stop sign, she could make a run for it. Push open the door and leap. They'd have to stop sooner or later, and even in the stupid wedding dress she could run like hell.

In the meantime he was on 495 and there wasn't a damned

thing she could do about it. Except wonder what the hell Richard was going to do when she didn't show up for the wedding.

And why she didn't really care.

CHAPTER TWO

So this had to be the dumbest thing he'd ever done in his life, Fitz thought as he headed north, the bride beside him. Hostages were always a bad idea—they usually ended up dead, and it pissed the cops off even more.

He should know. He'd been a cop for the last twelve years, and he came from generations of Boston cops. He wondered if any of his cousins were in on the manhunt. Or if they knew Jimmy Fitzpatrick would never have shot and killed his partner if he could have helped it.

The ice that had packed his wound had melted long ago, which surprised him, considering how frigging cold he was. He was trying hard not to shake—he didn't want the bride to realize how vulnerable he was. He just had to find out what she knew and then get far enough out of Boston to let her off at a Wal-Mart or something. Except then she'd tell the cops exactly what he was driving, and that he'd been shot, and he couldn't afford to let that happen. Not until he found Spinelli.

Max Spinelli had been his first partner, a crusty old cop who took crap from no one, and he'd scared the pants off Fitz when he'd been a young recruit fresh out of the police academy. But Spinelli had been solid, no-nonsense, as trustworthy as the Pope, and he'd told Fitz to come to him if he ever had any trouble with his boss. Spinelli had known enough about Connor O'Bannion to stop him if he needed to be stopped, and the old man would have the proof to back it up. Spinelli had always believed in insurance.

He glanced over at the bride. At least she wasn't screaming or crying. She sat beside him in the tiny car, her stupid white skirts billowing out so wide that they were covering his right leg. He was tempted to push the stuff away, but it wouldn't have done any good. There was too damned much of it.

She must have felt his eyes on her. "Why are they after you?" she said.

She had an accent—Australian, he was guessing. Just like the murdered Erica Devlin. He'd seen Dr. Eloise Pollard from a distance at the funeral, and she'd been the only one he'd been unable to place. She was his last hope of finding out what kind of dirty mess he'd stumbled into, and it was fading fast.

"Are you part of the mob?" she asked.

"Which mob?"

"I don't know. Is there more than one?"

His laugh was without humor. "There's the Irish mob, the street gangs, the Mafia, the Triad, the Yakuza…"

"You have Yakuza in Boston?"

"We have everything in Boston. And no, I'm not part of a mob. I'm just a guy who was in the wrong place at the wrong time."

"I'd say that was more my situation. If I hadn't come out of the store…"

"Not really. I was waiting for you."

She stared at him. "Why?"

"What do you know about Erica Devlin?"

"Erica? What does this have to do with Erica?" She looked truly bewildered.

"Everything. What's your connection to her?"

"I don't really have a connection to her. She and her husband died in a car crash six weeks ago," she said. "What makes you think…?"

"What were you doing at her funeral?"

"Not that it's any of your business," she snapped. "Her brother and I were friends back in Australia. We sort of grew up together, and when she came to live here, he asked me to check in on her. So I did. We talked on the phone a couple of times."

"And that was it?"

She frowned. "A few weeks before the crash her brother rang and said he thought she might be in some sort of trouble. She'd rung him sounding really edgy. I went to see her but Erica didn't have any interest in talking, so I gave up."

"You went to her funeral. You cried."

"Her brother's a friend. Her death left three kids orphaned. Babies. Of course I cried."

"And I'm supposed to believe that?" Fitz said.

"It's the truth. What do you think I am—some kind of crazy Australian terrorist?"

"How about a diamond thief?"

Her expression said it all. "Why would a family doctor be involved in a diamond robbery? You can do a background check on me. My only connection with Erica was through her brother—I was in foster care with him for a few weeks after my parents were killed. And, no, they weren't murdered. They died in a plane crash."

"I already did the background check," he grumbled. Another freaking dead end.

"And what about you? Besides kidnapping me, what else did you do? Did you really kill that cop?"

He was feeling light-headed. He couldn't remember when

he'd last had something to eat, and his side was hurting like a son of a bitch. He worried that the bullet was still lodged inside him, but he'd seen the exit hole in his leather jacket. No, he was just bleeding again, which to a certain extent was a good thing. It would wash the wound clean.

"Did you hear me?" the bride said again, a little annoyed.

"I heard you. I just didn't feel like answering."

"Will you at least tell me where we're going?"

"If I tell you that, I'll have to kill you," he said, ironically, then realized how it sounded. He'd kidnapped her at gunpoint—she probably didn't have any doubts that he'd shoot her at the slightest provocation.

Which was a good thing. It would keep her on her best behavior. She wouldn't go running off into the night the first chance she got for fear he'd put a bullet in her back.

He blinked. It was snowing, and the oncoming headlights were giving him one hell of a headache. The traffic was heavy—Christmas shoppers on their way home, laden with overpriced crap. It wasn't looking like he was going to make it home for Christmas. Suddenly the big old house in Woburn seemed as if it was on another planet.

"You know, you really should let me take a look at your wound," she said. "You might have internal bleeding."

"Then I'll pass out and you can get away. Don't sweat it."

"If you pass out on the highway while you're driving so fast you'll kill us both and probably whoever we hit."

"Cool your jets, bride. I'm fine." It was a lie. The traffic was thinning out a bit, and he slowed down just a fraction. Wouldn't do to get popped for speeding. He wasn't sure what he'd do if he had to face another cop with a gun.

"Look," he said, "we're driving south. I'll drop you in Connecticut...."

"We're driving north," she corrected him. "I happen to live here."

"Okay, we're driving north," he said, irritated. "Don't you know how to act like a hostage? You shut up and pretend you don't know anything. You don't act like a smart-ass. If you know where I'm going, I can't dump you."

"Dump me? Or my body?"

He began to curse, beneath his breath, low and profane and heartfelt.

"That's quite a bunch of words you've got," she said. "And I'm Australian, remember? We know how to curse down there."

"Would you just shut the hell up?" he said. Her calm voice was rattling around his head, making it even harder to pay attention to the road. "I'm trying to concentrate."

"Just answer me one thing."

"What?" he snarled.

"Are you one of the bad guys or one of the good ones?"

His answering laugh was without humor. "Don't be naïve. Everyone thinks they're one of the good guys. Even the worst criminal thinks he's got reasons for what he pulls."

She said nothing, and he could only thank God and Mary and all the saints that she'd decided to be quiet so he could figure out what the hell to do.

And then the words came out of his mouth when he wasn't expecting them. "I've been framed."

She turned to look at him. "Isn't that what they all say?"

"Lady, it's really pretty simple," he said, forcing out the words. "I'm a police detective with a dirty partner. Barber was involved in covering up a multimillion-dollar jewel robbery, and your pal Erica and her husband were part of it. Barber and his buddies had every intention of making me the fall guy. When he pulled a gun on me, I shot back, and I killed him in self-defense. Unfortunately I think my boss is in on it, along with God knows how many others, maybe even you, and if I don't find proof of their guilt and my innocence, I'm going to be shot on sight." Why was he telling her this? He had to be nuts.

"And I'm supposed to believe that? It's pretty lame, if you ask me."

"I didn't ask you," he said. "You wanted to know what I did, and I'm telling you. Now shut up if you want to live." He could feel his eyes drooping. He hadn't slept in thirty-six hours, not since he first figured out what O'Bannion and his pals were doing. The blood was soaking into his clothes, and he couldn't remember when he'd last eaten. And the bride was giving him nothing but a headache. He was going to have to pull off the road and find something, anything, before he passed out entirely.

He took the next exit, heading toward the strip mall. It was after eleven—most of the stores would be closed, but there was an all-night Wal-Mart up ahead. He could find what he needed there.

He pulled into the parking lot, way over to the side. This close to Christmas the stores were still crowded at such a late hour, but back away from the lights they could disappear. He came to a stop and turned off the car, leaving them in darkness.

"What now?" the bride asked.

"Just give me a minute. You got any rope in the trunk?"

"Why would I have rope? And if I did, why would I give it to you?"

He still had his knife tucked in his pants beneath the baggy Santa costume. He pulled it out, wincing as he realized it was covered in his own blood, and opened it, turning to her.

She just looked at him with unnatural calm, waiting.

He picked up the edge of her stupid skirt and slit it with

the knife, then ripped, yanking at the frothy stuff so that it came off in one large ring of fabric. He closed the knife and set it on the seat, blinking away the fogginess that was threatening him. "Hold out your hands."

He was half expecting her to refuse. But she did as she was told, and he began wrapping the torn fabric around her wrists, tight enough to hold her, not tight enough to cut off circulation. "I've gotta rest for an hour, and I don't...want you going...anywhere." Damn, he was sounding punchy. He finished tying the knot, then fell back against the seat. "Just stay still and quiet and you'll stay...alive..." he mumbled, trying to sound like the badass he was. For some reason it wasn't coming out right. He blinked, shook his head, then blinked again.

He was cold, exhausted. He could close his eyes for just a few minutes, just long enough to get his strength back. Just a few minutes...

The darkness overtook him, and he finally passed out, falling forward over the steering wheel in the midnight-dark parking lot of Wal-Mart.

ELLIE REACHED FORWARD and gently pulled Santa back from the steering wheel, so that he was leaning against the seat. His color was awful. He'd left the pocket knife on the seat before he'd passed out, and she picked it up, fumbling with it. It required a fair amount of dexterity to open it and saw through the tulle and lace that bound her wrists together, but she'd always been good with her hands. She flexed them when she finally cut through, then turned to look at Santa.

She kept the knife open, just in case, and pushed the white wig aside to feel his forehead. Not hot, which was a good thing. Cool and slightly damp, which wasn't great, either.

She pulled off the cap and wig, then unhooked the beard and tossed them all into the backseat as she put her hand against his neck to check his pulse.

And then she froze. He was out, solidly unconscious, and he wasn't going to come to anytime soon.

He was also a lot younger than she'd thought. Maybe only a few years older than she was, in his midthirties. He had a rough growth of stubble on his face, beneath his hollowed cheeks, and ridiculously long black eyelashes that matched his black, curling hair. Black Irish, she thought dazedly. He'd have either blue or green eyes, and his stubborn mouth was the one thing that was no surprise. Except for the fact that it looked ridiculously sensual.

She sat back in her seat, astonished. So Santa was a hottie. He was still a gangster of some sort, no matter what he said, and he'd kidnapped her and threatened to kill her. She needed to get the hell away from him before he decided to go through with it.

Except that he didn't look like a killer. Maybe even Al Capone looked innocent when he slept. Santa looked positively angelic, except for that stubborn mouth.

She rose on her knees on the tiny seat and began unfastening the costume, pushing it back. It was hard to see in the darkness, but she kept a flashlight in her glove compartment, and she turned it on to examine his chest.

A black T-shirt, soaked in blood. She lifted the cotton and winced. The bullet had gone straight through him, which was a blessing, and the bleeding had slowed. The wound was in a relatively good place, away from any major organs, but she had to make sure it didn't get infected....

Hell, it was none of her business if it got infected. If she had half a brain, she'd take off before he came to, call the police and have an ambulance come and get him.

His body was slack, and she felt for a wallet. Nothing. He'd been carrying a sack with him, and she reached in the backseat for it. There was a trashed leather jacket in it, and in the chest pocket she found his badge.

James Fitzpatrick, detective of the Boston Police Department. The photo on his ID looked a lot more menacing than he did as he lay sprawled on the front seat of her stolen car. And his eyes were blue.

She folded the wallet and tucked it in her purse, sitting back on her trashed finery and looking at him. What if he were telling the truth? She could turn him in, hope that justice prevailed and he'd be cleared. Assuming he was innocent.

Or maybe whoever had framed him was just too powerful to fight?

She'd always trusted her instincts. Of course, her instincts had told her marrying Richard was the right thing to do, and she'd been fighting off a major case of cold feet for the last month. But right now her instincts were telling her that this man was one of the good guys.

She took the open knife and sliced through her skirts, higher up, pulling off a wider ring of fabric. Skinnying out of the hoop skirts and crinolines was a little trickier in the front seat of the car, but she managed, tossing them into the back, along with the long, pouffy sleeves. She looked down at the ruined dress. It was now knee-length, short-sleeved and virgin-white. She grabbed his black leather jacket to cover up some of the blood on the top. She looked like a punk prom queen, and the turquoise Crocs completed the outfit.

She grabbed her keys from the ignition and stuffed them in her purse, then opened the door. James Fitzpatrick didn't move, and if she weren't so well-trained, she'd be worried he was dead.

But he wasn't. Not even near it. He was passed out from loss of blood and exhaustion, if she could judge by the purple smudges beneath his eyes. And there was no way she could abandon someone in need.

The night was growing colder, the snow still swirling overhead, and she shivered inside the leather jacket. There was blood in the lining, smearing her white dress, and she zipped it up to hide it before heading toward the brightly lit big-box store with the flashing green and red lights, the crowds of people. The normalcy of Christmas, peace and love and happiness.

And a gunshot victim in her stolen car who thought she had the clue to a diamond robbery. Tugging the jacket down, she braced herself, and then merged with the late-night shoppers in search of bargains, hoping everyone would be too busy to take a good look at her.

She moved fast, throwing things in her basket, and ended up at the pharmacy. The druggist looked askance at her, but her ID was solid and he had no choice but to fill her hastily written prescription. He also let her pay for everything there, which was a good thing—the checkout lines were endless. By the time she'd hauled all the stuff back to the car she was half-expecting her kidnapper to have disappeared.

He was still passed out on the front seat, and the bleeding had almost stopped. He didn't wake when she maneuvered him over to the passenger side, and she drove out of the parking lot quickly, barely missing an oncoming SUV.

They were out past Cape Ann, somewhere in the Gloucester area, and she could smell the sea. It was a good smell—snow and salt water. She drove until she found a backstreet, pulled over and parked, turning off the headlights. She kept the car running—they needed the heat—and turned to survey her patient.

He looked like holy hell. She stripped the Santa jacket off him, then used the knife to cut off the T-shirt. She concentrated on the wound, only allowing herself an occasional covert glance at the rest of him, lean and muscled and gorgeous. And smeared with blood, she reminded herself, cleaning the wound with calm efficiency. The exit would be messier, and it was hard to turn him over on the front seat, but she somehow managed. She'd left the radio on, and in the background was the soothing sound of Christmas music. She hummed beneath her breath as she stitched him up, trying to keep calm in case he woke up with a roar of pain, then bandaged him, moving him back carefully to finish up the entry wound.

And she had to clean the blood off his chest, didn't she? Using the alcohol-soaked towels was nothing more than she'd done as an intern, and the smell should have reminded her of operating rooms and trauma centers. She let him rest back against the seat while she stripped off her ruined dress. The buttons hadn't gotten any easier, but the knife made short work of it, and she took a certain vicious glee in destroying the damned thing. The jeans and flannel shirt she'd bought herself were a little stiff but a hell of a lot warmer, she thought, fastening the buttons…only to realize that bright blue eyes were watching her.

Her patient was awake.

"What the hell do you think you're doing?" His voice was nothing more than a weak croak.

"Getting changed. It's a good thing you're awake—you're a little big for me to be dressing." She tossed him the packaged T-shirt, then reached for another of the oversized flannels.

He just looked at her. "We're going to be twins?" he said, eyeing the red-and-black checks.

"Kidnappers can't be choosers," she said, reaching for the

bottle of water and the antibiotics she'd grabbed. "Take these, before you become septic and die a horrible death. Not that you don't deserve to, but I have professional ethics."

"And those include taking care of someone who steals your car and threatens you?" He was moving slowly, pulling the T-shirt over his head. "I prefer black."

"If you don't wear white I can't see if you start bleeding again. Not that you will—I did an excellent job of patching you up if I do say so myself."

He glanced down at his side, at the neat white bandage on his tanned skin. "So you did. Why?"

She didn't have an easy answer for that. She'd decided to help him before she realized how freaking gorgeous he was. She shrugged, untwisting the top of the water bottle and handing it to him. "I was looking for an excuse to ditch my wedding. You provided it. I figure I owe you. And if my best friend's sister was in to something bad, was murdered, then I want to find out what I can. For his sake."

He still looked at her as if she were out of her mind. "You could have just told your fiancé you changed your mind."

"Count your blessings, Detective Fitzpatrick. I'm going to keep you alive long enough to find your proof. Then it's up to you."

She expected him to make some kind of protest, but he said nothing, taking the water from her and pouring half of it down his throat before holding his hand out for the pills. He swallowed them, draining the bottle, and she reached in back for more water for both of them.

"I don't suppose you got any food?" he said finally. "I don't remember when I last ate."

"There's fast food up ahead. Just tell me where we're going—you're too weak to drive."

For a moment he said nothing. And then he seemed to make some sort of decision. "Camden, Maine," he said. "And I'll have a burger and fries."

"You'll have what I order for you. Cholesterol doesn't help the healing process."

"You're going to be a pain in the ass, aren't you?"

She smiled at him. "Count on it," she said. And, flicking on the headlights, she headed north.

CHAPTER THREE

FOOD HELPED. Closing his eyes while the bride drove was his only choice. If he'd still been a traffic cop, he would have pulled her over and lectured the hell out of her. Right now, as she said, kidnappers couldn't be choosers, and anyone who bandaged him up and bought him a grilled chicken sandwich and an eggnog milk shake was entitled to drive any damned way she pleased. As long as he didn't have to watch.

The Christmas music was still coming from the radio, and almost every damned song seemed to have sleigh bells in it. The sound was making his head throb, but she hadn't responded well to his suggestion that they turn off the radio. So he'd closed his eyes and endured, letting the memories play around inside his head.

He'd known something wasn't right for months. He'd never trusted Connor O'Bannion, and neither had Fitz's first partner, Spinelli, but for some reason O'Bannion and Tommy Morrissey, Fitz's second cousin, had suddenly become as thick as thieves, and Fitz couldn't figure out why. Or why his current partner, Grady Barber, had become more and more sullen. Not that that was much of a change from Barber's usual mood. Someone had paired the two of them together, probably O'Bannion. Fitz was supposed to keep an eye on Barber, but now he was thinking that it might have been the other way around. Grady had a brutal reputation and pairing him up with Jimmy Fitzpatrick had supposedly been the last step before being kicked off the force.

He was off the force for good now. Fitz had great instincts—they'd saved his life more than once, and they'd saved it a few hours ago when Grady had shot at him. He'd sensed the tension in the air, moved fast and avoided being shot in the head, dropping Grady with a bullet to the throat. He'd bled out as Fitz reached him, and even as he held his dying partner, Tommy Morrissey had emerged from the shadows, gun in hand. Tommy never could shoot straight—he'd only managed to wing him as Fitz dove out the window. Under the circumstances there was nothing he could do but run.

He turned his head to look at the bride. "Why did you decide to believe me?"

"I found your badge and your wallet." She turned the windshield wipers on to brush the gathering snow away. "I figured you were telling the truth. And if you were, turning you in would get you killed, and I didn't want that on my conscience. I'm supposed to heal people, not deliver them to their executioners."

"I could be a dirty cop. Maybe I shot my partner because he found out I was part of a jewel heist."

"Maybe," she said. "Why don't you explain it to me?"

He was still trying to work it out in his own mind, what the hell had happened to people he'd known all his life. "I can boil it down to three sentences. The way I see it, my boss got word of a major diamond theft going down. The cops interfered, killed the thief and took the diamonds for themselves. I found out, so they framed me and they're trying to kill me before I can find proof. That clear enough?"

"Crystal," she said, switching the wipers on to a higher speed. "So what's our timetable?"

He stared at her. "Lady, you're out of your mind. You need to drop me off in the next town, and I'll steal another car. If you feel so moved, you could fail to tell the police about being kidnapped and your car being stolen, but that's up to you."

"No."

"No, what?"

"I'm not dropping you off anywhere." She sounded maddeningly practical. "I'm not letting you out of my sight until I know you're not going to keel over from loss of blood. You should probably have a transfusion, but that would involve going to a hospital and I don't think you're going to be co-operative."

"You've got that right. And don't worry about me being down a few quarts. It's not as bad as it looks. I've survived much worse."

"Listen, James Fitzpatrick, I happen to be the doctor here, and I know just how bad your wound is. You're right, it's not life-threatening. Unless you decide to keep driving in this lousy weather and pass out behind the wheel." She flicked on the turn signal and started toward the exit.

"Where are we going?"

"To find some place to spend the night. The weather is lousy, I can barely see, and if I go off the road, people are going to be asking questions. There's a lot of blood in this car. We'll find a motel, I'll change your bandages and we'll get some sleep."

"Honey…"

"Ellie," she corrected him. "Or Dr. Pollard if you want to be formal. I'm not leaving you until I'm sure you're okay, and there's nothing you can do about it."

"Wanna bet?" He reached down, ignoring the searing pain in his side, and when he sat up he had his gun in his hand. "You're going to pull over right now and let me out."

She glanced at the weapon, then turned her attention back to the snowy roads. "Or you're going to shoot me? I don't think so. That's a hell of a way to treat your doctor."

"I don't need a doctor…" He could feel the wetness at his side again—he must have pulled at the wound to start it bleeding again.

"You don't have a choice. Now put that stupid little gun down and behave yourself."

"I'll have you know this is a Glock."

"I don't care what it is, you aren't going to shoot me. Now put it down and behave yourself."

"You've got a hell of a bedside manner, Doc," he said.

"When I have to deal with recalcitrant adults, yes."

"What do you mean?"

"Recalcitrant. It means balky, uncooperative…"

"I know what the hell *recalcitrant* means, lady. I went to college. What did you mean by adults?"

"I'm a pediatrician. Fortunately I don't usually have to deal with gunshot wounds."

"Great," he said. "I have an amateur taking care of me."

"Top of my class, Fitzpatrick. You're in safe hands."

"People call me Fitz."

"I imagine they do. Do they realize it's shorthand for bastard?"

She was a cocky creature. And to think he'd been glad she wasn't the weeping, trembling type. He could have gone for some hysterics about now. "Tell that to half of Ireland," he grumbled.

"Illegitimate children weren't called by their parents' name, they were called the Fitz-somethings. Illegitimate son of Patrick. A bastard."

"In more ways than one, babe," he snarled, leaning back

carefully. "Believe it." His side was on fire, and he'd been an idiot to try anything.

She glanced over at him. "Okay, Fitz, here's the way it's going to be. We're stopping for the night because the roads are too bad and I can't drive any longer. You'll get a good night's sleep to recover from your wound and you'll have several doses of the antibiotic in your system. If I think you're in good enough shape, then I'll go out and rent a car for you to finish your drive up into Maine, and I'll go home and deal with the mess I've made of my life."

He considered it. She was right. He was weak and exhausted and the driving looked like utter hell—each snowflake was divebombing the windshield and he could barely see the oncoming traffic. He'd be in better shape tomorrow, and if she kept her word, he'd have a legal car to make it the rest of the way up to Hidden Harbor. He'd lied about Camden—she didn't need to know everything. His destination was about three hours farther up the east coast, and it was going to be one hell of a drive.

"All right," he said finally. "But you'd better rent me an SUV. The roads along the coast are treacherous when there's snow."

"Humph," she said.

"You mind telling me where the hell we are?"

"Just over the New Hampshire border. I figured you'd be in a better position if we crossed state lines. The Boston police would have no jurisdiction outside of Massachusetts, right?"

"They have no jurisdiction outside of Boston, but they could get the staties involved."

"Staties?"

"State police."

"But not the New Hampshire state police, right?"

"In theory. In fact, every law-enforcement official in the northeast is going to want to bring down a cop killer."

"Even if it's a fellow cop?"

"Even more," he said in a bitter voice. "Right now I'd like nothing more than to blow a hole in O'Bannion's thick skull. And Tommy's going to break my second cousin's heart."

"Who are O'Bannion and Tommy?"

He considered whether he should tell her. Right now he was so cold and wiped out he wasn't thinking too clearly, but he couldn't see any reason not to.

"O'Bannion's the chief detective. My boss, and I'm betting he's behind the whole scam. Tommy Morrissey is a cousin, and he's up to his neck in it, as well. They've got to be the ones who framed me."

"Why?"

"Because I stumbled across what they were doing and they knew I'd turn them in the moment I got proof." He blinked. She was looking like someone in a movie—all soft focus and backlit. And he could feel himself beginning to slip away again. He closed his eyes, listening to the soft sound of the windshield wipers battling the snow, the whisper of Christmas music coming from the radio, the sound of the tires on the slushy roads. He needed to get rid of her—she was in danger, and as a cop his first duty had always been to protect the innocent. It had been drilled into him from childhood, growing up as he had in a family of cops and firefighters, and in kidnapping this very bossy woman he'd betrayed his code of ethics, just on the slight, unlikely chance that she knew something.

Of course, he'd only meant to take the car and dump her someplace safe as soon as possible. But all that had taken a flyer when he'd passed out and she'd gotten all medical on his ass.

"If you want me to be able to make it into the motel on my own, you better find it soon," he said, groggy.

He didn't hear her answer. Things weren't making much

sense—he was cold and he needed a bed. He tried to fight it—he needed to keep it together long enough to get rid of her, or she'd be a sitting duck. But he could barely focus enough to form words.

The car stopped moving, and suddenly all noise was gone—the jingling music, the comforting whoosh of the wipers, the soft purr of the engine.

He heard her voice from far away. "I'm going to get us a room. Don't move until I come back."

Yeah, like that was going to happen. He needed to get away from her, for her own sake. He waited just long enough, and then fumbled with his seat belt. It took him forever to unfasten it, and he reached for the door handle, pushing it open as a blast of snow hit him in the face. It took too much effort to swing his legs out of the car, and he lifted himself up from the seat, determined to get away from her.

A moment later he was facedown in snow, and the darkness began to close in for good.

"BLOODY HELL," Ellie said, moving around to the side of the car. Her patient lay sprawled in the snow, and he'd probably pulled his stitches loose. Irish cops were even more stubborn than Aussie men—she was going to have her hands full keeping him alive.

Fortunately the cheap, no-tell motel was practically deserted—it was a ways off the main highway and the snow was falling so thickly people were just staying home. She'd parked in front of one of the tiny cabins, and while the sullen teenager minding the front desk had warned her the heat left something to be desired, she took the room anyway. There was no guarantee she'd find another place on this back road, and she was on her last legs. She just had to hope

Norman Bates wasn't about to pop around the corner with a butcher knife.

She hauled Fitzpatrick to his feet, careful to favor his wounded side, and he was just conscious enough to help with the effort. He was bigger than she'd realized, and he was lucky she didn't have to drag his sorry ass through the snow. It probably would have left a trail of blood, making their situation even worse, but he managed to stay on his feet while she steered him toward the tiny cabin.

He collapsed on one of the twin beds, out cold, while she quickly fiddled with the space heater. The temperature in the room was icy, and she took the covers from the second bed and piled them on top of him before she went out to the car to get their stuff.

There was a patch of blood on the snow, and she quickly kicked at it, spreading more snow around to cover any traces of blood. She squinted up at the night sky—the snow was still coming down hard and fast. With luck there'd be no sign of the blood by morning.

The room was marginally warmer when she went back in, and she double-locked the flimsy door behind her before she turned to look at her patient.

He was still, his eyes closed. His color was slightly better, and she was going to need to wake him in a short while to get another pill in him and change his bandages, but for the time being he was better off huddling beneath the blankets until she could warm this place up.

The cabin was tiny—barely enough room for twin beds and a couple of uncomfortable-looking chairs. There was a television on the rickety table, and she turned it on, keeping the sound low as she sat on the floor near the heater and pulled off his wet sneakers. She'd kept his leather jacket around her, but it didn't provide much warmth. She thought of her sterile apartment back on Beacon Hill. It wasn't much but at least it was warm and had one hell of a shower. Right now she would have killed for that shower.

She just wouldn't have killed her patient, and if she left him, there was a good chance that would happen.

She channel-surfed while the room slowly filled with a surly heat, pausing at WSBK for a news report. A terrorist bomber had been suspected of planning an attempt on Farnham's, the store had to be evacuated but the terrorist had gotten away.

Ellie shook her head. The perfect way to manipulate people—play on their fears and they'd shoot first and ask questions later. She half expected to see a police sketch of Fitz dressed up in Middle Eastern clothing, but they stopped short of that. She pushed up from the floor, feeling stiff and sore, and moved to look at Fitz. Her patient, she reminded herself. She'd bought orange juice and crackers at the store, and she poured him a glass of juice and fed him another pill. He opened his eyes for a moment, then closed them again, but he'd looked relatively lucid. She hated to uncover him in the still chilly room, but she had no choice.

"I'm going to have to check your bandages. I think you're bleeding again."

He grunted, but made no effort to stop her as she pulled the layers of covers away. Blood had seeped through the white T-shirt, and she rolled it up, leaving it to cover his impressive chest and shoulders as she redressed the wound. It wasn't bad—the new bleeding had stopped, and she got him rebandaged in record time.

"Go away," he muttered, shifting restlessly in the narrow bed.

"Dream on, Fitzpatrick. I don't abandon patients."

"I'm not your patient, I'm your kidnapper. Abandon me."

"Get some sleep. You'll feel better in the morning."

He continued to grumble under his breath, but eventually he stopped, and his breathing grew even as he drifted into sleep.

She sat down on the other bed, now stripped of everything but the bottom sheet. It was still cool in the room—she could strip off that last sheet and wrap it around her but it wouldn't provide much warmth. She leaned against the wall, pulling her knees up to her body and hugging them to her for warmth. It was just as well she didn't sleep—she needed to keep an eye on Fitz, make sure he didn't start bleeding again.

But damn, she was tired. She put her head on her knees, just for a moment, and closed her eyes, listening to the sound of his breathing.

She awoke with a start, to realize she was freezing. It was three in the morning, according to her watch, and Fitz wasn't much warmer. He was lying swaddled under all the covers, but he was shivering. Blood loss would do that to you, she thought. And there was only one thing she could do about it.

She stripped down to her bra and panties in the chilly room, her body shaking, and slipped under the covers beside him before she could chicken out. She eased off the rest of his bloody T-shirt.

"What the hell are you doing?" he mumbled between chattering teeth.

"Trying to warm us both up. Trust me, it works." She wrapped her arms around him. She should probably strip off his pants as well, but that would require too much effort, and besides, the trunk of the body was more important.

He shifted slightly, groaning, as he made room for her on the narrow bed, and she burrowed her face against his shoulder, trying to will the heat to build between their bodies. She unfastened his jeans, pushing them down his hips so more of their flesh could touch, and they could heat each other, when his voice broke her concentration.

"You know, this would probably work better if you took off your bra," he said, somehow managing to drawl between chattering teeth.

"Shut up or I'll bite you," she said, shocking herself. She was feeling elemental, physical, beyond rational thought. All that mattered was that they warm each other.

"I wouldn't if I were you." He seemed to be shaking less. "I'd retaliate."

Warmth was beginning to flood her belly as she pressed up against him. "Dare you," she said.

Big mistake.

He moved fast for a man who'd just suffered a gunshot wound, and she found herself underneath him on the sagging, narrow mattress. And now she was finally warm, hot even, with the heat of his bed beneath her, the heat of his body pressing her down. His mouth was dangerously close, and for a moment the two were lost in time, frozen except for the heat searing between them.

"Bite me," she said, finding one last comeback.

"I've got a better idea," he said.

And he kissed her.

CHAPTER FOUR

YEAH, HE WAS thoroughly out of his mind, but right then Fitz didn't care. The heat from her body was sinking into his bones, and her gray eyes were calm and fearless. He just wanted to kiss her stubborn mouth and see what came next.

For a moment absolutely nothing happened. She lay trapped beneath him, warm flesh and cold lips, and he decided to put more effort into his kisses. He let his mouth trail to the corner of her lips, using his tongue to soften them, and a moment later she kissed him back, slowly, opening her mouth to him, responding. Her body flowed into his, and he was hard and needy and ready to tear the flimsy clothes off her when she suddenly shoved him, hard.

He was caught off guard, and he fell back, sliding onto the floor with a grunt of pain.

"What the hell are you doing?" she demanded. In the dim light she looked shaken, her mouth damp, trembling.

He sat up gingerly. His jeans weren't making his condition too comfortable, and his side hurt like hell, since the floor was cold and hard. "Kissing you. I must be out of practice if you didn't recognize it. Or maybe you're out of practice."

"I'm not out of practice, I'm engaged," she said. "And you had no business kissing me."

"Then you had no business kissing me back," he pointed out.

She looked like the kind of woman who threw things. Which wasn't a problem—he'd grown up with fierce women and an all-out brawl was good for releasing tension. Sex was even better, but the bride didn't look as if she were in the mood for sex.

Which was a shame, because she looked absolutely… No, he shouldn't be thinking in those terms. His sainted mother would smack him upside the head.

She said nothing, and still looked at him warily.

"Sorry," he said finally, not sorry at all. "I was half-asleep. I thought you were someone else."

As far as lies went, that was a pretty weak one, and she certainly wasn't about to believe it or forgive him, but there wasn't much she could do about it.

"Get back in bed," she said finally. "You'll freeze your butt off on the floor. Did you tear your stitches?"

"I don't think so." She wasn't moving, and the other bed was stripped. "You want me to get back in bed with you?"

"We don't have much choice. I don't want you dying on my hands, and with the blood loss you're in a weakened condition. If you start thinking I'm someone else again I'll slap you."

He pushed himself up from the cold floor, wincing dramatically. In fact, the pain had subsided from burning to a dull throb, and his head was becoming more and more clear. He slid back into the narrow, concave bed, coming up against her almost-nude, blessedly warm body. He pulled her into his arms, pressing their bodies together, and the warmth began to build again, accompanied by a low, erotic burn.

She lay stiff in his arms, making everything a hell of a lot more uncomfortable. "Don't worry about it," he said. "You're not my type."

Another blatant lie. She was exactly his type—tall, strong, with lush curves and a full, rich mouth. She was a fighter, unsentimental, practical and, he sensed, reluctantly turned on. Her body wasn't as obvious as his was—women were lucky that way—but he had no doubt she was as aroused as he was.

Why the hell did he always fall for the stubborn ones? Couldn't he once find a sweet, passive girl to fall for? Why was it always the difficult, powerful ones that got him going?

And the bride was one hell of a powerhouse. She was relaxing now, her skin up against his, her head resting against his shoulder, and he could move his head down and kiss her again, but he didn't want to risk having her punch him. She wouldn't pull her punches, either, even with a wounded man. Hell and damnation.

He was wide-awake, and even as her body softened against his he could still feel the tension that ran through her. "So tell me about your fiancé. What kind of man would make you wear such a monstrosity?"

"I'm not going to talk about Richard with you."

"Why not? I need to hear something boring so I can fall asleep."

"What makes you think my fiancé is boring?"

"Instinct. I bet he's old Boston money—safe and secure and docile."

"Then you'd be wrong."

He couldn't see her face, could only hear her muffled voice. "So what's he do for a living?"

"He's a doctor," she said.

"What kind?"

He could feel her hesitation, and for some reason it made him feel good. He wanted her to have doubts about her fiancé.

"He's a plastic surgeon," she said finally. "And don't say anything. I can feel you trying not to laugh, and I'm already annoyed with you."

He did his best. "So you're marrying a rich doctor who pushes wrinkle filler for a living."

"There's nothing wrong with keeping up your appearance," she said, without the heat of a true believer.

"There's nothing wrong with letting your face show what you've learned in life," he replied. Which made him want to look at her face again, but it was tucked against his chest, so he had to make do with his imagination. She had the softest mouth, once she relaxed, and a full lower lip that he really wanted to bite. Her curves felt lush and warm against his bare chest, which was almost as good as looking into her steely gray eyes and seeing whether she was really as unaffected as she wanted him to believe.

Odd that he could remember her eyes were gray. He'd hardly been in any condition to pay attention. But he'd noticed when she'd stripped off that ruined horror of a wedding gown, and even on his deathbed, with people out to kill him, he'd still wanted her.

His brothers would laugh. Fitz was notoriously picky when it came to women—he had the black Irish good looks and the soul of a Jesuit, his brother Brian had said. But Brian was wrong. He just had a tendency to take relationships seriously.

Which made his uncharacteristic lust for the pain-in-the-ass bride even more unlikely. "So where do you and your plastic surgeon plan to live?"

"He's got a house on Beacon Hill."

Fitz snorted. "I told you, old money. Don't you think you'll be bored by all that silver-spoon crap?"

"After the last twelve hours I could do with a little boredom." Her voice was tart, matter-of-fact, but he could sense a faint note of tension beneath it.

"Having second thoughts, are you?" he murmured against

her tangle of hair. He wasn't even sure what color it was—a sort of brownish blond with red streaks that were maybe put there by nature, maybe by a hairdresser.

Her body tensed against his again, and he waited for her to deny his question. "None of your business," she said instead. "Now stop talking and go to sleep, or I'll take my half of the covers and let you freeze."

"But then you'd freeze, too," he pointed out with great reasonableness.

"It might be worth it," she muttered.

She smelled like cinnamon and cloves, wonderful scents from his childhood, and while he wanted to keep arguing with her, bantering with her, annoying her, he found his energy flagging once more. And in the end, just holding her body in his arms was good enough. In the morning he'd be his rational self, and the hours of darkness in the narrow bed wouldn't have existed. She'd still be the same annoying woman, he'd still be on a run for his life. And the sooner they parted company the better.

But in the meantime…

He pulled her closer, letting his chin rest on her hair, and closed his eyes.

In the meantime…

SHE WOKE BEFORE he did, thank God, and slid out of bed, padding across the chilly room in her underwear. She grabbed the change of clothes she'd bought at Wal-Mart and headed into the bathroom, praying for hot water. For once the lousy motel came through, and she stripped off her underwear and stepped beneath the hot stream. She stayed in as long as she could, then dressed quickly in the tiny, steam-filled bathroom before moving back into the small bedroom. Fitzpatrick was still asleep, but his color was much better now, and to judge by his friskiness in the middle of the night, he was no longer at death's door.

Which meant there was no reason to stay with him anymore.

Which was a relief, right? She could go back to Boston, finish getting ready for her wedding, with the added bonus of not having to wear that hideous concoction. So it was all good, right?

Wrong. Even Fitz knew she was having second thoughts about her marriage, which wasn't surprising considering the way she'd kissed him. She'd done her best to resist, to be virtuous and distant. But damn, that man knew how to kiss. And lying skin-to-skin in that narrow bed was enough to tempt a saint.

Who'd have thought being kidnapped was just what she'd needed? Once she'd known Fitz wasn't going to hurt her, she'd almost welcomed the breathing space. Her priorities had narrowed down to two—keeping him alive and safely out of the hands of the men who were trying to kill him.

He'd do better without her. She moved to the window, pushing aside the dingy curtain. The snow had stopped, blanketing everything with a coat of white, and her small car was trapped in a field of thick snow. Someone was going to have to shovel it out, and that wasn't going to be her wounded patient.

She pulled her cell phone from her purse. She'd turned it off when she'd been in the dressing room—Richard had a tendency to call her every fifteen minutes to check up on her. She almost hated to turn it back on, and prayed there'd be no signal at the back end of beyond.

There was a signal, all right. And seventeen messages. She didn't bother to check who'd called—Richard was getting uneasy about the wedding, and his horror of a mother was pushing his buttons.

She took the phone back into the bathroom so she wouldn't be overheard, and dialed Richard's number. He came on the other end at a controlled bellow.

"Where the hell have you been, Eloise? I've been frantic! I thought you were off the road in a ditch somewhere, bleeding to death!"

"I'm fine, Richard," she said in the voice she used for over-anxious mothers. "I just decided I needed a little time to think. I'm…" It was a good thing she didn't know what town she was in. She decided to lie about the state, though she wasn't quite sure why. "I'm in Vermont," she said.

"You pick the night of a snowstorm to go for a drive? Do you realize how irresponsible that is? I was imagining all sorts of disasters. Jackie said you were at Farnham's when they had that terrorist scare—I was afraid you'd been kidnapped."

"I didn't think you had that wild an imagination, Richard," she said lightly. In fact, she hadn't thought Richard had any imagination at all. "Wasn't that jumping to conclusions?"

"The police took my concerns seriously enough," he said, his voice huffy. "I called them last night, and they were very interested."

Oh, crap. "Well, you can call them back and tell them I'm perfectly fine. I just decided to go walkabout to consider a few things." She threw in the little Australian slang in an effort to distract him. He tended to get annoyed when she did it.

"Drive-about in a blizzard is more like it," he said, still sounding fretful.

"I'm fine, I told you. I just had to think a few things through."

It was finally sinking into his thick, handsome skull. "Think what things through?" he asked, suspicious.

"I think we should postpone our wedding for a few months. Maybe next summer. We don't want to be rushing in to anything...."

"Don't be ridiculous! That's utterly impossible—everything's already planned. My mother has worked herself into a state of exhaustion seeing to all the details. The bridesmaids' dresses, the church decorations..."

"Those can be used in summer just as easily."

"Don't be ridiculous! Bridesmaids can't wear dark colors in summer!"

"Richard..."

"And the gifts have already begun arriving. My mother would have a fit. You know she's never been all that enthusiastic about the marriage, and if you pull a stunt like this, she's going to be even more difficult."

"Pull a stunt, Richard?" she echoed, her voice wintry.

But poor Richard didn't realize he was dancing on a razor's edge. "Really, Eloise, it's time you grew up and gained some sense of responsibility. Putting off the wedding is childish and ridiculous. I won't have it."

Ellie slowly banged her head against the Sheetrock wall, quietly enough so Fitzpatrick wouldn't hear her. She took a deep breath. "You're absolutely right, Richard," she said. "We're just delaying the inevitable."

"I'm so glad you see it my way." Richard's tones were plummy with satisfaction.

"I do. I'll have the engagement ring delivered back to you as soon as I return to Boston. I'm afraid there's been a little problem with your mother's wedding dress..."

"What are you talking about?"

"We're not getting married, Richard," she said, using the worried-mother tone once more. "Not in a week, not this summer, not ever."

There was a long silence at the other end. "And what has brought about this change of mind?" he said in a stiff voice.

"I don't think I'm cut out to be a doctor's wife, Richard. I'm not cut out for Beacon Hill, not cut out for private hospitals and paperwork. I'm thinking of moving to Canada."

"That's socialized medicine!" he said in tones that equated it with devil worship.

"Or back to Australia. All I know is I'm not cut out to be your wife, Richard. I'm sorry. I just wish I'd come to my senses sooner."

"You really expect me to just simply cancel everything?"

"Yes, I do, Richard. Goodbye," she said gently. Because she had no choice. If she'd been on a traditional phone, she would have slammed it down.

"So no honeymoon?"

Fitzpatrick was leaning in the doorway, watching her. He was wearing only his jeans, which rode low on his narrow hips, and the bandage looked good. Hell, everything about him looked good, but that wasn't any of her business.

"No honeymoon," she said with a shrug. "I think the realization came when it was a relief to be kidnapped at gunpoint rather than wear his mother's wedding dress. That's not the appropriate reaction."

"And you're always appropriate?"

She looked up at him. Appropriate would be not to notice how damned good he looked in those low-slung jeans and a bandage. Appropriate would be not to notice his black hair was a little too long and curling down his neck, and that his eyes were a bright winter blue. Or that his stubborn, sexy mouth looked like it could do amazing things to hers.

"Always," she said. "You can take a shower if you think you're strong enough to stand. Just don't get your bandage wetter than you can help."

"What if I fall down?" He looked about as likely to fall down as the Prudential Center.

"I can always help you bathe. I've done worse in my life."

"Tempting though that sounds, I think I'll decline the kind offer. The sooner I get on the road the better, and you might prove…distracting. Hand me your phone."

"Hey, I'm on roaming," she protested.

"You're a doctor—you can afford it better than a cop," he said. "Besides, my phone has got to be bugged. I don't want to do anything to lead them to me." He paused, looking at her. "What's the expression for?"

"Richard called the police last night when he couldn't get through to me. He knew I'd been at Farnham's, and he was afraid something had happened to me."

Fitz's reaction was brief and profane. "Did they blow him off or pay attention to him?"

"Paid attention."

"Hell and damnation."

"I'm sure he's going to call them back, tell them never mind." At least, she hoped so. Richard had never been terribly concerned about the needs of those he considered his underlings.

"Did you tell him where we were?"

"I said I was in Vermont. Alone."

"Thank God for small favors," he said.

She rose, but the area was far too small, particularly considering how little he was wearing and how damned cold the room was. "Take your shower and I'll go see about renting you an SUV."

For a moment he didn't move out of the way, blocking the doorway, and she was acutely aware of his size, his strength. He was just a few inches taller than she was, with the kind of lean, wiry frame she'd always found sexy. But she couldn't afford to find James Fitzpatrick sexy—he was just too much trouble.

She waited, and for a brief moment he moved toward her, and she had the insane thought that he was going to kiss her again. And that she wanted him to.

But instead he pulled back, moving out of the way. "I can find my own car."

"You mean, steal it? Hijack another innocent holiday shopper? I don't think so. If the car is rented legally by a woman, no one's going to think you had anything to do with it."

"Unless the police find out that Eloise Pollard rented a car less than twenty-four hours after she went missing from the last known site where James Fitzpatrick was seen. They'll be on me like flies on manure."

"How apt," she said sweetly. "Take your shower and tell me what you want me to do."

"I'd like you to go out and get in your car and get the hell away from here before you bring me any more attention."

For some ridiculous reason that hurt. She could point out to him that he was the one who'd drawn her into it, mention that if it weren't for her, he'd be passed out behind the wheel somewhere, or dead in a hail of bullets.

But he was right. She needed to get the hell away from him as quickly as she could. "Fine," she said briskly. "Take my cell phone—you need it more than I do. If you survive, you can always return it. Your antibiotics are on the beside table. I hope you make it to Maine."

"I'll make it," he said grimly. "Nothing could stop me."

She waited until she heard the sound of the shower. She put on the heavy socks she'd bought, then slid into her turquoise rubber shoes. Her coat was still in the car, and she figured, what the hell, and grabbed his ruined leather jacket. He could damn well freeze as he made his solitary way to Maine.

Zipping it up, she pushed open the door to the cabin and started trudging across the snow-packed parking lot toward her car.

And then she looked up.

The black car blocking hers was unmarked, with Massachusetts official plates, and she had no doubt it wasn't a coincidence. Especially when two men got out, one tall and burly, the other a paler, weaker version of Fitz. It must be his cousin, Tommy Morrissey. The men who wanted to kill him.

She froze, wondering if there was a chance in hell she could run for it, get back and barricade Fitz and her inside the cabin, warn him that they'd been found.

Damn Richard! It was just too bloody easy to trace her car. Maybe she could bluff, tell them she was here alone.

But then the taller man started toward her. "Are you Dr. Pollard? Dr. Eloise Pollard?" he said, his voice firm and friendly. "We've been looking for you."

Fight or flight? She still couldn't move. Fitz would have the brains to look before he decided to stroll out the front door the way she had, wouldn't he?

If she ran, they'd follow her, and find him. She really didn't have any choice in the matter. So she plastered her best smile on her face and started toward the approaching man. She hoped to God that he wasn't holding a gun in the hand she couldn't see.

Because as hot as James Fitzpatrick was, she had no intention of dying for him, or anyone else.

"Yes, I'm Eloise Pollard," she said. "Can I help you, Officer?"

The man coming toward her frowned. "How did you know I was a cop?" he asked. And she waited for the arm to come up, and her life to be over.

And the only thing she could think of was, *I should have kissed him back.*

CHAPTER FIVE

FITZ SHOWERED QUICKLY. The hot water ran out, thanks to the bride, and he cursed as he banged his elbow on the rusty tin stall in his hurry to get out of the suddenly icy blast. She'd bought him boxers with Christmas trees on them, probably out of sheer malice. He pulled them on, cursing. The jeans were too small for him—probably on purpose, as well—but he could get away with the black jeans he'd been wearing when everything had gone south. At least they wouldn't show the blood.

He prodded the skin around the wound. It was tender, but not agonizing. The bride was a pretty good doctor—he'd lucked out when he'd grabbed her. Except that she was a pain, and tempting, and he had too much on his plate just trying to stay alive to even be thinking about her that way.

But hell, he was a man. There was always time to think about sex.

He looked around for his All Stars. She'd had the presence of mind to put them by the space heater, and the canvas had dried out, at least for the time being. She was someone who paid attention to details—he liked that in a woman.

She'd also stolen his leather jacket, leaving him with nothing but a hooded sweatshirt, also with a freaking Christmas tree on it, and his appreciation faded fast. Shoving his gun in his waistband, he started for the door, planning to catch up with her and get his damned jacket back, and maybe, just maybe, kiss the hell out of her simply because he wanted to and because maybe he wasn't going to make it through the day, when something stopped him.

The instincts that had made him spin out of the way when Barber raised his gun, the instincts that had kept his sorry ass alive for so long were on full alert.

They'd found him.

He moved toward the window, slowly, so that his shadow wouldn't be noticeable through the dingy curtains, and looked out. O'Bannion was there, towering over her, and Morrissey was skulking around the car.

She was on her own. They'd have no reason to hurt her, but if they thought she knew anything about where he'd gone, they wouldn't hesitate to…

He couldn't think about that. He backed away from the window, slowly. He'd already wasted too much time. He had to get to Maine, find out what kind of proof Spinelli had. Find a way to stop O'Bannion and Morrissey and clear his name.

The bride would have to fend for herself.

IT WAS ALL Ellie could do not to turn and run. The man was big, tall and husky, with a smooth smile and the eyes of a sociopath or a politician. "You've got official plates on your car," she said reasonably. "And I'm a doctor—I've dealt with the police before when I've done work in the E.R. Am I wrong?"

"You're absolutely right, Dr. Pollard. I'm Senior Detective Connor O'Bannion and this is Detective Morrissey. Your fiancé has been very worried about you."

"I've been in touch with him, Detective. He knows I'm

fine—he just overreacted when I decided to take some time away. It's awfully nice of you to go to all this trouble. How in the world did you find me?"

"We have excellent resources, Dr. Pollard. Now why don't you tell me where he is?"

She blinked. "Where who is?"

"There's blood in the snow under the car," Morrissey called out. "I knew I'd winged him."

"What are you...?" Her words trailed off as she stared into the barrel of a gun. This was the second time in twenty-four hours that a stranger had pulled a gun on her, and she didn't like it any more this time than she had outside of Farnham's.

"Let's not dick around, Dr. Pollard. Just tell me where he is and you can go back to your fiancé and never think about it again." O'Bannion's voice was smooth, deadly. And she didn't believe him for one minute. "You don't need to worry—he's not going to hurt you again. We know Fitzpatrick car-jacked you at the department store and forced you to help him at gunpoint. We're here to protect you."

Yeah, right. "I don't know what you're talking about."

He hit her, slamming his hand against the side of her face, and he grabbed her arm in an iron grip before she could fall. "This isn't a game, Dr. Pollard. Where is he?"

"Her tracks lead to that cabin, Connor," Morrissey said. "Just one set of tracks. He must still be there."

"He's gone," she said rapidly, trying to ignore the throbbing on the side of her face. "I got away from him last night, but I was too freaked to drive home, and I..."

"Don't lie to me, bitch," O'Bannion snarled. "We'll just go see." He started dragging her across the parking lot, ignoring her struggles.

"He'll have a gun," the other man warned.

"That's why she's going to be our shield," O'Bannion said grimly, pushing her in front of him, twisting her arm behind her back to keep her under control. "Come along, Dr. Pollard. You don't want to be interfering with a policeman in pursuit of a suspect, now do you?"

There were a hundred things she could say, but only one came out. "Get out of there, Fitz!" she screamed, a moment before O'Bannion's meaty hand slammed down over her mouth.

She bit him, and he cursed, jerking her arm up harder. A little bit more and he'd break it, which would be the least of her worries because he was already going to have to kill her. He hauled her up the steps, his partner close behind them. "I've got your hostage, Fitz!" he called out. "Now I can put a bullet in her brain or you can get your ass out here."

No answer. O'Bannion kicked the door open, keeping her as a shield, but the room was empty. "Check the bathroom, Tommy," he ordered.

"He's gone, Connor," Tommy announced a moment later. "He went out the window. I can see tracks leading toward the street...."

"What are you waiting for? Go after him!"

"What about her?" He jerked his head in Ellie's direction.

O'Bannion released his agonizing grip, and she tore herself away, trying to rub the circulation back into her shoulder. "I think poor Dr. Pollard was in the wrong place at the wrong time. She was taken hostage by a fugitive and murdered by him before the police closed in."

"Sounds good," Morrissey said. "You want me to cap her?"

"Cuff her for now, while we find the son of a bitch. We can use his gun just to make things neat and tidy. Put her in the back of the police car. She can't get into trouble there." He leaned down, breathing on her, nasty, coffee-drenched fumes. "And if you make any trouble, we'll just shoot you now and have things a little less tidy. You got that?"

"Yes," she said, glaring at him. *He got away.* For some reason that mattered, even though there was a good chance she wasn't going to survive.

They force-marched her across the snow-covered parking lot and shoved her in the back of the unmarked car. The handcuffs were hooked into a bar on the back of the seat, so even if she could get the door open, she wouldn't be able to run. And considering there were no handles on the inside of the door, getting it open was an unlikely scenario.

"You want me to knock her out, Connor?" Tommy was just full of good suggestions, Ellie thought.

"We don't want her too bruised, now do we, Tommy? This is the back end of beyond—no one will be able to hear her if she screams, and even if they do, she's in the back of a police car. Everyone's gonna steer clear."

"You son of a…" The car slammed shut on the beginning of her string of curses. She yanked at the handcuffs, kicking the seat in sheer frustration as the two men disappeared behind the cabins. Where was Fitz when she needed him? She couldn't think of half the bad words he'd come up with.

She'd seen enough in her years as a doctor to know that death could come quickly and unpredictably, and there was no rightness or sense to it. She might very well die today. But she wasn't going down without a fight.

It had to be very early in the morning—the December sun was barely visible, and the roads were empty, except for a battered-looking tow truck heading into the parking lot. She tried to pound on the windows, but her cuffed hands couldn't reach, and she angled back, trying to kick at the door to get the driver's attention. Instead she slid onto the floor, wrenching her arms. She tried to get back up on the seat, but she'd somehow managed to get totally tangled up with her arms and legs going in opposite directions. She wanted to scream, she wanted to cry, she wanted to…

There was a bump, and the car jerked forward, then began to slide sideways. She finally managed to get to her knees on the seat. The tow truck had hooked onto the front of the police car and was towing it out of the parking lot so quickly the back tires were fishtailing in the snow, throwing her back and forth in the seat.

She wasn't sure whether to laugh or cry. The bad cops were foiled by something as simple as a tow truck, probably moving the car out of the way for plowing. Assuming the idiot driver got her out of there in time and didn't end up losing the car off a cliff in the slippery conditions, she was going to make it.

She fell back against the seat, her arms stretched out in front of her as they sped along the empty highway. Whoever was driving wasn't used to a tow truck—this was possibly more dangerous than being trapped by two killer cops. She closed her eyes and prayed, she wasn't sure for what, but she kept at it until the truck took a sharp turn, sending the car spinning behind it like crack-the-whip on ice skates, and a moment later it crashed up against the back of the tow truck, throwing her onto the floor again.

She didn't know what she was expecting when the back door opened, exposing her sprawled on the floor, but somehow Fitz came as no surprise. "Stop messing about," he said. "We have to keep moving."

She managed to flip around enough to glare at him. "I'm in handcuffs, Einstein."

Fitz swore. "They should have gagged you, too." He unfastened one cuff and pulled it through the bar, then undid the other one, shoving them in his pocket before hauling her out of the smashed car.

"What do you need those for?"

"In case you annoy me. Aren't you going to thank me for saving your life?" he said.

"Considering I wouldn't have been in danger if you hadn't pulled a gun on me in the first place, you'll have to forgive me if I'm a little less than grateful," she said. "How are we going to get out of here?"

"In the tow truck. We'll drive up into Maine and ditch it first chance we get."

"We?"

"Obviously I can't leave you alone. Look at the trouble you got yourself into."

Within five minutes they were back on the highway, the smashed police car left behind in the woods. The heater in the truck didn't seem to be operational, and when she reached out to turn on the radio and find some Christmas music, he said, "Don't you dare."

She looked at him for a long, thoughtful moment. "You didn't need to come back for me," she said. "Why did you? Why didn't you just keep on running?"

She thought he wasn't going to answer. She'd already learned that James Fitzpatrick wasn't the talkative sort, and she expected nothing more than a grunt.

"Because even though you're annoying and bossy and a pain in the ass, you're still innocent in all this. And that's what a cop does—protect the innocent, even at his own risk. And I'm a cop, the son of a cop, the grandson of a cop. I'm going to keep you safe, and if the only way I can do it is to take you with me, then you're coming with me. Got it?"

"Got it," she said. "How's your side?"

"Fine, thank you," he snapped.

"Good." She fastened the seat belt, leaning back and rubbing her wrists absently. In her struggles they were rubbed raw, and she tucked them into the overlong sleeves of his pilfered jacket. "Do you still have my cell phone?"

"It's back at the cabin. They'll be tracking that now, as well Spinelli already knows I'm heading his way. I was calling him when Grady decided to pull a gun on me."

"I don't suppose you're going to feed me?" Suddenly she was ravenous. Maybe running for your life did that to a girl.

"Eventually," he said. "Right now I'm more concerned with saving your life. I should have known they'd plan to kill you. O'Bannion isn't the type to leave any loose ends."

She reached forward again to turn on the radio, and this time he let her. Some sleazy lounge singer was crooning "Silent Night" and she resisted the impulse to turn it off again, instead leaning back in her seat. All is calm, all is bright. At least for now.

She had to admire his talent for grand theft auto. By the time they were halfway up the Maine coast they were on their third car, this one a muddy Jeep Cherokee, and she'd eaten the best fried clams she'd had in her entire life. And somewhere along the way they began to talk, really talk, as old friends do instead of natural enemies. He told her about his huge Irish Catholic family on the outskirts of Boston, his powerhouse of a mother, his seven brothers and sisters, his terrifying Aunt Agnes, better known as Sister Mary Joseph, his first girlfriend and his first dog. She told him of her years growing up outside of Sydney, of that dark time when her parents had been killed and she'd been left alone, with no one to turn to but Ruby, her very temporary foster mother. Ruby was only set up for boys, and Ellie's stay with her had been short until her aunt could be found, but it had been long enough to forge lifetime relationships with Ruby and with fellow foster child Joe Cartland. She told him of the long years of slogging through medical school, her decision to leave the rough, beautiful country and the warm, practical people to find a new life in the States, and her recent longing to return. By the time they reached the tiny town of Hidden Harbor he knew more about her than Richard ever did. And she knew more about him.

It was pitch-dark and bitter cold, but at least the Jeep had decent heat and a CD player full of holiday music. "We're getting close," Fitz said, the temporary lightness in his voice vanishing. "Spinelli lives three blocks over, but this town isn't exactly a bustling metropolis. I'm going to need to scout it out on foot."

That sounded reasonable. "Okay," she said. "But I think I'd better check your bandages before you go walking into trouble."

He turned right, following a narrow road. There were no lights on in the houses that lined it, no Christmas lights decorating the old cottages. Snow had begun falling again, drifting down gently, but this time they were in a four-wheel-drive vehicle and she didn't have to worry.

The road came to a dead end beside a closed and shuttered restaurant that looked out over the harbor. Fitz pulled up beside the old building and killed the engine. "Let's see what we can find. This looks like it's part of the vacation community—no one's driven down that road since the snow started yesterday. You should be safe enough here while I go check on Spinelli. They might even have some food, and I know how much you like food."

"Hey," she protested. "I don't always tend to order extra

large—today was the first time. I just haven't had a normal meal since you decided to abduct me."

The grin flashed on his face for a moment, then vanished once more. "A man's gotta do what a man's gotta do," he said with deceptive ease.

He was planning something. In the hours they'd spent together she'd gotten to know him very well, and all that calm signaled something devious going on. And he wasn't going to tell her until he was good and ready.

She slid out of the Jeep onto the light covering of snow. Maine hadn't gotten as big a dumping as Massachusetts and New Hampshire, but there was still enough to get between her Crocs and her socks, and a shiver ran across her. The salt scent of the ocean was rich and icy—she'd forgotten how much she loved the smell of the ocean. Even one surrounded by ice.

Fitz was as good at breaking and entering as he was at grand theft auto, and she wondered just what he'd omitted from his tales of his wild youth, but she was more interested in finding some heat than giving him the third degree. The inside of the restaurant was cold and empty. Chairs and tables were stacked in one corner, but there was a huge stone fireplace on one wall and enough firewood to last them for days if need be. After that they could start smashing the chairs.

"I'll start the fire while you find us something to eat," he said, heading for the fireplace.

"Hey, I know how to start fires as well as any man," she protested.

"Yeah, but I can't cook."

The place was loaded—canned fruit and vegetables, industrial size—and the locked chest freezer was probably just as well stocked. There were even pillows and blankets in the corner closet—all the comforts of home. She grabbed a couple of the blankets and headed back into the dining room to the bright warmth of a crackling fire. Fitz had dragged one of the big wicker chairs close to it, and he held out his hand.

"Come and sit for a while," he said. "Get warm."

She should have suspected him, but she'd been lulled by the long afternoon and evening on the road, and she sank down in the chair gratefully, trusting him.

He knelt in front of her and took her icy hands in his, warming them, and she felt the heat go straight to her stomach, a longing that she couldn't fight.

And a moment later he'd clamped the handcuffs back around her, and she was imprisoned once more.

CHAPTER SIX

ELLIE'S REACTION WAS immediate and angry. She tried to head-butt him, but he moved out of the way quickly, and she realized he'd threaded the handcuffs through the arm of the chair. "What the hell do you think you're doing, Fitzpatrick?"

"Keeping you safe while I go reconnoiter," he said. "You can kill me when I get back."

"Don't you think you could have just asked me to stay put?"

"I could have. But I don't trust you to stay out of trouble. I'm going to see if I can get to Spinelli, and you're going to sit there and behave…" His voice trailed off, and his eyes grew hard, his mouth grim. "What's wrong with your face?"

It wasn't like she'd forgotten. Her cheek had been throbbing from O'Bannion's blow during the long drive north, and she'd deliberately kept it turned away from him. "Nothing's wrong with my face," she snapped. "I think it's quite a nice face. Maybe not classically beautiful, but not bad, all in all."

"Don't play games with me." He caught her chin in one hand, turned it to survey the damage. She hadn't had a chance to look in a mirror but she imagined the bruises had already begun to form. "O'Bannion do this?"

She didn't answer. She didn't need to. "I'm going to kill him," Fitz said, his voice calm and flat. He grabbed one of the blankets she'd brought and tossed it over her, carefully.

"Fitz…"

"I'll be back in an hour or so. I built up the fire so you'll stay warm."

"What if they come for me? I'm not going to be able to get away if I'm handcuffed to this bloody chair."

"It's me they're after."

"And if they kill you?"

He leaned over her and kissed her full on the mouth. "No one's going to kill me," he said. "I've got too much to live for." He kissed her again, and she felt her body rise into the kiss, wanting more. "I've got you."

And then he was gone, the bastard, leaving her bound to the chair.

At least she was warm. She could sit there in relative comfort and figure out how she was going to kill him when he got back.

She looked at the fire. She should have put ice on her face, but for some reason she hadn't wanted him to notice. His furious reaction was probably part of his "protect the innocents" thing. It was nothing personal. He couldn't be feeling the extraordinary pull that she was. Of course, she wanted to kill him right now, but that was the least of what she wanted to do to him, with him.

Illogical as it might be, she knew he was just where she was. Wanting, no matter how crazy it was. He'd kissed her, and when he pulled back and she looked into his eyes she'd recognized that same longing, that same, crazy sense of belonging. Of finally finding his way home.

Her face throbbed with the heat, but her body began to relax. Too much adrenaline flooding her today, and there was no way she was going to be able to stay awake until he came back. In fact, it was better she be well-rested for his return, because she was going to kick his ass from here to Sunday.

And then maybe she'd kiss him back.

FITZ SLIPPED BACK into the old restaurant as silently as he could. She'd fallen asleep by the fire, which was a good thing, since she was going to be as mad as a hornet when she woke up. He'd had no choice but to cuff her—she was just too damned stubborn. It was one of the things he liked about her, but he couldn't risk letting her follow him into trouble. The bruised face was a reminder of what he'd gotten her into, and he was damned if he was going to let her get hurt again.

"I'm awake." Her dry voice carried to the doorway where he stood, hesitating. "Come and tell me what's going on and take these stupid handcuffs off me. I promise not to beat you up."

He laughed. "I'm trembling in my boots."

"You're not wearing boots, you're wearing runners."

"Runners?"

"Sneakers, running shoes, whatever you call them. In the middle of a snowstorm, no less."

She was sounding reasonable enough, so he approached her, still wary. Her head-butt had been impressive—she wasn't the type to pull her punches.

"Next time I'm shot and have to run for my life I'll try to plan better," he said. Her hair was in her eyes and her mouth was set in a stubborn line, and he wanted a thousand things that he couldn't have. "You're not going to hit me, are you? Remember, I'm a wounded man."

She snorted. "I have every confidence in my skills as a doctor. Your color's good, you aren't favoring your right side and you didn't scream when I whacked you."

"I'll have you know I don't scream. I just manage a manly grunt." She was holding out her cuffed hands, and he unfastened them, still ready to duck if she came at him.

She simply stayed in the chair, rubbing her wrists, and a

wave of guilt washed over him. "Why did you struggle and hurt your wrists? You knew I'd come back."

"This was from earlier. When I was cuffed to the bar and then tossed all over the backseat of the police car," she said. "Of course, you forgot to consider that."

He sat back on his heels, looking at her. The fire was putting out waves of heat, and he stripped off the stupid Christmas sweatshirt and tossed it on the floor, his eyes still looking deeply into hers. Not believing what he saw, not caring. How could he be wanting this, so badly, when men were trying to kill them?

"Did you talk to Spinelli?"

"I didn't. There are two undercover cops staking out the place, and I couldn't just stroll up the sidewalk and knock on the door. The back of the house leads onto the beach, but it's private and fenced in. At least O'Bannion and Morrissey are out of the picture."

"They are? How can you be sure?"

"O'Bannion's supposed to be getting married in Texas around now, and Morrissey's his best man. They were already cutting it close when they followed us to New Hampshire, and I'm willing to bet they're on their way to the wedding to keep from arousing suspicion. I happen to know the men who are staking out Spinelli's. They're in O'Bannion's pocket and they'll do what he orders, no questions asked. They'd shoot me even if they weren't ordered to—to them I'm a cop killer. But those two are dirty cops, and I'm betting they're part of the whole mess."

"So what are we going to do?"

"I don't know," he said wearily. "Figure out a way to get to Spinelli before the cops get tired of waiting for me to come to them and decide to search for us."

She pushed away from the chair, moving closer to the fire. She was a big woman, tall and strong, no shrinking violet. He looked at her, silhouetted against the fire, and he couldn't think about O'Bannion and Tommy, about the two cops parked down the street from Spinelli's, about stolen diamonds and dead partners. For the moment all he could think about was wanting her.

He was going to hell for sure.

She, of course, was entirely oblivious to what he was thinking. "What time is it? It feels like the middle of the night."

"Just after six. The sun sets early this time of year. There's a diner in town where we can get something to eat if it seems safe enough. The cops won't leave their stakeout and I'm starving. Otherwise we stay here until I come up with something."

"Stay here?" She turned to face him. "Stay here and do what? Wait to be killed?"

He said nothing, rose to his feet and moved toward her. She didn't back away. She just looked at him.

"We're not going to be killed." He had to be imagining the heat, the strong tide of longing that stretched between them like a lava flow.

"You can guarantee that?"

"I can't guarantee anything."

She took a step closer. "Well, if I'm going to die, there's just one thing I want to do before that happens."

"What?"

She closed the gap between them, put her arms around his neck and yanked his head down to hers, none too gently. "This," she said. And kissed him.

It was crazy. It was dangerous. And he didn't give a rat's ass. He pulled her body tight to his, so that she could feel his erection, and she tried to get even closer. In a matter of moments he had her down on the pile of blankets in front of the fire, in a matter of moments she'd stripped off his T-shirt and was reaching for the snap of his jeans. And then it was just a blur, of mouths and legs and hands and sweetness, and when he pushed inside her she was wet, and she arched beneath him as a climax swept through her, so fast and powerful that it almost brought him along with it. He pushed up on his arms, so he could look down at her while he thrust into her, and she looked so beautiful, so strong and passionate and fierce, and he wanted to keep on doing this forever, never stop.

And then she opened her eyes and looked up into his, gray into blue, with heat and possession and total abandon, and it put him over the edge, and when he came she did, too.

He wasn't quite sure what happened next. He must have collapsed on top of her, but his brain didn't return until he'd rolled off her, taking her with him, holding her against his body and flipping one of the blankets over them.

He kissed the side of her neck, the still-racing pulse beneath her skin, breathing in the scent of her, rubbing his face against her tangled hair. He wanted to sink into her, dissolve in her, and he was out of his freaking mind.

"This is crazy," she muttered, kissing his shoulder. "We shouldn't be doing this."

"Nuts," he agreed, turning his head to kiss her mouth, slowly, lingeringly. He was getting hard again, that fast, and he could blame it on the danger, blame it on the circumstances. But he knew the truth. It was her. This was a hell of a time to meet his soul mate.

Unfortunately he hadn't realized he'd said it out loud. "Soul mate?" She went suddenly very still.

"Don't worry about it. Probably just temporary insanity,"

he said, not believing a word of it. "Danger's always an aphrodisiac."

"Not to me."

"Well, then gratitude," he said, frustrated.

"That was gratitude? It felt like something else."

"And what was that?"

She hesitated, and he wondered what she'd been wanting to say. Whatever it was, she'd thought better of it, and she shrugged. "Pure, irrational lust," she said, sitting up, pulling the blanket around her in an infuriating and ridiculous show of modesty. He wanted to yank it off her. He wanted to push her back on the makeshift bed of blankets and show her just how impure his lust was. And that it was a hell of a lot more.

But right now the best thing he could do was shut the hell up. Maybe she'd be willing to listen later, once they were out of danger. He could even court her—bring her flowers, ask her on a date. If she said no, he could always kidnap her at gunpoint again.

Hell, he was turning into a stalker. He rolled onto his back, closing his eyes and groaning.

She was immediately on her knees beside him, the blanket still wrapped around her body, her clothes scattered on the floor. "Did you tear your stitches? Let me look…"

His bullet wound was the least of his problems. "It's fine," he growled. "Why don't you get dressed and we'll pretend this never happened?"

He didn't catch her expression. "Fine," she said briskly, rising again and scooping up her scattered clothes. He waited until she stomped from the room with her clothes and her blanket and her dignity, and then began to curse under his breath.

So he could be a total idiot at times. That was nothing new, as his brothers would be happy to tell him. And there was nothing he wanted to do more than follow her into the darkened restaurant, strip off that blanket and tell her…

Tell her what? That he had the gloomy, irrational suspicion that he'd actually done the impossible and fallen in love for the first time in his life? Hell, no. If it was real, it could keep for the time being. Right now they had more important things to concentrate on. Like staying alive.

When she emerged, she was fully dressed, her hair tied back, her face freshly washed. Her eyes were slightly red, but he was going to ignore that for now. "You found a bathroom in this place? I would have thought they'd drained the pipes for the winter."

"Count your blessings," she said in a cool voice that only had the faintest note of strain in it. "And hurry up. I'm hungry and in a small town like this that diner isn't going to stay open forever."

"Ellie…"

"Yes?"

"Never mind." She wasn't in the mood to hear apologies, and he wasn't in the mood to give them. Once they were safe they could deal with what was between them. For now it could be ignored.

The moon was up, bright and full in the winter sky. She'd clearly decided on the silent treatment, which was fine with him. It made him feel guilty, and he deserved it, but for now it gave him time to think, to try to figure out how the hell he was going to get past the sentries and into Spinelli's house.

The diner looked like a thousand other diners, with great cheeseburgers and French fries and lousy salads. He and Ellie took a booth, eating quickly and without conversation. The place was fairly full—a surprise, and everyone was wearing some kind of festive gear, like reindeer sweaters and Santa

Claus hats. There was ketchup-splattered plastic holly along the counter, Christmas music played over the sound system and the waitresses were wearing elf hats. He wanted to groan.

But Ellie was loving it. She was a Christmas junkie, just like his mother, who decorated everything that wasn't moving and a few things that were, including the ancient springer spaniel with his very own Christmas sweater and Christmas collar. She'd love Ellie, and Ellie would love her.

And what the hell was he thinking of?

"We need to get going," he said.

"You figured out how you're going to get inside Spinelli's?" Her voice was deliberately casual.

"Not yet. Maybe it'll come to me."

"Maybe not. It's a block away, right?"

"Spinelli's place? Yeah. But don't suggest you try to get in there instead of me—Spinelli won't trust you. Hell, it took him years before he trusted me."

"You go ahead but just wait for me on the corner. I'll be there in five minutes."

He didn't bother pointing out to her that five minutes on a street corner in the middle of December in Maine was not going to be too comfortable, and he'd only just be out of sight of the cops keeping watch at Spinelli's. But he figured he owed her that much.

The town, which consisted of one tiny little block with the diner, a restaurant, a sports store and a bunch of empty store-fronts, was deserted. All the holiday merriment seemed to be confined to the diner. He could see Spinelli's place up ahead. One black sedan was parked on the opposite side of the street, the windows smoked, the motor still running. Just past Spinelli's on the same side was another unmarked car. Just waiting for him to walk into their trap.

He heard the singing first, freaking Christmas carols, and he growled, turning… To see Ellie standing there, surrounded by most of the people in the diner, including two of the three waitresses, and they all were bellowing "Hark! The Herald Angels Sing" with more enthusiasm than tunefulness. She came up to Fitz and tucked her arm through his. "Sing, Fitz. It's the only way a stranger is going to be able to walk up to Spinelli's door."

He had to hand it to her, she had more balls than his brothers put together. She had launched into the second verse of the Christmas carol, and the rest of the makeshift carolers were struggling to keep up. He said to hell with it and started singing, as well, as they made their way up the narrow, shoveled sidewalks to Max Spinelli's modest little ranch house.

The cops had gotten out of their cars, watching the procession warily. He knew both of them—they were from a different precinct but well known for their brutality and their corruption. Internal Affairs Division had been after them for years, but so far nothing had happened. Probably because they'd had O'Bannion's protection.

They probably had two guns each—one in a shoulder holster, a smaller one on their ankles. Same as he usually had, but there were two of them, and now about a dozen innocents, singing their stupid hearts out.

"'Hail the heav'n born prince of peace, hail the lord of righteousness,'" he sang, and Ellie looked at him in surprise, then joined back in. "Twelve years of Catholic school, baby," he said in her ear. "I know all the verses."

They stopped at the three houses on the street before Spinelli's, which had a blow-up rock-and-roll Santa smack in the middle of the front lawn. He expected Ellie's draftees from the diner would have started flagging, but they were singing with the same enthusiasm they'd started with.

And then they headed up Spinelli's walkway. As the winter moon shone down, the armed cops waited for their chance, Christmas carols filled the air and the woman he loved had her arm through his and was holding on tightly. Totally surreal, and he was going to remember this for the rest of his life. Whether that was ten minutes or fifty years remained to be seen.

Ellie stepped forward and knocked loudly on Spinelli's door, and the choir switched to "Do You Hear What I Hear?" which Fitz thought was particularly prescient. The door opened, and Spinelli stood there, dressed in a Santa suit, no wig on his balding head, smiling at them with benevolence until his eyes narrowed and he recognized Fitz.

It was only a blink, and everyone else would have missed it, thank God. Spinelli, the old ham, immediately joined in the singing, louder than anyone, and then bellowed loud enough for half the town to hear him, "Come in, friends, and let me get you something to eat!"

Like the freaking ghost of Christmas present, Fitz thought. The choir surged closer, blocking the doorway, and Ellie yanked his arm and they ducked into the house while the others kept singing like lunatics.

"No?" Spinelli bellowed, playing to the audience. "Well, merry Christmas, friends. Don't stay out too long." He closed the door behind them and turned to face Ellie and Fitz, a gun in his white-gloved hand.

CHAPTER SEVEN

"DAMN, SPINELLI, you're not going to try to shoot me, are you?" Fitz said, sounding exhausted, while Ellie stood there, frozen.

"Hell, no," the balding Santa Claus said, shoving the gun in the wide black patent leather belt of his costume. "Who's she?"

"The bride."

"You got married?" Spinelli said, clearly shocked.

"Not my bride," Fitz clarified.

"Not anyone's bride," Ellie snapped, annoyed by all this. "I'm Ellie Pollard, Fitz's hostage."

"You don't look that unwilling," Spinelli pointed out. "And is that a love bite on your neck?" He turned to Fitz. "What the hell you been doing, son?"

The noisy caroling was growing fainter as the carolers moved away, and Ellie didn't have much hope that they'd keep up the charade much longer. And sooner or later the cops staking out the place would realize the group of carolers had gotten smaller and they'd come looking.

"What the hell have you been doing?" Fitz demanded. "Why are you dressed up like Santa?"

"I volunteer at the senior center every Christmas. Bet you didn't know your old partner had such a sentimental streak. I know you'd rather be caught dead than dressed up like Santa Claus."

"I wouldn't say that," Ellie said. "Shouldn't we be getting out of here?"

"Good point, little lady." He was looking at her approvingly, though Ellie had no idea what he was approving of, and at six feet tall she'd never considered herself a little lady, but what the hell. "I don't know if I've got enough to nail O'Bannion for anything other than being a dirty cop. I've got documents, records of all the sleazy crap he's been pulling for the last ten years, but that's not gonna convict him of murder and grand larceny."

"Why didn't you turn him in?" Ellie asked, mystified. "If you knew he was a crook, why didn't you tell someone?"

"She needs to understand about cops if she's going to marry one," Spinelli said. "We don't rat on each other if we can help it. We handle these things internally. It's only because things got this bad that I knew I had to make a move."

"Who's going to marry a cop?" Ellie demanded, as Fitz quickly interrupted.

"I owe you, Max," Fitz said, taking the manila envelope and shoving it under his sweatshirt—the one with the Christmas tree that she knew would annoy him. He looked adorable.

"Hell, no, you don't owe me. You saved my life at least a half a dozen times over the years. I'm just sorry things had to get to this point. Tell you what you should do—the two of you head out the back onto the beach. There's a break in the fence about half a mile up. You can circle around and get the hell out of here while I figure out the best way to handle this. Until we have proof of what O'Bannion's been doing we'll have to lay low."

"Are you going to be okay?" Ellie asked.

"Hell, those boys wouldn't dare…" A look of surprise passed over his face, and his words stopped midsentence. She heard the belated sound of the window shattering, and clutching his chest, Spinelli fell. She tried to catch him, but Fitz was ahead of her, lowering the old man to the ground with surprising gentleness. Outside the cops were shouting, and she could hear them pounding on the door. Fitz jumped up, dragging her with him.

"We have to get the hell out of here."

"I can't leave him," she said. "I need to see how badly he's hurt."

"He's either too far gone for you to make any difference or a few minutes won't matter. He wouldn't want you to endanger yourself. Come on."

He wasn't giving her a choice in the matter—he was hauling her through the darkened house, through what must have been the kitchen and out the back door, onto the moonlit stretch of sand.

She could hear voices shouting behind her, and then nothing but the rush of icy wind in her ears as he dragged her across the sand in a forced run. She heard something zip past her, and she looked back for a moment to see the two cops struggling through the sand, coming after them.

"Keep going," Fitz said, breathless, not slowing for a moment.

There was another gunshot, this one louder, and she knew the cops were gaining on them, knew they'd be aiming for Fitz. They'd go for a headshot, and there'd be nothing she could do for him, and she couldn't let that happen.

Another crack, and Fitz stumbled. Without thinking she threw herself at him, knocking him to the ground, covering him as gunshots filled the air. She buried her head in his shoulder, expecting him to put his hands on her arms and shove her off, but he didn't move, and she was afraid he was already dead.

And suddenly all was silence. She kept her eyes closed,

breathing in the night air, and then she realized Fitz's chest was rising and falling beneath hers. She opened her eyes, and he was looking up at her, an odd expression on his face.

"Why did you do that?" he whispered.

"I didn't want them to kill you," she said.

He managed a slow, bemused smile. "Bride, you still manage to surprise me."

"It's Ellie," she said.

"It's Bride," he said, cupping her face with his hands and kissing her.

"That you, Fitzpatrick?" a voice called out.

She jerked away in panic, but Fitz simply sat up, still holding on to her. "It's me, Harry. How did you know where to find us?"

Fitz scrambled to his feet, pulling Ellie with him. The man standing there was older, relaxed, and behind him she could see the two cops down on the sand, with half a dozen uniforms moving around. "Ellie, this is my uncle Harry. He's with IAD."

"Internal Affairs," the older man clarified.

"How's Spinelli?" Ellie asked.

"He'll be fine. He was wearing a vest—an old cop never forgets his tricks. I'm afraid those two scumbag cops aren't saying a word, and I wouldn't hold my breath waiting for them to spill. So far we haven't got enough to touch O'Bannion."

Fitz cursed. "What else do you need?"

"It's not up to you anymore. You need to take this little lady and stay low for a while. Get the heck out of Dodge."

"Dodge?" Ellie echoed. "I thought we were in Maine?"

Fitz's uncle chuckled. "She's cute, Jimmy-boy. Better than you deserve. You treat her right or your ma will have your ears. Take her somewhere safe and warm while we clean up this mess. O'Bannion's going to want to shut you both up if he can."

He looked at Ellie. "You're Australian. It's summer in Australia, isn't it? Great place for a honeymoon, out of danger and all."

"What the hell are you talking about?" Ellie demanded, incensed. "He's not taking me anywhere."

Harry beamed at her. "She's a firecracker, isn't she? Any Irish in her?"

"I forgot to ask," Fitz said, sounding bemused.

"I'm betting on it." He took Ellie's cold hand and shook it vigorously. "Nice to meet you, Ellie. Welcome to the family."

"What?" she shrieked, but he was already heading back to the group of men waiting for him. She turned to Fitz. "What was he talking about?"

"He seems to have gotten the impression that you're my girlfriend. Actually, it sounded more like he thinks I'm going to marry you. I have to warn you, Uncle Harry is well known to possess 'the gift.' No one argues with him when he makes one of his pronouncements."

"But that's ridiculous. You're not going to marry me...."

He was shaking his head. "You don't argue with Uncle Harry," he said again. "And besides, I've always wanted to see Australia. And you can still be a Christmas bride. Mine."

"Did a bullet hit you in the head when I wasn't looking?" she demanded, exasperated.

"No."

"Are you seriously asking me to marry you?"

He looked amused. "I guess I am."

"And you expect me to say yes?"

"I do."

She looked at him for a long, contemplative moment. He'd kidnapped her, insulted her, dragged her hundreds of miles at gunpoint and nearly gotten her killed. She needed to get as far away from such a crazy man as she could.

Except she wanted to stay right there. "I do," she said.

He looked at her warily. "You do?"

"I do," she said, moving closer, and he pulled her into his arms, kissing her.

There was a roar of approval from down the beach, a rushing noise in the back of Ellie's head, but it didn't matter. She'd found her way home, and she was there to stay.

* * * * *

CAUGHT AT CHRISTMAS

Tina Leonard

Many thanks to the wonderful Anne Stuart and the fabulous Marion Lennox for being awesome and kind to this "newbie"—this was the most fun project! Also great appreciation and a sincere thank-you to Kathleen Scheibling for pulling me, Marsha Zinberg for being wonderful and patient, and Margaret Learn for fabulous editing. Also appreciation to Alexandra Patrikios for her invaluable assistance, and Georgia Haynes for helping with last-minute reads. There are a lot of other wonderful people who deserve thanks at Harlequin, and gratitude goes to them, as well. As always, so much of my success comes from being supported by a wonderful family: my husband, Tim, and my children, Lisa and Dean. Happy holidays and blessings to all!

CHAPTER ONE

JEAN NORVILLE was dressed like a velvet grape, complete with purple hoop skirts and silver trim. Yes, she was a grape, bursting with Christmas cheer and wedding wishes.

Like hell. The tight-waisted Southern belle bridesmaid gown was hideous—it had to be viscose and not a good silk velvet. But she would have worn it with pleasure if any holiday spirit she'd possessed hadn't gone out the window when she'd met Connor O'Bannion, the man Molly, her best friend from college, was to marry. Ten days before Christmas was a terrible time to be thinking Scrooge-like thoughts, but from what she'd seen of the groom and his groomsmen, they looked more like bad elves hiding from Santa than detectives with the Boston P.D.

To be fair, since this was her second maid-of-honor role this year, her fourteenth lifetime opportunity to serve at a friend's big moment—but who was counting?—she wasn't exactly the poster girl for wedding enthusiasm. There was also a possibility she'd read one too many Agatha Christies in her career as a librarian and was seeing trouble where there was none. Yet she was pretty certain that despite the lightly falling snow and the white Christmas lights twinkling around the Southfork Texas Wedding Chapel, there was very little romance in the air. That feeling had intensified last night at the rehearsal dinner party when she'd overheard Connor in the gardens angrily talking to someone on his cell phone. "Find the diamonds, kill the kids, end of story is how I figure."

It hadn't seemed like a very warm and fuzzy thing to say at Christmas, or anytime. Jean had accidentally caught Connor's gaze, his eyes narrowing at her. She pretended she hadn't heard a thing, smiled and airily departed.

Since then, all kinds of horrible misgivings had risen in her imagination. Surely she had misheard. She shouldn't take a remark out of context when she hadn't heard the other end of the conversation.

Likely she was suffering from wedding jitters the bride should be having. She should have stayed in New England and sent an expensive gift if she was going to be such a grumpy attendant.

The wedding was late getting started. Molly had just arrived a few minutes ago and Jean had had to tell her that Connor was not here yet. The wedding guests were inside, the wedding party was about to make the triumphal entry into the rose-and-ivy-festooned chapel and the groom was a no-show. That was cause for real concern, not the fact that she had to wear the grape velvet dress that Letitia, Connor's pretentious mother, had chosen.

Jean faked a serene, maid-of-honor smile.

"Cheer up," she heard behind her. She turned to see Molly's brother, Sam Broadbent, looking down at her, no smile gracing his handsome face.

"Right back at you." Jean clutched her huge bouquet more tightly, ignoring the zing she felt at seeing the handsome Texas Ranger. Why did the man have to be so sexy in a formal tuxedo? Dark, delicious, tall and strong; just the way a hero in a Western should look.

She didn't know a lot about Sam—he and Molly hadn't been extraordinarily close as kids. Sam was a lot older to begin with, and though their parents had been wealthy, they'd fought a lot and there hadn't been much love to go around. Molly and Sam were working on their relationship now, finding new pleasure in forging sibling bonds. She knew Sam was independent. Molly had told her he was burned out, and was giving the job a break for a while. Maybe a permanent break. He planned on enjoying ranch life—and he wasn't dating anyone, her friend confided with a sisterly wink that Jean had ignored at the time.

Her attention was caught by sudden whispers, pointing fingers. Four or five police cars pulled into the parking lot in view of the wedding party, doors slamming as officers jumped out. Loud cracks like fireworks shattered the nervous chatter of the bridal party. Heads turned, then screaming broke out. The rapping pops continued, and people began running in every direction.

Too stunned to move, Jean felt relief wash over her when Sam grabbed her, dragging her away from the chapel. Her skimpy strappy sandals were only meant to look pretty, not actually be functional. The dreaded hoop skirts ballooned around her legs awkwardly. "Wait!" She jerked away from Sam. "What are you doing?"

Cries rang out behind them, underlining the urgency. Realizing she wasn't going to be a willing escapee, Sam scooped her into his arms. He did it without grimacing, for which Jean gave him high marks. The hoop skirts weren't made for hustling down the pebbled path toward the parking lot. "You're supposed to be giving away a bride, not hauling off a maid of honor."

He put her down and unlocked a silver Mercedes. "Think the plans changed. Get in."

She did as he asked. It wasn't easy, considering she had

to fight the skirts for every inch of the seat. "What's happening? Should we be leaving? Molly's supposed to get married in a few—"

"Don't think she'll be a bride tonight." Sam pulled out of the parking lot, swiftly heading away from the chapel. "Get down so you don't get hit by a bullet. Stay down until I've got you far away from the action."

She refused to accept that Molly's lovely fairy-tale wedding had turned into a nightmare. "I didn't see guns!"

"You weren't looking for guns. But trust me, there were plenty." He eyed the road behind them in his rearview mirror. She realized he was deadly serious. As a Ranger, he knew better than she the sounds of weapons being fired.

He was driving fast, his body tense. And then she got it: Sam was rescuing her from danger. "You left your sister! Turn around and go get Molly!"

His cell phone rang. He tapped the speakerphone on. "It's Sam."

"Molly's fine."

He breathed a sigh. "Thanks."

"No problem. Do you have the maid of honor?"

"I do. What's going on back there with the bust?"

Jean listened, her heart racing.

"Right now, we're just trying to make sure everybody's all right. Sorry about your sister's wedding. Wish it could have happened a different way." Whoever was on the phone sighed. "Hey, get the maid of honor somewhere far away, okay? We need her safe."

Sam was silent for a moment. "Can do."

"Three of the groomsmen were taken away in handcuffs, but a couple escaped, along with Morrissey. Everybody saw Tommy Morrissey shooting, but there were other shooters, mass chaos. Until we know more, we're keeping everybody in the wedding party protected."

"Where's Molly?" Sam demanded.

Jean leaned forward so she could hear every word.

"We've got her covered. She wasn't hit. Like I said, she's fine. We'll take care of your girl—you just take care of the maid of honor. Unfortunately, they're on to her."

Jean's breath left. She felt faint. Sam clicked the phone off.

"Feel better?" he asked.

"Why did you grab me and not your sister? You should've protected Molly!"

"Molly was covered. I trusted the men who were looking out for her. Our information suggested you had inadvertently become a problem."

He must be confusing her with someone else. She was in no danger.

"No one would want to hurt me!"

"We think Connor might have discovered his cover was blown at the rehearsal dinner. He ran, and his henchmen must have figured he'd left them holding the bag."

"None of that has anything to do with me."

He didn't answer, which infuriated her. He simply didn't understand that they needed to be worrying about Molly. She must be in shock—what bride wouldn't be with a shoot-out at her wedding? "Where are you taking me?"

"To my ranch. I can keep an eye on you there."

She started to protest, then remembered the person on the phone had requested that Sam get her "far away." Yet she wasn't exactly comfortable about being on a ranch out in heaven-knew-where. All she had was this stupid dress—not that clothes were the most pressing of concerns, but what she wouldn't give for a worn pair of jeans and maybe some UGG boots. And she was Molly's maid of honor, right? Supposed to be taking care of the bride on her big day? "There's no place else I could stay?" Preferably somewhere away from Sam's watchful vision, so she could go find Molly and make sure she was really all right.

He turned onto the highway and hit the gas, putting distance between them and the ruined wedding. "Until the coast is clear, you're my guest."

Guest. "Just for a day," she said, scrambling to sound normal, as if she hadn't just been at a wedding where guns were fired. It was the only way to calm herself.

He didn't say anything. "Poor Molly," Jean said. "Her wedding day ruined. What was that about groomsmen in handcuffs?"

"Several men at the wedding had concealed weapons. You didn't notice the bulges under the jackets?"

"I can't say that I did."

"We'd already made some phone calls," Sam said, "to check for gun permits. It seemed suspicious for firearms to be at my sister's wedding. I mentioned it to a buddy. Some cops were called in to quietly keep an eye on things. They were the guys who weren't wearing tuxes. They stayed out of sight until the shooting started."

"Maybe it was a mistake," Jean suggested. "It doesn't make sense that this wedding would be targeted. A wedding is supposed to be a happy, romantic occasion." She still couldn't accept that criminal activity had disrupted her best friend's ceremony.

He pulled into a truck stop. "We have a two-hour drive ahead of us, in case you're interested."

She glanced around at the packed truck stop. "What are we doing here?"

"I'm going to grab some water bottles and snacks in case you get hungry. There aren't tons of fast-food places along the highway, and I'm presuming you don't want to go out to eat in what you're wearing."

She glanced down at her dress and shook her head. "Nor you, I imagine."

He grimaced in agreement. "No man wears a tux willingly. I'll grab some food."

Sam might be unwilling, but he looked great as he walked into the truck stop in his tux. He had a strong, tall bearing, an easy walk. He was taller even than her surgeon father, which was saying something. *Dad's six foot one, just right for hanging the star on the Christmas tree,* she thought wistfully. She should be home now with her family, making holiday preparations. Her stay-at-home mom would be baking Christmas cookies with her younger twin sisters, Trudy and Starla, twenty-four and just learning how to take care of their first apartment, which was only an hour from the family home, of course. Gigi, the golden retriever, would be scampering around the house wearing her traditional loopy red bow. The stairwell would be trimmed with red and gold velvet ribbons….

She made herself quit thinking about holidays and home. There was no way she could get there just yet—Sam had said she wasn't going anywhere for a while.

A truck with Vermont license plates caught her attention. A large, strong blond woman got down out of the cab to check her tires. Jean wondered if she dared approach the trucker for a ride. Of course she had no purse and no ID since they'd left the wedding in a hurry. She didn't have a cell phone. *C'mon,* a small voice egged, *you're an independent woman. Don't let a silly purple dress slow you down!*

Wouldn't she be safer in New England than in Texas,

anyway? It was kind of dramatic to assume that she needed protection—no one had been shooting at *her*.

"Don't even think about it," Sam said, getting into the car. "When I saw those Vermont plates, I figured you'd consider hitching a ride."

She wrinkled her nose at him. "In this dress?"

He laughed and handed her a water bottle. "Just admit that's exactly what you were thinking and don't be annoyed you're so easy to read. You wear your emotions on your face."

"If you escorted me home, it would solve everyone's dilemma. I'd be with my family, and you'd still be doing your bodyguard job. Not to mention my mom's an incredible cook, especially around Christmas. We're nothing if not addicted to the season."

"And what if—just theorizing for a moment—what if you're part of something you haven't realized?" Sam said reasonably. "What if someone wanted to shut you up? And followed you home?" He glanced over at her. "Would you want to put your family in danger?"

"Of course not! But that's a Hollywood plot, Sam. No one is going to care that I was at the wedding. And everybody there was an eyewitness."

"But to what, exactly?"

She sighed. "I don't know what you're getting at, but you're being overly concerned. Molly always said you were a very cautious person who was hard to get to know."

For some reason that made him smile. "Molly was too easy to get to know."

He was right. Molly had had lots of friends in college—she naturally drew people to her. "You're a more likely target than me. Dark, cynical ex-Ranger, taking a leave for unknown reasons… Maybe you ticked someone off?"

Her voice sounded hopeful, and he smiled. "Dark and cynical? Did Molly say that?"

"It's an observation on my part." She wasn't going to expand the description by telling Sam that he was also handsome, sexy, smelled good, had nice hands... She tore her gaze away and looked out the window at the blur of lights. Very little else was visible in the darkness, just lights along the highway, marking how far she was from home.

"I don't think I was the target," Sam said. "There are too many chances to get to me besides following me to a wedding."

"True." Jean shook her head. "Anyway, Connor seems seedy to me. You don't seem to like him, either. Any particular reason?"

Sam shrugged. "I don't know. I think I always saw Molly settling down with someone more...caring. That's the word that keeps coming to my mind. I just never got the sense deep down that Connor loved Molly for Molly."

"That's interesting," Jean murmured, "I never got the sense that Molly loved Connor with all her heart. And I was uneasy from the moment I met him." She remembered his eyes when he'd stared at her...hard, cold and flat. "He didn't seem like the kind of guy who would want an outgoing woman like Molly."

Sam grinned. "You're not exactly a shy flower yourself, for a librarian. Shouldn't you be bookish and quiet?"

She looked at him. "Are you saying I'm talkative? By your definition?"

He chuckled. "I think it's fair to say that this Christmas season will be the most lively my ranch has seen."

"I'm not your Christmas party," Jean said, her tone unamused. "Even if this misunderstanding hasn't been straightened out, in forty-eight hours we're either flying or driving to New England to my family."

Sam was silent, ignoring her demand. Jean glanced out into the darkness. She felt as if they were traveling into a black hole—not a great feeling at Christmas. "So when you said you live out in the country, you meant far-out, uninhabited country."

"We have a stop sign in our town."

One stop sign. That meant there must be about ten residents, Jean thought glumly, not even enough for a powder-puff football game. "Is there a reason you live so far away from civilization, Sam?"

"I like it," he said simply. "It gives me peace."

She would never be happy with *that* much "peace." "I should thank you for being worried about my safety. I've just never been good with having my independence hijacked. Even when I was a child, I wanted to do everything myself. At least that's what my parents say."

"Molly says that's one of the things she admires about you. That go-getter thing you've got going on is energizing to people around you. And it's a warning that I'll have to keep a *very* close eye on you."

The warning sounded like a sexy promise to her. Jean felt her whole body unexpectedly heat. She reviewed her situation: Alone with a very good-looking man out in the middle of nowhere.

Women dreamed of Santa dropping a dreamboat like Sam under their Christmas tree—but she wasn't daring enough to consider unwrapping him.

CHAPTER TWO

SAM BROADBENT was well aware that Molly's maid of honor had misgivings about him. It was obvious that Jean was worried about Molly, more than anything. But if there wasn't going to be a wedding—and from what he could tell, there was no way in hell his sister was going to be O'Bannion's bride—Jean clearly wanted to be at home for the holidays with her family.

Being somewhat of a loner, he didn't share those sentimental feelings. He didn't send cards or get a tree. Most times he worked through Christmas, opting to let his fellow Rangers have a day with their families.

He pulled into the garage and helped Jean from the car so she wouldn't trip on the ridiculous gown. "I have a hard time imagining Molly condemning her best friend to that dress."

"She didn't. Her future mother-in-law did." Jean got out as gracefully as she could, seeming happy for his assistance.

"Yet another reason to reconsider her choice of groom," he said. "Poor taste in the family tree."

Jean smiled. "You and I agree on something."

"Finally." Opening the door, he motioned Jean inside. "This is a pretty standard ranch house. Here you have a laundry room, kitchen, family den, bedrooms down that hall."

She viewed all the rooms as he flipped the lights on, then

slowly turned to him. "You must have been too busy to start your holiday decorating."

He shook his head. "Nope."

She blinked. He had to admit that, despite the gown, she was an attractive woman. He'd like to know what her hair really looked like when it wasn't in that overdone shellacked twist. Even running from gunfire hadn't dislodged it. She was pretty, fine-boned and didn't wear a lot of makeup. It was obvious she was built well from the waist up, but the skirt definitely did a great job of hiding her other charms.

"*Nope* what? You haven't been too busy?"

He walked to the fireplace, tossed some logs in, reached for a fire starter. It was a bit chilly in the house; the weather was colder this December than usual. She was going to be very uncomfortable without boots and other warm gear. "I've never put up a tree."

She looked around the room, turning to meet his gaze. "Oh."

Her tone was so disappointed that he tried to put himself in her place for a moment. "I work a lot. Never had a lot of time. Plus, I always figured decorating was a woman thing. Molly sends me a box of holiday junk every year, though."

"Molly would. She loves the holidays."

He remembered. Despite their lack of closeness now, they had shared a few happy childhood holidays. "Let me get you a pair of my warm-up pants and some socks so you can get out of that costume."

"Thank you."

"This will be your bedroom," he said, leading the way, "and bath. There are towels in the cabinet, fresh sheets on the bed. You'll find new toothbrushes in the top drawer, as well as a hairbrush."

"I feel like I'm at a nice hotel."

Her smile was wobbly. He could tell she was trying to be polite. "I like to keep the amenities stocked for my friends." He disappeared down the hall, returned with some clothes. "This is the best I have that might fit you. It's at least warmer than what you have on, and I would bet more comfortable."

He handed the clothes to her and disappeared to give her some privacy. A moment later she came out wearing his sweats. She'd taken her hair down, brushed it free of spray, put it into a soft, attractive ponytail. "Better?" he asked.

"Much."

Nodding, he went into the kitchen to put a kettle on. "Coffee? Hot tea?"

"Tea, please."

Sam got out some mugs.

"You're not going to give an inch about taking me back to Vermont, are you?"

He shook his head. "Would you prefer something harder? Wine? Vodka and juice?"

"No thanks. I always reach for tea when I'm upset. I'm still rattled by what happened tonight, so I'll stick with my usual routine."

His cell phone buzzed. "My sister," he said, "checking on you, if I know Molly." He read the text, then grinned. "She says to tell you she's fine, which, given the fact that her wedding was ruined, is not entirely the truth. She got your belongings from the hotel and is sending them out tomorrow. She wants you to lie low until everything blows over, and says she's sorry she got you involved in this."

Jean frowned. "Molly didn't know criminals were going to be at her wedding."

He put his phone away. "It's pretty typical of Molly to put on a brave face."

Then he caught it, something he hadn't noticed right off: Jean was trembling. Ever so slightly. He didn't think it was because of the chill in the house. Quietly, he went to turn the heat up a couple of notches. He kept it low out of habit; until lately he'd been working a lot and rarely home. When he returned, he gave her his most unassuming, boy-next-door face. "Jean, are you all right?"

She rubbed her arms. "I thought I was. I think I am," she added, "but all of a sudden, I feel strangely overwhelmed."

Shock. She'd finally allowed herself to acknowledge the danger everyone had been in today and shock had taken over. It was a perfectly normal, understandable reaction. "Why don't you sit down, and I'll get you something stronger than tea?"

"No," she said, "I think I should just go to bed."

"Good idea. Down the hall, in the back." She knew where her room was, but he figured it didn't hurt to remind her.

She made it as far as the hallway before turning around to look at him. The expression in her eyes killed him. She was afraid, though she didn't want to admit it.

"I promise you're safe here," he stated.

"I know. And I appreciate everything you're doing for me. You should be taking care of your sister instead."

"Actually, since I'm technically not on the force anymore, I'm not part of the team assigned to my sister and her fiancé. Anything to do with this case would not be handled by me."

"Maybe tomorrow we'll find that everything has been a whopping big mistake."

He didn't want to give her false hope—there had been too much gunfire to make him believe that matters would be sewn up nicely in one day—but he also didn't want her more upset than she already was.

"So is this a pullout sofa?" she asked, looking at the leather furniture in the fireplace room.

"It is."

"I was just wondering," she said quickly, "because you said you frequently have guests, and I figured—"

"You don't want to sleep in the guest room?"

She shook her head. "It feels claustrophobic, for some reason. Not that I've ever had a panic attack, but when I think about going down the hall and being alone, I start to feel strange. Like I can't breathe. Is that a panic attack?"

He pulled out the sofa bed. "Sounds like symptoms of not being real happy that you got shot at when you were expecting to be throwing rose petals at a bride. Also could mean you have a fear of being alone with a man you don't know very well, in a place with which you're not familiar." Grabbing some pillows from a linen closet, he tossed them on the bed, along with some sheets. "This is a very comfortable bed. You'll be able to relax out here. The stars shine through the drapes, or if you don't like the light, you can close the—"

"Light sounds wonderful," she interrupted. "Thank you, Sam. I can make my bed."

"Okay, then. Anything else I can do to make you comfortable?"

She industriously shook out a sheet and spread it on the mattress. "I hate that I'm taking up your time with my panic attack. Please text Molly back and tell her not to worry about me." She drew a deep, bracing breath. "I'm fine."

"The only thing I'm worried about is that you might take the notion to leave."

She raised her head up as she stopped smoothing down the sheet. "The only way I'm leaving here is in your car."

He briefly made a note to keep his keys on him at all times, then realized she meant when he took her back to the city. He looked at her, gauging her emotions. "The thought seemed to have crossed your mind at the truck stop."

"Well, yes, but…where would I go? I don't even know where I am."

"You're in Penn County, Texas, in a town called Penn. Named after Mr. and Mrs. Carl Penn, who settled it with their German family in the 1800s."

She crossed her arms, unsuccessfully trying to hold in a shiver. "I have faith everything's going to be straightened out in time to get me home for Christmas."

"I'll drive you to the airport and put you on the plane myself," he promised.

"I'm holding you to that. I need to call my sisters, by the way. My family doesn't watch a lot of television, but by now they may have heard about the wedding from friends who saw the evening news. I don't want them to tell Mom."

He handed her his phone. "Maybe you could just reassure them that you've gone away with a friend for a few days until everything blows over a little, to keep them from worrying."

Jean hesitated, then dialed the phone. He left the room for a minute to give her privacy, knowing how hard this call had to be for her. Ten minutes later, when he couldn't hear the murmur of her soft voice, he went to check on her.

He had to admit Jean looked pretty crushed, and he hated to see her so low. She was reclining on the bed, her back propped up against the pillows, staring out the big window. "The view is so pretty," she said, her tone dispirited. "Miles and miles of uninterrupted peace."

He sat nearby, seeing the same landscape that held her focus. "The house faces north, so from this direction I get a wide view of unoccupied farmland and vast skies. I bought this house just for that reason."

"What will you do when someone buys that land?"

He shook his head. "I took care of that problem and bought it myself."

She sighed, then looked at him. "I feel so sorry for Molly."

He did, too. He felt for Jean, as well, noticing she still seemed unable to relax. He didn't know what to do to help her. "Would you mind if I pull up an armchair and sit here with you? Until you fall asleep?"

She gave him a grateful glance but disguised it by saying, "Keeping a close eye on me, Ranger?"

It didn't hurt to play along, act like he hadn't noticed she was as stiff as a poker. "Gotta do my job."

"Pull up your chair, then."

He did. "So what would you be doing right now in New England?"

"Well, at this hour, just breathing in the scents of home," she said wistfully. "Cinnamon, gingerbread, coffee. I'd be addressing Christmas cards. Wrapping gifts and hiding them in closets so no one will find them before Santa has a chance to put them under the tree. In the morning, my mom and I might go to Macy's looking for gifts and decorations."

He leaned back in the chair he'd pulled over to the side of the bed. "Sounds like fun."

She glanced at him, detecting the sarcasm that had accidentally rolled off his tongue. "You really are a Grinch, aren't you?"

He winked at her. "You just told me what the girls are doing. Fill me in on the guy activities, and maybe I'll be less Grinchy."

"My dad would be watching football on TV. He'd get called upon for various duties, like hanging the star on the tree, wiring the outside lights and unstopping the kitchen drain."

"That's a Christmas tradition at your house? Clogging the sink?"

She nodded. "The holidays haven't begun until Dad's gotten out the plunger."

He shook his head. "Go on."

"We stock the freezer with cookies—"

"You're supposed to be telling me about the guys' part in the festivities."

"Dad helps with the baking," Jean told him. "He loves eating cookie dough. Cookies fresh from the oven. All the treats my mom puts in front of him. Santa, she always says, needs his strength."

"Okay." He leaned back, closed his eyes. "You convinced me I'm missing out. Tomorrow I'll let you bake me some cookies. I'll eat the batter."

She gazed out at the stars, not replying. He thought she seemed less tense, so he opted to let her digest her thoughts. After a while, her eyes closed, then she snapped them open and stared at him in the dimness. "Thank you for everything."

He shrugged, not about to say it was his duty, because it wasn't. It was more like a favor to his sister. Besides, he was enjoying Jean's company.

"You don't really think…"

"What?" He watched her, waiting.

"You don't really think I could be in any danger, right? You're just being overly cautious?"

"It wasn't me being overly cautious. I'm sure you'll be questioned, though, so the appropriate law-enforcement officials can try to figure out exactly what happened."

"You were there, too. You saw as much as I did, maybe more."

She was trying to get out of staying for an extended period. "They'll want to be thorough."

She sat up. "I think I'd know if I heard something, saw something—"

"I understand you're nervous. And a little scared. It's a very weird situation you've been thrown into."

"This is my last maid-of-honor gig!" she exclaimed, suddenly defiant, shaking a mental fist at her fears. "Something bizarre always happens. I don't even want to think about what might happen if I were ever the unfortunate bride!"

He laughed. "Go to sleep. You'll feel better when the sun comes up." The moon shone in the glittery cold sky. He focused on that, reminding himself that this view brought him peace. It had always been enough for him: the country air, the freedom, the night sky. But the panicked female in his pullout sofa bed wasn't altogether a bother. She talked just enough—not too much, not too little—and she had grit and a sort of no-nonsense appeal about her. She was feminine, from her soft blond ponytail to her upturned, freckled little nose. "You're okay company."

"Well, thank you," she murmured, her eyes closing. "You're all right yourself. Which I find a little surprising, considering that Molly warned me that you…" She opened her eyes, stared at him.

"Yes?" he prompted softly.

"Can be a wee bit difficult to get along with."

He grinned. "I'll have to rib her for that when I see her."

"Why'd you quit the force?" she asked suddenly. "If it's not too personal."

"Needed a break."

"Ah. And yet here I am, another job."

"No." He shook his head. "You're a guest."

"Right." She sighed, sounding more content. "Suddenly, I could fall asleep on a bed of rocks."

He was glad she was calming down. "Go right ahead. Tell me if you need another blanket or anything." He settled back.

"Are you going to sleep in that chair?"

"For a while. Then I'll head to bed. I'll be just down the hall if you need something."

"Oh, for heaven's sake," she said, "this is silly. Nothing's going to happen, and I'm being a ninny. Go get in your own bed before you give yourself a backache sitting up in that chair. I think I've figured out this much about you—you'll tell me you're going to your own bed to lull me to sleep and then you'll stay in the chair all night."

"I'm used to snoozing in far worse places."

"Still." She waved a hand, indicating he should head toward the hallway. "As you said, I can yell if I get spooked."

A coyote let out a long howl, the sound curling into the room with intensity. Jean's eyes went wide. Sam tried not to smile.

"I thought you didn't have any neighbors close by."

He shook his head. "That's not a neighborhood pooch. Coyote."

"Coyote!" She sat straight up. "He's much too close to the house!"

"You weren't planning on taking a walk, were you?" He crossed his arms over his chest and closed his eyes, unable to wipe the grin off his face. "He wants no part of you, anyway, even if you did go outside."

"Well, I'm not planning to. You don't have to worry about that!"

She flipped over, her long hair trailing across the pillow. He could see her curves under the sheet and blanket; a lump rose in his throat. It had been a long time since a woman had graced his house. Too long. He missed female companionship. Jean was fun, and handling her circumstances well. As he'd said, he didn't mind her being here at all. "I always wondered why Molly chose Connor. They seemed to enjoy each other, but I felt it was more of a convenient thing than a real once-in-a-lifetime love affair."

"I'm not sure a woman always believes that there's a Mr. Right," Jean said.

"You're not suggesting she was just 'making do' with Connor because she didn't feel she'd meet Mr. Right?"

Jean shook her head. "I can't speak to Molly's emotions. She may truly love him. Of course, if he's truly Molly's Mr. Right, where was he tonight?"

"I have a bad feeling about that I'm not willing to share right now."

"You're thinking he might have been kidnapped by the goons who shot up the wedding?"

Sam frowned. "Perhaps he's behind the whole thing."

Jean gasped. She opened her mouth to deny his statement, then hesitated. "When we were at the restaurant Friday night for the rehearsal dinner, I went outside to get some fresh air. I saw Tommy Morrissey—the best man—and Connor outside arguing. I walked away, but later when I went back—it was cold outside and I'd had all the fresh air I could stand—I heard Connor talking on his cell phone." Jean's words were slow as she thought back to the night before.

"And?"

"He was angry with whomever he was talking to. He said something about—" She closed her eyes for a moment, remembering. "'Find the diamonds, kill the kids, end of story is how I figure.'" She opened her eyes, meeting Sam's dark gaze. "Those were his exact words." She sat up, worried all over again. "I should have realized something was wrong. But I was so shocked, Sam. I told myself he was joking, but he

seemed mad that I was nearby, as if he didn't want me to over-
hear. I smiled and acted like I hadn't heard a thing, because
it was Molly's wedding and I wanted her to be happy, and even
if she was marrying a toad, I would keep my opinions to myself." Jean's voice turned slightly panicked. "Only maybe I
shouldn't have."

Sam got out of his chair, pushed her down into the bed
gently, started rubbing her back like he would an upset child.
"Jean, Molly does what Molly wants. She's a big girl."

"True," Jean said, "but still—"

"Still nothing. Put it out of your mind for the moment. With
any luck, you'll be on a plane sooner than later."

"What if the kids Connor was talking about, and this is just
really wild and random, what if he meant his own nieces and
nephew? Charlie, Lily and Zoe? The little wedding attendants.
They were so proud of participating in Molly's wedding."

She stared at Sam, her blue eyes wide as her thoughts
raced. Sam let her talk, knowing that a good cop knew how
to listen at the right times—and sometimes the right time was
when a victim was talking. And remembering.

He shrugged. "Keep going."

She looked completely panicked now. "Maybe those children
were put in harm's way because I didn't speak up. I just wanted
everything to be so beautiful for Molly. But maybe I put Charlie,
Lily and Zoe in danger with my silence, because I would never
have suspected Connor would harm his own family."

He shrugged. "Who do you think would have believed you
if you'd told them what you heard? How would it have
changed anything?"

She shook her head. "I suppose you're right…although I'm
well aware you're trying to make me feel better."

"Not necessarily. I'm a Ranger, not the Good Humor man."

Sam narrowed his eyes. "I have to say I didn't pay much attention to the children, although I did notice they seemed to like my sister."

"There's Zoe, who's three. She was a flower girl. Lily is five, and she was also a flower girl. Then Charlie, who's eight. He's such a great kid—he looked so handsome in his little tux. Their great-aunt, Letitia, arranged to have them in the wedding party."

Sam nodded. "Because I haven't been properly branching out the family tree."

"So anyway—"

"Did Molly say that?"

"She said you were ten years older than she was and showed no sign of wanting to marry and have kids," Jean admitted.

The words struck an unexpected nerve. Had it bothered him that his little sister was heading down the aisle before he did? Maybe Molly was right. Had he ever really thought about being a dad? He was thirty-eight—maybe he should have considered fatherhood. "So back to the kids," he said, surrendering ground for the moment.

"This is going to be extremely difficult on them." Jean chewed on her lips, lips he realized were full and completely kissable. "Molly said they'd been through so much recently. They lost their parents in a tragic car crash...and Letitia thought being ring bearer and flower girls might cheer them up—or at least distract them. Molly was happy to include them, but they must be so shell-shocked from what happened tonight." She turned sad eyes on Sam that ripped at his gut. "Can you imagine how frightened they must be?"

"Don't think about it," he said gruffly, getting onto the bed next to her. He'd been hoping Jean wouldn't go there—as good a Ranger as he was considered to be, he was a little freaked that his sister could have taken a bullet. Just thinking about it made his gut churn acid; the cramps were slow in leaving him from the adrenaline surge. He wasn't entirely sure who'd been the target today, but the thought of losing his sister, the only person left on the planet he cared about, was not an option he wanted to consider.

If he ever got his hands on the SOBs, he'd kill them without even a twinge of remorse.

He worked the knots out of Jean's shoulders as much to comfort her as to keep himself from jumping back in his car and racing to Dallas to hand out a little vigilante justice. Yet he could not do that. No one, by the grace of God, had been harmed.

Only by the grace of God, though.

Slowly, Jean relaxed under his absent-minded massage. Five minutes later, he felt the tension ebb from her, and slowly removed his hands from her body. She had a gorgeous back, he realized, and soft skin. He wanted to touch her again, but it wasn't right; she was nearly asleep and he didn't have her permission.

He looked out the window at the moon and wondered what was wrong with him. Temptation didn't usually lure him this hard, this fast, and certainly not for a woman he was supposed to be protecting.

He forced his thoughts away from her. One thing that bothered him was the idea that Jean thought he and Molly weren't close—even Molly felt that way. But a ten-year age difference was not enough to keep him from loving his sister. He'd been an emotional coward. Taken off from home at the first opportunity, as was normal for eighteen-year-old boys. But the distance between them had never meant he didn't love her.

Reluctantly, Sam reclined against the pillow on the opposite side of the bed so Jean would feel protected. When he heard her begin to breathe in slow, rhythmic breaths, he sneaked a glance her way. The moonlight through the curtains gave a luminous glow to her face. He liked the shape of her body, the sensual slopes outlined by the blanket. Watching over Jean this closely wasn't really part of the job, but he decided he kind of liked it.

He thought again about what she'd heard Connor say on his cell phone. He'd known it was worth remembering the second the words had fallen from her bow-shaped lips. As her protector, he wasn't about to tell her she was probably on to something with those "random" thoughts of hers.

She was a witness, which she would realize sooner than later.

The anger pushed at him, and he jerked his gaze to Jean, forcefully reminding himself that she was just another assignment—not a smart, attractive woman he had a sudden overwhelming desire to hold.

Someone on the inside had known of Sam's phone call to the police, warning that Connor's buddies were carrying weapons. That same someone had let Connor know the wedding party was going to be crashed.

Which was why Molly's groom had developed *very* cold feet.

The question was…why the gunfire at the wedding? Who had been the true target? Morrissey seemed to be shooting at Jean. But what about the kids? He dismissed that. His sister? Hard to miss her in that lovely wedding gown.

Find what diamonds? Jean had mentioned overhearing Connor's threat. Diamonds and weddings were supposed to go together, but not accompanied by gunfire.

Jean rolled over in her sleep, throwing an arm across him as she snuggled against his chest. Sam stiffened. She felt wonderful lying so close to him.

He shouldn't be in bed with a possible material witness.

He was in heaven—and hell.

CHAPTER THREE

JEAN WAS ALONE when she awakened the next morning. Sam wasn't anywhere to be seen, which surprised her. She'd expected him to be hovering over her, making certain she didn't leave his watchful presence.

She had a distinct memory of feeling safe all night. In fact, if she hadn't been so bone-tired, she almost might think she remembered being safe and warm in Sam's arms.

She really had been dreaming.

Once she'd showered and dressed, she headed for the kitchen. The doorbell sounded. "Sam! It's Molly! Open up!"

Jean raced to the door, but Sam grabbed her from behind. "Oh, no, you don't," he said. "That's a great way for you to get hurt."

"It's your sister!"

"I'm aware of that." He moved her behind him. "Let's just make certain no one's with her that I reserve the right to welcome."

Jean rolled her eyes. Molly was right—Sam was totally overbearing. "Yes, sir, Mr. Ranger, sir," she muttered.

Sam opened the door. He didn't have a chance to scout the porch because Molly flung herself into his arms. "You're the best brother in the world!" Then with her typical enthusiasm, she hugged Jean tightly. "And you saved my life!"

"I did?" Just as enthusiastically, Jean returned the hug. "I'm pretty sure I didn't do anything."

"Molly, what are you doing here?" Sam demanded sternly. "Why aren't you being protected by someone? Shouldn't you be tucked away somewhere for safety?"

"I'm in good hands." She gave a little sniff. "A very nice older cop drove me out here. He says you and he go way back. I insisted Jean needed her clothes and her suitcases."

Sam sighed. "Any cop should know better than to bring you here. I have a feeling you wrapped him around your finger just to see Jean."

Jean smiled at Sam's obvious annoyance and Molly's obvious determination.

"He said not to worry," Molly assured Sam. "He's hanging around, checking the grounds."

"Great." Sam shook his head. "You're supposed to be safe somewhere until we get everything sorted out with your… with Connor."

"I'll be fine, Sam." She gave Jean a tight hug. "I'm so sorry about everything."

"Don't be sorry for me. I'm actually kind of enjoying myself." Jean didn't want her friend to agonize on her behalf.

"You can't be." Molly glanced around the living room, her gaze falling on the pullout bed. "This isn't exactly the Ritz, and Sam, where are all the Christmas decorations I sent you over the years? Boxes and boxes of them?"

Sam looked sheepish. "I'll be getting them down from the attic soon," he said apologetically.

"Did you ever even open the boxes?" Molly demanded.

"I'm going to, I am," Sam said, his gaze flicking to Jean as he headed out of the room. She grinned at him. His weak spot was definitely his sister.

"Well, I must be off," Molly said. "I'm only supposed to stay five minutes." She looked at Jean, her eyes serious. "Are you sure you're all right here? With my brother?"

"He's been the soul of good manners—really," Jean assured her. "I'm so sorry about your wedding."

"Strangely, I'm not," Molly said. "I'm worried about Letitia, and I'm worried about Zoe, Lily and Charlie."

"Where are they?"

"Right now they're with Letitia, who is either in her element with all the media attention, or having a dramatic meltdown. Depends on the moment, though I can't blame her for being upset. I'm still waiting to hear from Connor—Letitia's very worried about him, of course." Molly pointed to Jean's suitcases and purse. "Hopefully this will all be cleared up soon and you can be back in New England." She left after giving Jean one last hug. Tears filled Jean's eyes. It was just like Molly to be more worried about everyone else, instead of herself.

She was glad to have her things, though. She began hauling her cases back to her room when suddenly she realized Sam was behind her, carrying one. "You scared me!"

"Sorry," he said, "just trying to help. These things weigh a ton. Girl stuff is heavier than it should be, but I suppose that's not a gentlemanly thing to say."

She let that pass. "Molly left."

"I know. I said goodbye."

"Where'd you go?" Happily, she pulled her own jeans and a soft green sweater from a case.

"I went to talk to my buddy," he said a little too casually.

Jean turned and looked at him for a long moment. "You told him what I told you, didn't you? About what I heard Connor say?"

"Does it matter?" Sam's gaze narrowed on her.

"Well, now that he knows everything I know, can I go home? There's nothing else I can tell you. I promise you that."

"Actually, I'm supposed to stick pretty tight to you."

The thought was appealing—not that it should be, Jean reminded herself. The strong Ranger looked like he might eat her up as easily as he could eat a Christmas cookie. "I don't know that I'm any safer with you than I would be with the bad guys," she said, just to rattle his cage a bit.

Sam crossed his arms, leaned against the wall. "Really? The bad guys might want you dead."

"I wouldn't have figured you to be melodramatic," she said with a sigh.

He watched her with interest, his dark gaze inscrutable, and her body heated with longings she shouldn't feel. "I'd like to change my clothes," she said briskly.

His lips twisted in a smile she was certain he begrudged. "I'll leave you to it."

Jean heard his boots in the hallway as he walked away. A breath escaped her that she hadn't realized she'd been holding.

And then it hit her: She had the hots for that emotionally stunted Ranger...*bad*.

SAM DECIDED to give Jean a wide berth—she'd let him know when she wanted company. He knew she was eager to be home for the holidays, and he was aware that she didn't particularly feel comfortable around him.

He heard thumping in his attic and sighed. The woman wasn't very subtle.

She was after those damn Christmas boxes Molly had mentioned. The second Molly had said "boxes and boxes of Christmas decorations," Jean had looked positively electrified. He sighed, listening as more thumps sounded on the stairwell, the sure sounds of the Santa Claus effect being unleashed upon him. With a sigh, he got up to make some tea. If he had to endure this harbinger of the holidays, this ringing in of the meaningless season, he might as well put on his good-cop face.

"So, Sam," he heard from the living room.

"So, Jean," he answered.

"Why are you such a Scrooge, anyway, and your sister's not?"

He put the kettle on the stove and jacked up the heat. "Guys see the holidays as commercial. Girls see Christmas as the possibility of all their fantasies coming true. Instead of a fairy godmother, it's Santa to the rescue."

He heard a gasp from Jean and grinned.

"That's so Scrooge, Sam!"

That made him laugh. "Maybe." He set some tea bags into a teacup and a mug. The mug was black, and the cup was black. He liked black better than green and red, the traditional colors of the holidays. Black was nice and basic and served lots of utilitarian purposes. "Guess I don't believe much in fairy tales dreamed up by merchants."

She came into the kitchen, smiled when she saw the cup he'd prepared for her. "But you're not totally inconsiderate."

"No. I'm a gentleman," he said. "I'm just not looking to sugarcoat life."

She cocked her head at him. "Are you saying Molly does?"

"No. Molly has a right to be happy. I wish it had all worked out for her."

"Come out here with me," she told him.

"Can't," he said, knowing she was going to show him a bunch of doodly Christmas crap she'd spread all over his living room. "Have to make my guest some breakfast."

"What can you make?" she asked, clearly testing his

culinary talent. His grocery-buying skills were also under the microscope as she opened his fridge. "Ah. Well, let's see…we could have beer. Or…beer! Or even," she said, glancing at him, "a beer."

"Hey, don't make it sound as if I subsist on hops," he said, irritated. "There's only one bottle in there."

She closed the door. "Precisely. Your cupboard is bare."

"Well, I was planning to go shoot Bambi and bring her back here to make venison omelettes," he said, waiting to get his head handed to him.

"We could just snack on the stuff you picked up at the gas station last night and leave Bambi to roam," Jean said.

"I'm kidding, actually." He didn't want Jean to think he really didn't know how to cook. "I was planning on making a run to the grocery store. We'll need a few food groups, I would imagine."

"You're leaving me here alone?"

Sam nodded. "I won't be gone long. Your decorating should keep you busy."

"How do you know I'm decorating?" She gave him a sly look.

"I know the sounds of elves and their shenanigans. Anything special you want from the store?"

She sighed. "We could make Christmas cookies. And maybe some fudge. I can whip up a Godiva pie that'll have you—"

"Jean," he said, "no sugarcoating."

She blinked. "What do you mean?"

"I don't need all that holiday cheer stuff."

She looked at him with big blue eyes, drowning him in her innocence. "So…maybe you could just pick up more beer?"

"All I'm saying is this Christmas could be a lot different from any you've known before if the police don't find O'Bannion and Morrissey."

Her face fell for a moment before she quickly regrouped. "Look, Scrooge, that doesn't mean I can't bake some cookies. And you can eat them without all your Christmas issues ruining my holiday."

She reminded him so much of Molly; he could see why the two of them were so close. The truth was, if she wanted "sugarcoating" right now, she deserved all that he could give her. "Hey, maybe I'll go get some cookie stuff and even some milk," he said in his best Boy Scout voice, as if the thought had just occurred to him.

"That would be wonderful, Sam," she said, playing along, "and maybe even get one of those Christmas CDs they always have in the aisles for the convenience of people who like a little music with their baking?"

"It would make the occasion just that much more festive," he said agreeably, putting his hat on, shoving his keys in his pocket, telling himself he wouldn't ask her if maybe he should pick up some coal and switches to go in a certain little Miss New England's stocking, as well. "And you be waiting right here so that when I return, we'll have so much holiday fun even Santa will be impressed." He waited for her to promise him there'd be no funny stuff, no hitting the road with the ol' thumb-out ticket. The store was only five minutes away—Martha could fix him up with the proper ingredients they needed for baking something. But still, he wanted to know that he could trust Jean.

She smiled at him, and his heart dropped into his boots.

"Thank you, Sam."

"Don't mention it," he said gruffly. The cop guarding Molly wasn't the only sap who'd been wrapped around a woman's finger today, and the funny thing was, it didn't feel as bad as Sam had thought it might.

WHEN SAM RETURNED, there was no escaping Christmas. "Wow," was all he could say as he walked into the living room to find Jean. The holiday beckoned him with a vision of lights and color. "Holy Christmas."

Jean laughed. "Molly's quite the elf. You've got enough decorations for the entire house."

"I see that." He walked slowly around the room. A small tree stood on a tabletop, its branches adorned with tiny felt candy canes, silvery tinsel and gold ornaments. On the top was a gold star, opened like a locket with a picture of Sam and Molly inside, when they'd been much younger. It was a black-and-white photo, but he remembered this pigtailed Molly, the one he'd read stories to, the one who'd followed him around like an adoring puppy. Unexpectedly, he felt the sentimental fog of the season creep over him, its tendrils reaching for his heart.

He turned away, noting the manger on the coffee table, angels hanging from the roof. Inside, the typical scene: baby, Mary, Joseph, barn animals. But what was different about this manger was that there was a small sign nearby that said *Room at Sam's Place,* which had been hand-painted by Molly. He'd said that to Molly a hundred times—*there's always room at my place if you need somewhere to stay*—but she'd never taken him up on it.

Still, it meant a lot to him that she'd known his offer was sincere.

There were stockings hanging from the mantel of the fireplace. All the stockings matched except one, and that one had his name on it. That stocking had been empty for a lot of Christmases, but now it had books bursting from the top of it. He went over to look at them. They were small versions of *The Night Before Christmas* and other classics.

He felt startled tears jump into his eyes.

Beside him, he noticed Jean move. He couldn't face her just yet, so he didn't say anything. Quietly, she placed on the mantel three silver-framed pictures of him and Molly: one as children, one as young adults and one when Molly had graduated from college. She looked beautiful in her cap and gown, and his breath hitched in his chest as the full force of her gifts tugged at his heart.

He wasn't going to get mushy in front of Jean, though. He was supposed to be her protector, not an emotional washout, so he walked into the kitchen and began unloading the grocery bags he'd set on the counter.

She came to stand beside him; he felt her gentle presence.

"She's going to be all right, Sam."

"Let's just worry about you, New England, and these cookies you wanted, okay?"

She looked over his shoulder. "What did you bring me?"

"Chocolate-chip rolls and Frank Sinatra."

"Rolls?"

"Well, yeah. The cut-and-bake things. That's what you wanted, right?"

She laughed. "Sure, Sam. They'll be great."

He looked at her to judge her sincerity. "Besides Sinatra, the only other choice was the Dixie Chicks."

"*Sinatra sings Christmas* will be perfect." She wandered off to put the CD into his player, and the soft sounds of "White Christmas" began filling the air as she returned. "Now, we just preheat the oven and—"

He surprised her and himself by taking her in his arms. "I'm hoping it's just the holiday spirit screwing me up, but I've been thinking about kissing you since I met you. I'm only able to withstand so much temptation, so call this a warning."

"A warning?"

He nodded. "I even brought mistletoe." He held a sprig above their heads. "Martha insisted on it, although I'm pretty sure it's just a parasite." Slowly he touched his lips to Jean's, and to his surprise, he could have sworn he felt a spark of Christmas magic.

But he didn't believe in that and he didn't want Jean to be uncomfortable, so he pulled away from her and tossed the mistletoe in the trash. "Definitely not a healthy plant to have around, in any case."

Jean's expression turned stoic. She handed him a knife and a roll of cookie dough, clearly ignoring his attempt to quash the romance and the holiday spirit. "Cut and bake, Scrooge."

CHAPTER FOUR

"YOU'RE GOING to have to give me a break here," Sam said, putting the knife down. "I'm trying to do the Christmas thing, like you would have had back home. I'm well aware it's going to fall a bit short, but I'm not Ranger Claus, you know."

"Your pants are buzzing," she said, changing the subject.

He took out his cell phone. "Hello?"

Jean shook her head. His kiss had been a lot more gentle than she would have imagined. She had wanted to kiss him back, which was not a great sign. All she needed to further complicate her life—really goof it up—was to fall into some type of relationship with Molly's brother.

Talk about getting lumps of coal in your stocking.

"Are you sure?" he demanded of the caller. "One hundred percent positive?"

After listening a moment more, he hung up and stared at Jean.

"What? Is Molly all right?"

"Molly's better than all right. She's going far away to a safe place, and the Texas Rangers are pretty sure Morrissey and O'Bannion have both left the state. The Boston police are on the alert—they figure the two will head back home to the Boston area. So—" he shrugged "—I can take you home."

"Take me home?" Her heart jumped wildly.

He nodded, but she caught a slight hesitation.

"Wait, why do you have to *take* me?"

"You're Molly's best friend and I owe it to her to get you safely out of here. The immediate threat seems to have passed, so there's no reason for you to be stuck here."

"Oh," she said, suddenly realizing she hadn't felt that "stuck" after all. "That's great."

"Yeah. It's great." He nodded. "You'll want to call your folks and let them know you're on your way home."

"My cell phone has no charge left on it." She could barely look at Sam. Her thoughts were in such a snarl. She was happy to be leaving Texas, wasn't she? And Sam?

He silently handed her his phone. Taking it from him, she thought about how she'd just found herself in his arms—quite willingly—and knew the best thing she could do was leave temptation behind. Especially since he seemed to be eager for her to go.

She dialed her mother, averting her gaze from Sam. "Hi, Mom. It's Jean."

"Jean!" her mother caroled in her ear. "How was the wedding?"

"The wedding?" For some reason, it seemed like a long time since she'd been wearing the dreadful purple pouffy gown. "Oh, Mom, Molly decided not to get married after all."

"Oh?" Her mother's voice fell, but then she perkily said, "Well, that's good news. Molly's such a practical girl! If she's decided to take some more time to think things through, I'm sure it's for the best."

"I'm sure that's true," Jean said, electing not to burst her mother's bubble at this moment.

"Where are you?"

"I'm…in Dallas, with Molly's brother, Sam."

"Molly's brother? That's lovely! I'm sure he's every bit

as nice as Molly!" her mother exclaimed with abundan
enthusiasm.

She glanced at Sam, who was clearly enjoying the conver
sation since he could hear her mother's less-than-dulcet voice
"He is nice," she said reluctantly, knowing what was coming

"Is he good-looking?" her mother asked.

She wanted to groan. "In a dark sense, I suppose."

"Oh, I hope he looks like Patrick Dempsey on *Grey'
Anatomy!*" her mother exclaimed.

Sam nodded enthusiastically. Jean raised a brow, thinking
he was awfully sure of himself. Perhaps he did look a bit like
the handsome actor, but when did Sam have time to watch TV
anyway, she wondered crossly.

"What's Sam doing for Christmas?"

"I'm not sure, Mom." She worked to keep the edge from her
voice. Her mother was way too interested in the Ranger—and
Jean didn't need well-meaning motherly interference right now

"Does he want to come home with you? Since there's no
going to be a wedding? I'm sure that's upset his holiday plans."

"I don't think so, Mom. He's not quite like Molly." Sam
was looking altogether too confident. "Not as outgoing."

"Oh, good, then he can keep your father company and
watch football. They can keep Gigi from pulling the bows off
the packages."

Sam grinned. "Love to."

She put a hand over the phone. "You'll be bored stiff."

"Doesn't sound like it. I have to protect the Christmas presents from the lovable family pet. And help your father eat all the
good food you were telling me about." He rubbed his stomach,
which, Jean couldn't help but notice, was extremely flat and no
doubt washboardlike. A misty craving rose inside her, which she
sternly told herself to ignore. "This is not a good idea."

"Why not?"

"Because you just kissed me."

"So?"

She wrinkled her nose. There was practically a tripped alarm system the size of Fort Knox's going off inside her, though why, she wasn't exactly certain. Neither she nor Sam was the type to fall blindly into a relationship. But a kiss was a kiss, and it wasn't exactly something she'd say no to if it happened again—

Yes, I would. I could make sure Mom understands that there can be no mistletoe in the house. Who am I kidding? She'll have that parasitic plant in every nook, cranny and doorway.

"Jean?" her mother said.

"Just a moment, Mom." She covered the phone with her hand again. "Sam, you're Scrooge in jeans. My family's more like a Hallmark card."

"Maybe I could use that in my life right now."

He was being obstinate. "You're going to get my mother's hopes up," she warned him. "She's not very subtle about wanting me married. Like every other mom, I suppose, she'd like grandchildren one day."

"I've had women try to catch me before."

"I'm not trying to catch you! Just the opposite!"

"I'd feel better if I was with you," Sam said, very serious now, reminding her without saying so that the coast wasn't exactly clear. Not until O'Bannion and Morrissey were caught. "And your family."

Great. He'd been playing at Romeo, and she'd been guarding her heart. "Mom expects everyone to help with the dishes," she warned, her last attempt to discourage him from what she just knew was a very bad idea. But with a mischievous grin he put the cut-and-bake cookie roll into the refrigerator next to the lonely beer, clearly not worried in the least.

SAM WATCHED Jean walk out of the kitchen, presumably going to pack up her things. Or maybe to kick something. He couldn't fail to notice that she wasn't exactly thrilled about him coming to her family's house.

The thing was, he really wanted to go. Sam didn't have to protect Jean anymore. Someone else could do the job.

He wanted to be with her, plain and simple.

Oh, yeah, honesty required him to acknowledge that he wanted to spend more time with the Christmas-loving, bossy little Miss New England, even if it meant stepping into a Hallmark-card existence as she'd warned. It wouldn't kill him—and it just might kick his Scrooge-butt into the holiday spirit.

She poked her head into the kitchen. "I'm sure this is an obvious question, but are we driving or flying?"

Whatever gets me alone with you. She was right about the kiss—something had gotten started there, although he wasn't quite sure what. Now that he knew how soft she was—and yet a bit on the spicy side with her temperament—he craved more. "Driving," he said, "definitely driving."

"It'll be about a twenty-eight-hour haul," she told him, "and the road conditions may not be entirely favorable."

"At this point, getting plane tickets would be difficult and expensive, and let's not forget the waits in the airports. The weather's bad, already meaning passenger pileup. I think our best bet is the open road."

She nodded. "We could likely drive in the amount of time we could wind up sitting in uncomfortable chairs in an airport. And I bet the drive north will be really pretty at this time of year. I just hope you're good with a map." She fixed deep blue eyes on him, her gaze hopeful.

"I have a GPS system. I'll have you home in plenty of time for Christmas," he said, feeling every inch the big bad wolf.

SAM PACKED Jean's things into his car and handed her his keys. "You drive."

"Me?"

"Aren't you a good driver?" He grinned at her and got into the passenger seat.

She slid into the driver's seat. "I've been told I drive like a grandma."

"Would never have guessed that. Start the engine, Granny."

She did, giving him one last wary glance. "Are you planning to nap or something?"

"Not quite yet. Drive to the end of the driveway."

"Thank you, I think I could figure that much out."

He couldn't help a smirk. "Just making sure you don't head to Mexico."

She slowly went down the drive, getting used to the feel of his car. "I just want to get home before you change your mind."

It would be best not to tell her that he was going to play lookout. Ranger-caution was second nature. From here, he could keep one eye out for danger and one eye on Jean.

The eye he had on Jean would definitely be the happiest. He'd never seen a woman look so gorgeous with so little makeup. She seemed completely comfortable in sweatpants, a sweater and boots, with her hair up in a ponytail. It started to snow, and fat wet flakes splatted against the windshield.

"We're not leaving a moment too soon," he said. "I heard on the radio that there's a major storm blowing in."

"Let's get out of here, then. I don't want any delays."

She wanted to get home. It was also clear she didn't want to spend any more time alone with him. "Hey, if it upset you

that I kissed you, I'm… Well, I'm not sorry, but I'll be respect
ful of your wishes not to duplicate the action."

She glanced at him. "Thank you."

"Just wanted to get that straight in case we get stuck in a
cabin somewhere due to the weather."

She came to a complete stop at the end of the street. "We're
not getting stuck *anywhere*."

"I agree, it wouldn't be much fun," he said, picking at her
just a little to keep things friendly between them. He thought
he detected a motion reflected in the passenger-side mirror,
but when he turned and looked, the street was empty. He was
overly cautious, he decided.

What am I doing here? he asked himself. Why not just put
Jean on a plane, say goodbye and tell her she was now the
problem of the Boston police?

The only answer he had, and it wasn't really a good one,
was that the whole Christmas thing was sneaking into his
heart. He'd been shocked by his emotions when he'd come
home and found his den decorated with holiday spirit—he'd
never expected the rush of warmth and good cheer and all that
utter nonsense. The tide of sentiment had taken his breath
away. It was as if by opening those boxes and dragging out
the contents Molly had so lovingly packed, Jean had shown
him all the things he'd been missing in his life. She'd shone
a light in his very lonely existence, and frankly, it had felt good
to clean out the ol' emotional closet just a bit.

So now he was intrigued. Was it ingrained cop instincts that
wouldn't let her go until he knew she was delivered safely into
her family's arms?

Or was it just plain selfishness and curiosity about how
much Christmas spirit she could bring into his life?

The adventure wouldn't kill him. And he had no other plans

THREE HOURS LATER they were at the Texarkana border. Snow was falling more heavily here than it had in Dallas. "I didn't know Texas got this much snow," Jean remarked.

"White Christmases are rare except in the panhandle."

She looked at him as she passed into Arkansas. "Did you enjoy your nap?"

"I wasn't napping. I was thinking."

"About?" She turned on the windshield wipers, making sure the defroster was on, as well. No amount of snow was going to keep her from getting home.

"The diamonds."

"Really? Did your Ranger friend have anything more to share about that?"

"It seems Boston's Internal Affairs Department is investigating the possibility that O'Bannion and Morrissey and a few other bad cops got wind of a diamond theft and in the takedown killed the real thief and kept the stones for themselves. The reason for all the drama at Molly's wedding, best as the Boston police can figure, is that no one's quite sure who's got them. So you have bad cops suspicious they're being double-crossed." He shifted in the seat, eyeing the passenger-side mirror, which made her nervous, though she didn't say so. He'd been monitoring it regularly, almost as if he expected O'Bannion and his buddies to show up behind them at any second.

The very thought of the possibility sent shivers over her skin that had nothing to do with the cold. Still, she turned the heat in the truck up a notch. "I feel so sorry for Molly."

He shrugged. "I'm not worried about Molly at this point because she wasn't the one they were aiming for."

"Who was?" Jean still found it hard to believe there had been guns at a wedding.

"The target was you," Sam said, "which is why I'm sitting

in this car going to New England. Where in New England are we headed, anyway? Some quaint-sounding little—"

"What are you talking about?" Jean demanded. "What do you mean, *I* was the target?" Her heart sped up nervously. She wanted to stop the car and wring Sam's neck for not telling her sooner. "I don't know anything about any diamonds except the one Molly was wearing."

"True," he said, "but Tommy didn't know that, and when Connor didn't show for his own wedding, he probably thought he'd been double-crossed. He suspected Connor had the diamonds, and had every intention of skipping town with them on his romantic honeymoon. Or maybe Connor told him what you'd overheard. Where was it Connor and Molly were planning to go for their honeymoon?"

"Australia, I think," Jean said. "But what I heard was hardly enough to implicate him."

"Seems Connor might have thought so. He knew something had gone wrong at the point you overheard his conversation. All he had to do was put in a phone call to Tommy to take out the one person who'd heard him threaten the children and talk about diamonds. Whether it was suspicion on Tommy's part or Connor ordered a hit on you is something we'll know eventually."

Jean could feel a tremor start in her fingers and move down to her ankles. She told herself not to think about the danger she'd been in; there were bigger concerns to worry about. "Where are Charlie, Lily and Zoe?"

"Not sure yet. But they'll be safe and in good hands, don't worry. You're just lucky Tommy Morrissey is such a poor shot," Sam said cheerfully. "Apparently one of his nicknames is No-Hit Tommy."

She didn't think that was humorous. "If he was such a

poor shot that he couldn't even hit a grape-velvet, hoop-skirted maid of honor, why was he Connor's right-arm man?"

"Loyalty. Speed up a little."

"Oh, I can't," she said. "I absolutely never drive over sixty miles an hour, and as you may have noticed, the roads are going to be getting slick from all this snow. I really don't want traffic tickets on my record."

"Bend your rules and give me five or ten miles or more."

His tone had changed from teasing to tightly wound. "Why?"

"Just for grins, okay?"

He was such an autocrat. She eased the accelerator three miles higher, then five, then a reluctant ten, until she realized he was back watching that damn mirror again. "Just what are you looking at behind us?"

"Just making sure we're not being followed."

Cold chills snaked through her. "Sam, look. Maybe flying would be better. You're going to be a very tiresome companion if you're going to worry the entire way to New England."

"Sorry to be the rain on Miss Christmas's parade."

She was now up to seventy miles an hour and not happy about it. Relief washed over her when five minutes later, he said, "You can slow down now. And I'm not completely anti-holiday, by the way."

She met his eyes briefly as she eased to a more comfortable speed. "Sure you are. And a day around my family would probably scare you off them for good. Are you satisfied that we're not being followed?"

"Pretty much."

"What made you think we were?" The thought that he might have actually seen somebody made her feel cold all over.

"Instinct. Gut feeling."

This was ridiculous. He wasn't going to ruin her Christmas. "This theory about me being the target is silly," she said, marshalling herself for an argument that he richly deserved. "Perhaps if we don't talk anymore about the wedding and focus instead on being—"

"Romantic?"

That actually didn't sound half-bad. "Not unless you want Mom going into the stratosphere with plans. She'll call all her girlfriends and all the relatives if she even suspects I might have brought home someone special."

"You've never done that before?"

Uh-oh. She was the same age as Molly, and Sam was older, so he obviously wasn't any more intent on the altar than Jean was, but still the answer to that question made her feel awkward. "Guess I've just been waiting for Mr. Right," she said airily.

"I'm already out of my comfort zone," Sam said, pushing his hat down over his eyes and leaning back comfortably, lazily untroubled, "but if you want me to play at being Mr. Right, I'm game."

And Molly had always said her brother was so hard to get along with. Sam was being so accommodating, Jean wanted to scream.

CHAPTER FIVE

SAM WASN'T really asleep. He was giving Jean time to stew over his offer. He'd never thought about settling down. Bachelorhood had only taken on a strange connotation when he realized his baby sister would beat him to the altar—and then he'd begun to wonder if maybe it was time to start reconsidering life as he knew it.

Life as he knew it was very good—but it was also solitary. He *was* moody, dark, introspective. Not like Molly, and not like Jean. Jean wanted to analyze and categorize everything; it was the librarian in her. He just couldn't see himself waking up every morning, getting the newspaper and sitting down at the breakfast table with a woman who wanted to discuss the most recent literary work.

Of course, if that woman happened to look like Jean, he could consider revising his life's plans. He certainly hadn't had a negative reaction to being the Christmas hunk her mother was hoping would drop into her daughter's stocking.

"Hey, I'll drive for a while."

"That was a fast nap."

"I was thinking." He pushed his hat back. "Problem solved."

She glanced at him. "That fast? Must not have been world peace."

"More like family peace. Pull over at the next stop, please."

"Why did you make me drive in the first place? Just so you could look for nonexistent baddies?"

"A woman driving my car was one of my fantasies, all right?" he said. "And you looked great doing it, so now that I've lived the fantasy, I'm ready to drive."

"Whew, what a crab." She laughed and pulled off the road into the parking lot of an abandoned, long-closed gas station. "Maybe you need a little more time under your hat."

She was probably right. But he was beginning to realize that fantasies and Jean sort of went together. Okay, so he'd lied about fantasizing about a woman driving his car, but she'd done it so capably—and in bad weather—that sexy had come to mind. And then she was so darn pleasant about everything, coddling him emotionally, badgering him in his crusty moods—why wasn't she annoyed? Why was she totally sunny…and why did he find that so appealing?

"Don't fall," he said, as she came around to the passenger side. "It's as slick as hell—"

He reached out to catch her just as she slipped on ice neither of them saw.

"Thanks for the catch," she said breathlessly, but he didn't need thanks, because he had an armful of beautiful blond woman and somehow he'd gone quite warm despite the twenty-degree weather. She was close enough to kiss since he'd grabbed her tightly to him, and strangely, kissing her was very much on his mind, but he'd already done that once and she hadn't seemed too happy about it. They had many hours left to travel, and there was no point in having a mad companion.

"I'm good at catching things," he said lightly. "Get in the car before you knock both of us down."

"That would not be good," she said, climbing into the cab. He shut the door and headed around to the driver's side.

And then it hit him: the strangest sensation that they were being watched. It was impossible, though. He'd kept a careful eye on every mile of the road behind them.

He was, as Jean liked to say, suspicious.

"What are you doing?" she asked when he got into the car. "You stood out there so long I wondered if you were getting cold feet about your decision to come home with me."

"No, I'm still in for Christmas-hunk duty," he said, unable to dispel the strange sensation prickling the back of his neck.

"Good," she said, "my mom's really going to like you."

He turned to look at her. "Is that a good thing?"

"Oh, yes. She despairs of my love life. Seeing you will let her know that I am totally capable of meeting sexy men with good manners." She smiled at him.

"I would think there are tons of guys out there who would make a mother's heart melt."

"Not mine." Jean shook her head. "My mom and dad have only been married to each other. They don't argue, they don't even squabble. If they do, my sisters and I never hear it."

"Oh, boy," he said, "that's a pretty tough one to live up to."

"You're just playing at being the hunk, you don't have to sacrifice yourself for Mom's sake. She'll just be happy to see that there's someone I know who's very…you know, eligible."

He hadn't really thought about his eligibility. Molly had always teased him about girls and whom he was dating. She'd warned him he'd best be careful or he'd get caught by some sweet woman and the next thing he knew, he'd be hanging stockings for a large family—but he'd always known in his heart her teasing was nonsensical. Grouchy Rangers who lived alone in the country didn't get married. They dated occasionally, but they never gave up their personal freedom. "How does your father stand living in a house with four women? Oh, five, counting Gigi, the golden retriever."

"Dad says he's the happiest man on the planet," Jean said, and Sam had the feeling he probably was.

A sudden shot rang through the air. The car lurched and Sam knew a tire had been hit. "Get down!" he barked, crushing Jean to the seat and covering her with his body.

She was warm, she was still and he could feel her panicked breathing underneath him. And that was the moment he realized that if anything happened to her, he was going to lose his only chance at a woman he was really starting to care about.

"Get off!" she exclaimed.

Nothing rattled her. He liked the fact that she wasn't a nervous ninny. "Someone just took a shot at the car. Stay down."

"We're in the middle of Nowhere, Arkansas. I'd rather stand up and be shot than lie here and cower. Even though you're nice and warm, I want out from underneath you."

Jeez, this woman was fearless. "You're not going to like taking a bullet. I advise you to stay down."

"I wouldn't have liked it at the wedding, either, so I'm not going to be a crybaby about it. Besides, if they'd meant to hit either of us, they would have done it when we were out in the open. They only blew out a tire, so whoever it is is toying with us. I, for one, do not appreciate being toyed with."

She made a good point. Why would someone have shot out the tire and not taken him out so they could have had Jean to themselves, to question and whatever else?

It didn't bear thinking about.

An eighteen-wheeler pulled up behind them, and a burly driver with a cheery face got out and walked to Sam's window. "You've got a flat," he told Sam. "Need help changing it, or could you use a lift?"

Sam could change his own tire, but accepting a ride in the hauler would preempt any more shooting. Jean was right. Whoever was stalking them hadn't meant to hit them, just slow them down, make them feel hunted. "Stranger, I'd be obliged," he said, "but I should warn you we're being followed."

"Figured that by the bullet in your tire," the stranger said laconically. He shrugged. "Harder to take out a big rig, though, and I don't mind company at all. We can sing Christmas carols together." He grinned cheerfully, and Sam looked at Jean, thinking the plan was almost airtight.

"You'd be taking a lot on by giving us a ride."

The trucker stuck out a hand, grinning broadly. "Name's Len Hughes. You ever see *Smokey and the Bandit*?"

Sam nodded, getting a mental vision of car chases and wild truck escapes.

"My rig and I have a bunch of road-warrior stories to tell," Len said. "You'll be as safe as kittens with me."

FIVE MINUTES LATER, Sam and Jean were ensconced in the cab with the amiable driver who'd agreed to haul them as far north as Kentucky. From there, they'd have to get to Satterbury, Vermont, and the Norville family home, but this was definitely safer than being a sitting duck for a shooter who thought Jean knew enough to implicate Connor O'Bannion. Eventually, the guy was going to slip up.

"Hitching a ride wasn't in the plans," Sam said.

"My mother doesn't care how I get home, just so long as I do." Jean decided being this close to Sam wasn't a bad thing at all. She was warm and she was with him—her holiday still felt very shiny. And the driver, she had to say, looked an awful lot like Santa Claus. She could just imagine him wearing a red cap with a white ball of fuzz on the end rather than the red gimme cap he wore. His truck cab was even painted red, and he had a sprig of holly hanging from the rearview mirror and a wreath on the silver grill.

"I like working for myself," Len Hughes said, in his friendly way. "Means I'm only responsible for me."

"It's a good thing," Sam said.

"Which means I won't mention to anyone that a bullet flattened your tire." He glanced at them in the mirror. "But I do have to wonder just for the sake of curiosity why anybody would be shooting at such a nice couple. You folks on the run?"

"No," Sam said, clearly deciding he could trust their driver, "we're not in trouble with the law. In fact, I'm in law enforcement, and Jean is a librarian. However, there's trouble in the family tree."

Actually, no, Jean thought, *it's your family tree, not mine that was marrying into trouble.* And then she realized he was including her in the Broadbent family, and it felt kind of good.

"Well, one little pop gun can't do any damage to my rig, so you two just relax," Len told them. "I've got a place not far from Mom's where you two can spend the night if you want. We'll be there by nightfall."

Not far from Mom's? This big man still lived close to "Mom"? Jean decided that any man who wanted to live that close to his mom deserved a medal in his Christmas stocking this year. "We'd like that," she said.

"It'll doubtless be pretty cozy," Sam said softly.

"I'm good with cozy."

"You might just let Ma think you two are married," Len said, "just for the sake of propriety, if you know what I mean, because it's a one-room place. But you'll be safe, I guarantee you that."

"We can go for safe," Sam said, and Jean told herself that the tingling in her fingertips was because she'd just been shot at for a second time and not because Sam's warm fingers had briefly squeezed hers when she'd jumped at the word *married*.

"THIS LOOKS MORE honeymoon than getaway," Jean told Sam when they were shown into the "one-room place" of Len's. "I feel like we're in a four-star hotel instead of hiding away from someone who's trying to scare me into having a bad Christmas."

"I texted Mom and told her I was bringing home a honeymooning couple who were down on their luck," Len said, his broad face a trifle sheepish. "I hope you won't mind the small fib."

"Thank you for all your kindness," Jean said, and Sam shook Len's hand. "And please tell your mother, as well." The room was lovely, not a place she would have imagined as Len's. Beside the bed a pitcher of ice water was placed; nearby was a crystal decanter of wine. A plate of cheese and crackers was set on the table, as well, with mounds of glistening grapes. Just looking at the fluffy bed made Jean want to crawl in and forget the past forty-eight hours.

"We're four miles from the road and hard to get to," Len said. "So no worries that your friend'll catch up with you. On the property I've got a couple of dogs that roam. They're gentle but not with trespassers, so don't feel like you're unprotected. They'll let you know if anyone's out there." Len grinned. "No one would want to meet up with Ma's shotgun, anyway, but be sure to telephone the house if you get worried."

"We will. Thank you." Sam looked around the room as Len left them in the cabin. "This is great. I want one of these places."

"You already have one. You just haven't decorated it as nicely. Besides," Jean said, industriously digging into her suitcase and trying not to think about sharing the inviting bed with Sam, "Len said he doesn't really live here. He uses this place as a bed-and-breakfast hideaway for travelers. You can always come back."

"Wouldn't be the same without you," Sam said. "You keep things lively."

"Because someone keeps shooting at me?" She shook her head. "I'll be delighted when all the criminals are in jail. Right now, I'm going to bed, and I'm dreaming of nothing but sugarplums. I'll leave the cop stuff to you."

He smiled. "You realize this is the second time we'll have slept together? We're two for two."

"Yes, but you're on your own tomorrow night. Mom will have your room a decent distance away from mine." It was a pity, Jean thought. *I should have kissed him thoroughly when I had the chance—I'll never be able to work up the nerve at Mom's with my sisters spying around every corner.*

Strange how kissing him today seemed much more tempting than it had yesterday. But today she felt she knew this man better than she had yesterday. In some ways it seemed like she'd known him for years.

"I didn't tell you how much I appreciate you putting up the ornaments that Molly gave me," Sam said suddenly. "It made me sorry I've been so stubborn all those years about decorating."

She closed her suitcase, glancing at him. "Guys don't decorate as enthusiastically as women do."

"I just didn't want to. I didn't want to clean up the mess after the holidays. I didn't want to feel sad when I packed everything away. Molly has her own life. Why would I decorate just for me?"

"If you missed your sister so much, how come you just never told her? You've always been Molly's shining star, you know."

His heart leapt at those words. "Once you've closed the

door on the past, it's hard to reopen it. I'm much better at leaving things closed."

"Most men are," Jean said. "Women, too."

"It wasn't until I saw those framed pictures of the two of us that I realized I do want to remember the past. I want to remember her, not our dysfunctional parents. I'm sure Molly told you there was lots of money in our family but not a lot of fun. Still, Molly was my best friend."

"She'd say the same, Sam. Now turn around so I can get in this bed. I'm beat."

"How about some wine?" he asked, pouring himself a liberal glass. It was going to be a long night if he had to ward off the temptation of being in bed with Jean, listening for trouble.

"Not for me. I'm going to click my heels three times, fall asleep, and dream of home and shopping at every department store in town. I haven't even started my list," she said sleepily.

Sam heard the bed shift. He waited a few more moments, then swallowed half the wine he'd poured to give himself strength. He didn't dare make a move on Jean—she was tired and not in the mood to be swept off her feet. All she was dreaming about was home.

He heard even breathing and turned around to see she was already asleep. She looked like an angel, a very sexy angel.

But not for him. He shook his head, and went to sit in the rocker by the window to gaze out into the night. The police had said they'd send some guys to pick up his car and take it back home for him; they'd also told him Molly was fine. But Sam knew that until O'Bannion and Morrissey were found, he wouldn't be able to let down his guard.

IN THE NIGHT Jean awakened, and realized Sam wasn't in bed with her. She couldn't see much in the dark, but she could see him silhouetted near the window. "What are you doing?" she asked softly.

"Nothing. Thinking."

"Don't you think you should get some sleep?" To be honest, she wanted him in bed with her. She was getting used to the warmth of his big body beside her.

"Nah."

"The bed's very soft," she said, well aware she was luring him, and she saw that he turned to face her.

"Are you inviting me into your bed, Jean?"

She giggled. "It's not my bed."

He walked over beside her and her pulse sped up, almost making breathing painful. She wanted him, in the worst way.

"And 'Mom's' up the street," he said with a sigh. "As much as I want to get in bed with you, I don't think I can get over the specter of Mom."

Frankly, some good rousing sex would keep her mind off the goons that had decided she was Job #1, but Jean knew she didn't dare say that to Sam. He'd never relax. "It is daunting," she agreed. "Let me see if I can massage some of the tension out of you."

"I guess that's okay since we're supposedly married," he said, and she laughed.

"Just lie down so I can help you unwind a little."

He did, slowly lowering himself into the bed.

She admitted that she was a bit disappointed he didn't bother to take off a single layer of clothing. Since he had on three—a fleece-type jacket, a nice cotton shirt and some thermal underwear—it was pretty obvious he intended to sleep just as he had last night, fully clothed.

Big hands suddenly cupped her shoulders, kneading the tension from her own body. "That feels wonderful," she said on a surprised sigh. The best part was the feelings flowing inside of her, womanly feelings, making her glow with desire.

Of course her Ranger wasn't about to let himself be seduced. She wanted to cry into the pillow with frustration, then froze as Sam suddenly stood.

"What are you doing?" she asked. "Did you hear something?"

"I'm undressing," he said, "That's the only way to test this marriage thing out."

Her eyes widened. She heard layers peeling off, clothes hitting the floor. She held her breath, waiting to be enveloped by Sam's warmth.

He finally slid in next to her and framed her face gently with his hands, kissing her the way she'd always dreamed of being kissed. "Don't stop," she murmured. "Don't stop kissing me." She didn't think she could stand it if he didn't pull her cotton T-shirt off—okay, it wasn't romantic, but she'd been going for modest.

"Are you sure you're okay with this?" Sam asked.

She pulled the T-shirt off. "Every girl should get a pretend husband once in her life." She smiled in the darkness when he trapped her hands above her head and kissed down her throat, along her breasts and then each nipple, sending pleasure washing over her. Everything was going oh, so, well—this was going to be the Christmas present of her dreams—until the window shattered and all hell broke loose.

CHAPTER SIX

"RUN!" SAM COMMANDED, so Jean grabbed her clothes and her purse out of habit and headed off into the cold Kentucky woods barefoot. She stumbled into her jeans, pulled on her boots, then stopped in her tracks. "Why am I running? I don't want to spend my entire holiday running from some creep!"

"Let's have bravado later," Sam said. "Someone's out there, and for some reason, Len's dogs didn't sound an alarm. Run first and ask questions later."

It was four miles to the road, Jean remembered, and they were heading that way. She could make four miles easily, but she wished she were still in bed with Sam—that pleasure seemed a distant memory.

"Did someone shoot out the window?" she gasped, running, hoping she didn't brain herself on a tree in the black night.

"It was a rock, which is why I wasn't too worried about leaving the cabin. But why hang around to be target practice? If they want to shoot, they'll have to do it in the dark. The rock was thrown from the north—we'll go west to the highway. But not to Len's, which is what I think they'll suspect."

"I'm getting tired of this," Jean said. "I've got a good mind to stop and yell that I don't know anything about their silly diamonds and I don't want to know anything about them."

He pulled her over a fallen log. "But you did, unfortunately, hear something about a plan to kill some kids, which makes you a problem. I think that's what this is all about."

"That's a problem for me, too. If they think they need to take me out in order to keep me from letting the whole world know that some children might be in danger, then they'd be right on that score."

"C'mon." Sam grabbed her hand as they dashed through a clearing.

Behind them they heard dogs barking, a sudden eruption of sound in the dark, frigid night. "Sounds like Len's dogs are on the case," Jean said.

"They sound pretty fierce. And God help them if Mom finds them." The very thought made him grin. If the dogs were after their attacker, it would buy him time to get Jean far away.

"I feel bad for Len. We should never have accepted a ride from him." She gasped as a burst of cold wind stole her breath.

"We'll send him a ham for Christmas and some chocolate for his mother." Sam was pretty certain gifts were in order, and some money to pay for the window and damage to the lovely cabin. "Hey," he said, stopping suddenly to allow Jean to catch her breath, "I've got a wild-and-crazy idea."

"Really? Just one?"

He cupped his hands around Jean's face. "This one's a doozie."

"What?" She looked up at him.

"When this thing is over and far behind us, we come back here and finish what we started."

The breath she'd needed to catch left her completely. "There are plenty of other places to go."

"I know. But this hideaway has sentimental value."

"How?"

"First kisses count, even for New England wildcats, don't they?"

"You did kiss me before—"

"But not naked," he said, kissing her again, taking possession of her mouth and making her want him more than ever. "Not naked and pretend-married. So…deal?"

"I thought the marriage part would have you running scared," Jean said.

"I'm running and I'm mildly scared," Sam said, grabbing her hand and pulling her with him again, "but it's not because of a kiss."

"Ask me again after you meet my parents," she said, and he laughed.

"If your mom's anything like Len's description of his mom, I'll probably be fine."

AT THE HIGHWAY, Jean's teeth were chattering and she was nervous, but she would be fine on her own, as she tried to assure Sam many times. She was almost desperate for him to get back and make sure Len and his mother were all right. But Sam stayed put, his arms around her, trying to warm her.

The man was terrible at listening, but secretly she admitted he felt wonderful.

He had called his police contact to say that Jean needed to be picked up, and also that he'd need the help of the local law enforcement. She wasn't surprised a few moments later when a squad car pulled up to drive her to the airport. She *was* surprised and a bit sad when Sam didn't kiss her goodbye. He looked at her, then saluted the two cops in the front of the car.

"Take care of her," he said, and they nodded, pulling onto the main highway again. Turning, she craned her neck to watch Sam disappear up the road toward Len's place.

She wondered if she'd ever see him again—and had the oddest, sinking feeling that despite his "wild-and-crazy ride idea" she wouldn't.

JEAN SAT ON THE tiny plane, awaiting takeoff. She hadn't wanted to call her mother and scare her to death, but if she said she was being put on a private plane courtesy of the police, her mother would erupt with questions. She needed to think through a careful story plan. Nothing would escape her mother's sharp gaze, and the lack of luggage was going to be questioned, not to mention Jean's disheveled appearance. It wasn't every daughter who came home from a wedding in which she was to have been the maid of honor wearing no makeup, dirty jeans, scuffed shoes and hair that hadn't seen a brush since morning. She still had her purse, though, so as far as Jean was concerned, everything was peachy.

Except for worrying about Sam. She couldn't help it. Even though she knew he was an experienced lawman, they had no idea exactly who was after them.

She accepted a Bloody Mary from the single flight attendant and closed her eyes. Connor's mean gaze appeared like a bad omen in her memory. She replayed his threatening words as clearly as if he were sitting next to her, and now that Molly's wedding was no longer on her mind, she could hear the menace in his tone.

What had he meant by killing kids? Shivers ran up her arms. How heartless did someone have to be to even consider harming children?

If Sam was right, and all this trouble had come because she'd accidentally overheard some terrible plan Connor had, she was okay with it, as long as the children were safe.

The airplane's engines roared to life, a comforting

sound. Jean laid her head back, not afraid any longer. She was on her way home for Christmas, and everything would be all right.

FOUR HOURS LATER, when Jean knocked on the door of her mother's house, everything was *not* all right. Her sisters opened the door and started screaming melodramatically at her appearance. It was not a Hallmark-card moment, and she was glad Sam wasn't with her to witness it. "What is your problem?" she snapped at her sisters.

Her mother came to the door, took one look at her and snatched her daughter inside the house. "Come in where the neighbors can't see you! Was it a wedding or a war zone, Jean? For heaven's sake!"

"Well, now that you mention it," Jean said, trying to glance at a mirror as she was dragged into the warm kitchen. She could smell brownies and maybe a chicken being browned, which meant tonight they were likely having chicken spaghetti for dinner. Her stomach rumbled, but she couldn't eat. Not right now. Not until she knew Sam was safe.

He might not call her to let her know, she realized. He didn't have her cell-phone number, he didn't know where she lived. Jean could feel her heart sink despite the warmth of her mother's kitchen and the utter pleasure of allowing her mom to fuss over her.

It wasn't going to be the merriest of Christmases without knowing Sam was all right. Maybe she could call the police herself and track him down. Jean sank into a chair at her mother's kitchen table, the enormity of all that had happened over the past forty-eight hours weighing her down. She wanted to tell her mother everything, wanted to sort out her feelings about Sam, but the fact was, she really needed to keep her mouth shut…for their sake. From what she could tell, her family had no idea what had really happened at Molly's wedding.

"Hot cocoa, Jean?" her mother asked as Gigi skidded into the room, staring at Jean as if she was a total stranger.

"Yes, please," Jean said meekly, "you have no idea how good it is to be home."

SAM LOOKED AT THE thug Len had tied onto a metal chair just off to the far side of his patio. "It's going to get down to around fifteen degrees tonight," Sam told him. "Mighty cold."

The man didn't want to talk. Sam shrugged. He could stay out here all night, especially since he was sitting under the covered part of the patio close to the outdoor heater and a lighted fire pit. Len's mother, Sally, had made him and the other officer some mulled cider, which was warming and delicious in the chilly night. And he was in a really good mood from kissing Jean. "I can stay out here for days," Sam said, as icy rain began to drizzle from the sky.

Questioning the suspect was really the job of the local police, but since Sam was determined to stay until the backup car came to pick up the guy, he wanted to find out all he could. The officer with him had no objection.

"I'm not talking," the shooter said, and Sam nodded. "That's fine."

He thought about Jean then and how soft her body was, and the rain fell harder, and he thought about how much he'd enjoyed holding her in his arms, and an hour later, when his prisoner was seemingly frozen to the bone, Sam heard him say, "Connor wants her dead."

"Why?" Sam asked mildly as Sally brought him out some warm chicken soup. He could completely understand why

Len and Sally's little cabin hideaway was popular with tourists. Sally, it seemed, knew her way around a kitchen and could whip up all the good comfort foods.

"I don't know why. I just do what I'm told."

The growled admission sounded a bit desperate. The conditions were getting pretty miserable, so there was a chance Sam might get the truth out of him the first time. "Were you at the wedding?"

"No."

Sam didn't think he'd seen the guy. "What's in it for you?"

"The pay is good. Whaddya think?"

Sam nodded. "Would the pay be diamonds?"

"I was only paid half up front, but it was fresh, clean bills," he snarled, which didn't sound so menacing since the guy was half-drowning from the heavy rain. "That's a strange question, even for a cop."

Sam sipped on the soup, warmed by the savory taste. This rat wasn't one of Connor's tight circle or he'd know about the diamonds—he was merely a hired hand and not really useful. "Are you supposed to follow anybody else? Hurt anybody else?"

"Just your girlfriend."

He started to say Jean wasn't his girlfriend, then closed his mouth because Len's mother was nearby and he and Jean were supposed to be "married." Yet the idea of Jean being his girlfriend had appeal, Sam realized, his insides warming for reasons other than Sally's delicious soup.

How would a man from a small dot on the map in Texas convince a woman from genteel New England that everything she ever wanted was far from her home? There was one stop sign in Penn, when she was used to bright lights and stores that stayed open late into the night. Shopping malls, fashionable clothes, Christmas parties.

"Thanks for the info," he said, finishing up the soup. "Anybody else with you?"

He received silence and then a negative head shake. "Connor said it wouldn't be that hard to take out one of Molly's pampered little friends. Said it was a one-man job."

And for that I should beat you senseless.

When the police car showed up, Sam considered his next move. The police would have undercover cops watching Jean's house while Connor O'Bannion was still on the loose. Sam's presence wasn't really needed there. It was Christmastime and Jean was with her family, and the last thing they'd want was a Texas Ranger horning in.

He said goodbye to Len and Sally, and headed off into the night.

CHAPTER SEVEN

"So what was it like?" Jean's sisters asked her.

Jean had hugged her father—good old Dad never worried about a girl's appearance, he was just happy to see her—and reacquainted herself with Gigi, then gone to shower. The woman staring back at her in the mirror had been a trifle scary. Perhaps her mom's reaction was justified. Jean was just glad to be home among the people she knew and loved.

"What was what like?" Jean repeated softly. She was now seated near the fireplace, drinking cocoa. The soothing roar of her father watching football games on TV kept the last two days from her mind. "You mean, Molly's wedding?"

"Running off with Molly's brother," Trudy said, her expression one of shock. "Mom says you eloped with Molly's older brother."

"It was a pretend elopement, so we could stay at this lady's cabin in Kentucky." In glossing over the events, Jean had told her mother that she and Sam had to leave quickly, and she wasn't even sure where Molly had gone. Jean was just glad her family had missed all the media coverage. During the holiday season, they only listened to Christmas music on the radio and her father's sports on TV.

"Mom says you shouldn't have caused such a stir at

Molly's wedding," Starla offered. "She says it's not like you to be an attention-grabber."

Jean had to giggle at that. She thought about being the target of gun-wielding groomsmen and figured she'd love to never be the focus of anyone's attention again. "You know how Mom is. Flair for the dramatic."

Trudy nodded. "So, you and this Ranger—"

"I'm pretty sure it was just one of those job things," Jean interrupted. "His job was to get me home safely. And here I am. End of story."

"Oh." Starla was clearly disappointed. "We were sort of hoping for a Chuck Norris, 'Walker, Texas Ranger' type of brother-in-law."

Jean shook her head. "Sorry. All you get for Christmas are endless shopping sprees with Mom."

Starla looked at her. "We just want you to know that if you get a second chance at him, and you need some quick bridesmaids, we're on standby."

Jean smiled. "Thanks. Just comfort Mom, okay? I didn't mean to ruin her Christmas."

"She's baking. She'll be fine." Trudy sighed. "Texas is awfully far away."

Jean nodded, thinking about how much home meant to her. There was just something safe and secure about being in the place where she'd grown up. On the other hand, it had been so exciting to live in Sam's world for a while. "Maybe I should travel," she said.

"You just got home," Starla said. "Mom'll be upset if you dash off again."

"I meant, take some time off." Recuperate from being a maid of honor with hitmen after her. "See the world. Japan, maybe Ireland."

Would seeing the world make Penn, Texas, seem dull by comparison? Or would being with Sam be excitement enough for her?

"Did you fall in love with him?" Trudy asked, sitting at her sister's feet. Starla scooted in next to her, all three of them soaking up the warmth of the log fire.

There were some things even a big sister should be able to keep to herself, Jean thought. But Trudy and Starla were looking at her so expectantly, she couldn't tell even a white lie. "Yes."

They giggled, delighted that she'd confessed.

"Mom said you had," Trudy offered. "She said no single woman came home from a wedding without being disappointed unless she already had her own man."

"Oh, I don't have a man," Jean told them. "Falling in love with a man and being with him forever are two very different things." Look at Molly: one minute her friend was at the altar, and the next she was on the run.

Not exactly a happy ending.

"Not to be a party pooper, but I think I'll go to bed." Jean stood and hugged her sisters. "Let me rest up, and then tomorrow we'll go get Mom and Dad their Christmas presents."

"We're glad you're home, Jean," Trudy said, and Starla nodded.

"When Mom said the wedding had been canceled, we were worried about you. And then when you showed up looking like you'd been running through a forest all night—"

Jean laughed. "Mom's letting her imagination run away with her."

"You won't get married and move away, will you?" Trudy asked, her voice anxious.

Jean shook her head. "Now you're starting to sound like Mom."

JEAN HAD NEVER BEEN so warm and toasty and comfortable. As good as being at home was, this was a different kind of protected feeling—something only twelve hours of sleep, her own familiar bed and a nice hard body holding her could make her feel.

Her eyes went wide in the darkness. Nice hard body holding her? In her parents' house? She started to squeal and leap from the bed but an equally hard arm held her down.

"Hang on, wildcat," rumbled a deep voice she remembered well. She relaxed, her heart slowing down its crazy hammering because Sam was holding her.

But then she thought about her sisters sleeping down the hall. She tensed up all over again. "What are you doing here, Sam?" she whispered urgently. "How did you get in the house?"

"I came in just like Santa Claus, down the chimney." He kissed her throat and let a hand roam over her hips. "There was no way I could wait until morning to hold you."

"You came this far to get in my bed?"

He kissed her palm, then nipped at her fingertips. Slow heat burned up through her body. If she wasn't careful, she was going to end up giving in to Sam's special brand of persuasion and never know what was really going on. "You're not telling me everything."

"I had to know that you were all right."

She straddled him, holding him down and keeping his hands prisoner so he couldn't romance her into fast, delicious submission. "Tell me how you got in the house."

"Your dad snoozes by the fireplace. He hadn't locked up yet."

Her father's nighttime routine: nap first while Mom cleaned the kitchen, then when Mom went to bed, Dad made the rounds of locking up the house. "What makes you think I want you in my bed, Ranger?"

"You're not screaming, and believe me, I figured I was taking a chance. There are two unmarked cars patrolling the neighborhood."

She felt fear tighten her muscles. "Didn't you catch the bad guy?"

"That was the easy part. Catching you may prove harder."

Her heart was jumping around in her chest. "Please be serious, Sam. I can't stand the thought that you're still worried someone has followed me and aren't telling me."

It seemed forever before he spoke again. Jean could tell he was weighing how much to tell her.

"The police have lost Connor's trail."

Her muscles went slack from shock. "How did that happen?"

"Connor O'Bannion is a cop. Dirty cops have a lot of practice at outthinking the system. Even good cops can get caught off guard, and O'Bannion knows the ropes."

"So you're saying Molly could have been followed."

"I don't know."

"And possibly my family's in danger because I'm here. Hence the patrol."

He removed his hands from under her knees—which wasn't too difficult since she knew what magic he could do with those hands—and cradled her to him.

"It's a lot of guesswork," Sam said. "My only assignment was protecting you. It was a job I certainly enjoyed doing."

And then he made love to her, obliterating all the worries and fears Jean had, and replacing them with wonder and delight as she let her body melt into his…for the moment.

In the morning when she awakened, she wasn't surprised at all to find that Sam was gone. Somehow she'd known that something so perfect could only be a dream.

SAM DIDN'T WANT to scare Jean. He didn't want to ruin her Christmas. But he was worried, no question about it. If O'Bannion thought Jean had information that could be used against him, and he'd put a hit on her, there was no reason for him to suddenly change his mind and play nice.

So Sam was here in his role of bodyguard. He shouldn't have made love to Jean—that was definitely crossing over the line of professional conduct. But was he falling in love?

She had this strange effect on him, making him think dumb stuff like how bright this holiday season was. Why would he think that, when the two women in his life were in danger?

And that's when Sam knew he was done like a Christmas turkey.

When a man started thinking about the two significant people in his life, his sister and the woman he had made love to, in the singular sense of *in his life,* it was all over but the Christmas caroling.

Yet there was no way to make a happy ending out of it. Molly was off running from Connor, and Jean should be doing the same. He was going to tell her and last night would have been the perfect time. But greedy guy that he was, he wanted to make love to her and burst her bubble afterward, and then he'd chickened out altogether.

But the fact was, Jean couldn't stay here.

Not until Connor O'Bannion was caught and put in jail, his cronies with him.

Great. It's really going to warm the cockles of her little Christmas-loving heart when I tell her she can't celebrate Christmas with her family. She's gonna love that.

And Jean was also going to know that he'd held off telling her. Make love to Jean, forgo bad news, leave like a coward in the night…then what? How the hell was he going to tell her?

She might not ever forgive him for either of his transgressions.

But it really didn't matter. He couldn't afford to let emotions get involved. The fact was, he had to do his job. He had to tell her she couldn't stay here. The nightmare wasn't over, and he didn't know when it would be.

CHAPTER EIGHT

"THERE'S SOMETHING I have to tell you," Jean announced to her mother in the kitchen the next morning.

"Like the fact that we had a visitor last night?" Her mom smiled. "A gentleman caller?"

Jean froze. "How did you know?"

"He left roses." She pointed to a vase on the sideboard table. "Santa doesn't leave roses. Well, he used to," her mom said with a girlish giggle. "But I happen to know my Santa was snoozing in his recliner last night, so it had to have been the one you know."

Jean stared at the full-blossomed, red roses.

"Why didn't you at least introduce your friend to your father? He was almost certainly still awake."

"It didn't occur to me." Jean doubted her father had been awake when Sam crawled into her bed. She went to look at the flowers, a trifle amazed. Sam hadn't struck her as the roses type, but if he was turning romantic on her—and at Christmas—that indeed must mean something.

"There was a note."

Jean took the handwritten envelope from her mother and opened it. *"Dear Jean, I hope Santa is good to you…Sam,"* she read out loud.

"Oh, that's sweet," her mother said, with all the pleasure

of a mom who thinks her eldest daughter has finally found someone who just might be "the one."

It was certainly sweet, but not very illuminating. In the meantime, what was she supposed to do? Believe that she and Sam had a romance? Be happy that it was a one-night stand? Think that her life could just go on as it had before the wedding getaway and falling in love with Sam?

Gigi came over for a pat, which Jean was only too happy to give her. "You realize you're no good," she whispered into the dog's fur, enjoying the comforting feel of a girl's best friend. "You must have flunked Guard Dog 101. You could have at least gnawed on his leg a little before he walked out with my heart."

Gigi smiled a satisfied doggie smile, only too pleased to take in Jean's confidence as long as she was being cuddled. "Strangely, I feel depressed," she told her mother, and got a simple nod in reply.

"Shopping's the only cure for the blues!" her mother suggested. "Let's go get matching sweaters." And so they left with her sisters to find five red sweaters for the entire family for a Christmas photo. Gigi already had a red bow, and since she was useless, Jean thought, not even bothering to alert the family that an intruder had been in the house—sneaked into her bed!—the dog wasn't getting a new one.

However, Jean relented when she found the cutest bandana with green holly against a red background. "This would be perfect for Gigi," she said, and her mother and sisters agreed. Jean was beginning to feel better until she remembered that Sam would most likely insist she shouldn't be out shopping—in fact, she was quite jumpy—but she'd decided she couldn't allow her favorite time of the year to be spoiled by paranoia. Besides, Sam had rolled out of her bed and apparently out of her life— obviously he wasn't too worried about her safety anymore.

Men. All derring-do and then they disappear.

Even if he hadn't left, though, what would she have done with him? What was she really hoping for here? Jean wasn't certain. She simply knew that Sam had put the glow in her holiday season in a special way she had never before experienced.

"When do we get to meet Sam?" Starla asked.

"What are you getting him for Christmas?" Trudy wanted to know, and then ran on to the next thought. "Wonder what he's getting you?"

Her sisters seemed to think the possibilities were endless, judging by the delighted grins on their faces. Her mother had a secret smile, enjoying their sisterly badgering.

Jean hated to ruin their fairy tale, but her Ranger wasn't the average walk-up-to-the-door-and-introduce-himself-to-the-family kind of guy.

It would never happen.

IT WAS NOW OR NEVER, Sam decided, time to make everyone unhappy.

He stood on Jean's porch and rang the doorbell. To his surprise, she opened the door herself. "Hi," she said, not entirely enthusiastically, but since he wasn't smiling, maybe she knew this wasn't exactly a social call.

"Hi." He tried to swallow past a sudden lump in his throat. Jean had never looked more beautiful. She wore a pretty red sweater and cream-colored slacks. Her hair was long and straight, and he could just detect the twinkle of some sparkly earrings.

"Come to introduce yourself to the family," Jean asked, "by way of the front door?"

"Yes and no," Sam said. "Can I come in?"

She let him in, and he resisted the urge to pull her to him

for a fast, hard kiss. He didn't like it when she was so stiff and formal—and yet, she seemed to have realized something had changed.

"Is Molly all right?" Jean asked.

He nodded. "As far as I know."

They hesitated, awkward with each other.

"Thank you for the flowers," Jean said, but he shook his head.

"Don't thank me. It wasn't near as much as I wanted to do."

She seemed to think his words over. After a moment, she said, "So what's on your mind?"

"I need to talk to the whole family," Sam said.

"At your own risk." She walked into the living room. He followed, more nervous than he'd ever been in his life. Her family was involved in their Christmas preparations, putting bows on the tree and tinsel on the branches. Dr. Norville was hanging the Christmas star.

"Everyone, this is Sam Broadbent, Molly's big brother," Jean said, and the room went utterly silent.

"Wow," Trudy said, "he's hot, Jean."

"Trudy!" Jean exclaimed, but her father came forward to shake his hand and her mother rushed to envelop Sam in a hug. Sam's heart clunked like an old machine coming to life.

This was getting harder by the moment. What he had to say was going to ruin their Christmas.

"I'm not really here on a social call," Sam said, and the whole family seemed to freeze, even Gigi, who'd been sniffing around his boots.

"Oh?" Jean's mother said. "Do sit down, anyway. We want to hear all about Molly and what she's doing. Is she all right now that she canceled her wedding? I think it's so smart of her to do that. You know, it's much easier and cheaper to call off a wedding than to have a change of heart later."

Jean's eyes went huge. Sam realized Jean had told her family very little about what had happened.

That was going to make his job even harder. How could he tell them that Jean couldn't stay here, in fact, had to get away, far away, when they believed Molly had simply gotten cold feet?

Jean shook her head at him surreptitiously, and that's when he got it: He was to leave her family living in their uncomplicated, happy world.

There was something to be said for protecting people from the harsh reality of life, but that meant Jean had been bearing the burden of the danger she was in by herself.

"Well," Sam began, trying to think how to cover himself, "I haven't actually talked to Molly yet, but I know she did the right thing."

Jean nodded in approval of his hedge.

This wasn't going to work. The police had specifically suggested that Jean get the hell out of New England, and better yet out of the States until they figured out where Connor was. But this family lived a gentle existence, and it was their holiday. Dumping the news on them that their daughter had a price on her head wouldn't be anything they'd be prepared to hear.

Jean had to get away.

"Jean," he said slowly, "Dr. and Mrs. Norville, I wasn't going to do this right now, I wish I had more time but it's the Christmas season, and…" He realized he was doing this badly. In fact, once he'd realized what he was going to do, his heart had given a joyful leap. "I was wondering what you might think about me…taking your daughter away for the holidays."

Jean stared at him. They all stared at him, in their matching red sweaters. He felt like a black-cloaked ghoul among holiday cherubim.

"Well, it's up to Jean—" her father began, but his wife interrupted. "Do you mean on a vacation?" Mrs. Norville asked.

"I meant on a honeymoon," Sam said, looking into Jean's eyes. "A wedding getaway."

"Elope?" her mother said, stunned, and Sam nodded.

"Ohhhh," Jean's sisters chimed, and Trudy said, "Jean's always wanted to go to Ireland."

Mrs. Norville started to cry, and even Dr. Norville's eyes got misty, but Jean herself looked a little mad. She wasn't buying it—she was reading between his lines.

"Excuse me, everyone," she said, taking Sam by the arm. "Daddy, Mom, if you don't mind, we're going to go outside to talk."

"Take all the time you need, dear," her mother said, blowing her nose, and her sisters snickered. Jean ushered Sam outside and into a car he'd either borrowed or stolen—the plates were from Vermont. Then she realized it was an unmarked squad car and really got ticked. "How *dare* you make my parents think you were proposing to me?"

"Is there something wrong with that?" Sam demanded.

"You're going to get my mom all worked up! What mother doesn't dream of the day when one of her daughters gets a marriage proposal!" Jean looked as if she couldn't believe Sam could be so dense. "You're clearly here on business, so why don't you just give me the update instead of going through this charade? It's guaranteed to break my parents' hearts."

"The police think you should leave the country. Now," Sam clarified. "As soon as you can pack your bag."

"I'm tired of the police," Jean said. "I'm tired of running, and I'm tired of you popping in and out of my life."

"Precisely," Sam said. "That's why we'll elope."

"I don't need an eloping bodyguard," she snapped.

"Who better to run off with than me?" he said.

"I don't want to run." Jean crossed her arms. "I'm not going anywhere. It's Christmas, and I'm staying right here with my family, where I belong. I know you don't like celebrating Christmas, you like being out in the middle of nowhere, brooding in an empty house, but *this* is Christmas to me." She gestured to all the two-story, fully-wreathed and lit houses on the block—very traditional, very New England. "Why would I leave this?"

"Because if you don't, you could be dead," Sam said simply, "and that will upset your parents more than when you walk away from our elopement."

"Let me get this straight," Jean said slowly, "we're going to tell my parents we're eloping, and we're going to make a great escape. When the coast is clear, I'm going to reprise Molly's excuse that I just wasn't ready to be married, which you've already heard my mother say is a wise decision to make."

"No harm, no foul," Sam said, his heart tearing because he realized Jean hadn't gotten it. Marrying him was the furthest thing from her mind. "Everybody wins."

"It's not exactly what I had in mind," Jean said slowly, and Sam shook his head.

"Me, neither." He was sadder than he wanted to be. Jean clearly wasn't ready to think marriage; she'd gone totally pale when he'd begun to ask her father for her hand. It hurt, because it had taken a monstrous amount of bravery to utter those words in front of their red-sweatered clan. He didn't think he'd ever done anything more difficult than try to propose marriage.

He felt as if he'd misfired terribly.

Jean got out of the car. He got out, too, watching her walk away. She went up the steps, ignoring the snow and the ice patches. He could tell she was mad; the snow practically melted as she hurried to the door. She hesitated outside, thinking through her options. Sam could tell she was tempted to walk inside and slam that door in his face. But she couldn't do that because of her family.

He had to express his real emotions before he lost her forever. "Hey," he said softly, and she turned.

"Jean, I love you."

Those blue eyes he loved went wide; the breath that she'd been snorting like fire, making plumes in the icy cold, seemed to stop in that moment. "You do?"

He nodded. "Oh, hell, yeah. With all my heart." Suddenly inspired, he scraped a large heart in the snow with his boot heel. "Like that. Only better, because you melted my heart a long time ago."

She looked at him. "You're just saying this because—"

He bounded up the steps, sweeping her into his arms. "Nope. I'm in love with you. The thought of living without you isn't a thought I want to have."

Her lips curved softly. "Sam Broadbent, you don't know what you're getting yourself into. Years of decorating Christmas trees and hanging lights and being a family man."

He kissed her, his whole body singing with joy. "I like what I'm getting myself into."

"I love you," she told him, "even if you're the overly cautious type."

He laughed. "First we run, then we argue about who's the most cautious."

"Where are we running to?" she asked, wrapping her arms around his neck.

Sam grinned. This Christmas stuff wasn't going to be so bad at all. "Maybe we can run to Australia to check up on

Molly? Or we can go wherever you want. No matter where we are, it's going to be home as long as I'm with you," he said, kissing her.

"Australia sounds wonderful," Jean said, and with a joyous smile, Sam carried her inside to tell her family they had another reason to celebrate the season.

* * * * *

CANDY CANES
AND CROSSFIRE

Marion Lennox

With thanks to Alexandra Patrikios
for her assistance in sorting our muddle
and coming up with something spectacular.

CHAPTER ONE

HE DIDN'T DO Christmas, and he sure as hell didn't do weddings. But here he was, planning Christmas as he sat in on a wedding straight out of a schmaltzy fairy tale.

The Southfork Texas Wedding Chapel looked like a vast, shiny meringue with lace on top. It was every bit of kitsch you'd ever want to see, and then some.

Aaagh.

But he had to be here.

Charlie, his eight-year-old nephew, had met him with his grandparents at the airport yesterday and had soon found a way to give him the facts. "Mr. O'Bannion is…*was* Dad's cousin and he's getting married tomorrow to Molly. Grandma and Great-Aunt Letitia say it'll cheer us up to be ring bearer and flower girls. But it won't. Molly's nice but even *she* thinks the dresses and stuff are silly. Lily might stop crying if you come."

It was emotional blackmail at its finest. Charlie, eight, Lily, five, and Zoe, three, had lost their parents in a car crash six weeks back. Joe Cartland was their only uncle—their nearest relative apart from their not very paternal grandparents. He lived in Australia. They lived in the U.S. He hardly saw them.

He'd assumed their grandparents would take over. But Charlie had something to say about that.

"Grandma hates us being in the house. She says we get on

her nerves. Grandpa says if Zoe cries one more time, he'll take his belt to her."

So he'd come. He was here for Christmas.

When had he last celebrated Christmas?

Joe worked for Zanapag Aeronautics and his role in crash analysis meant he could be called on at a moment's notice. Christmas was therefore easy to avoid. He either spent it working, or in his bachelor pad overlooking Sydney Harbour. Alone. Which was the way he liked it. He and his kid sister had been taught early that family stuff like Christmas was for everyone else.

Only Erica hadn't learned. She'd fallen for a scumbag of a… Well, he shouldn't think ill of the dead, but thinking about his brother-in-law still made Joe crazy enough to want to haul him out of the grave and slug him.

Joe's sister met her husband when she was eighteen. Vincent was rich, arrogant and masterful, and Erica, who'd drifted without purpose since their parents died, thought he was hot. She also loved the money. But Joe thought Vincent's wealth was suspicious. His explanations for his income were always vague and unsubstantiated. He described himself as a financial planner, but he never seemed to work.

And now… Maybe Joe's suspicions were right, for Vincent and Erica were dead and the police were saying it was no normal accident. Something was deeply wrong. Drugs? Some sort of money laundering? Who knew?

But at least the kids were safe, left with a babysitter that fateful night. They'd been living with Vincent's parents since the crash.

And the three of them were currently magnificently attired in purple tulle and purple velvet. Bridal gear.

They were not happy.

This ceremony was taking forever to start. Joe glanced along the aisle, expecting to see Connor O'Bannion waiting for his bride.

O'Bannion wasn't there. Odd. The rest of the groomsmen were present, though, glancing at their watches and looking nervous.

Connor's mother, the ghastly Letitia, the kids' great-aunt, looked as if she was about to have hysterics.

He perked up. He was stuck with two weddings before Christmas, this one and his foster sister Ellie's. He hated weddings, but hey, if he had to be here it might as well be interesting. Groom jilts bride…

Whoever this Molly was, she'd be best out of it. Mind, the kids would be disappointed.

The kids were outside, waiting for the bride.

Maybe he ought to check.

MOLLY BROADBENT stepped out of the gleaming white Rolls-Royce. Six purple bridesmaids surged forward, ready to twitter over her veil and adjust her train. Two purple flower girls and one purple ring bearer were looking really uncomfortable in the background. Hot, itchy and, even at their age, aware they looked ludicrous.

She tried not to wince. Wincing was a bad look for a bride, but it was easy to do when her bridesmaids looked like over-ripe grapes. Each one was encased in a tightly waisted, Southern belle dress—hoops, flounces, velvet and bows—and their hair had been teased, primped and sprayed into artificial awfulness.

At least Molly had Jean—her best friend from college and maid of honor—to support her. She caught Jean's gaze and felt a huge surge of guilt for embroiling her friend in this. The other women were Connor's relations, women Molly's future mother-in-law insisted would be deeply offended if they weren't part of the wedding party.

"A Christmas wedding," Letitia had said in deep satisfaction when Molly and Connor had broken the news of their engagement. "Okay, ten days before Christmas, but it still counts. Now I know you don't have your own mama anymore, my dear," she'd said to Molly, "so I'll do it all. Oh, I see it all…."

Bemused, Molly let her have her way. What did it matter?

In truth, Molly could see little point to this wedding. She and Connor had been together for three years now—or almost together. As together as she ever wanted to get in a relationship.

Molly was a corporate lawyer. Connor was a cop with the Boston P.D., but he'd inherited money and his sideline was financial investment. He was doing very well; so well the cost of this wedding was waved away with an airy nonchalance.

"Whatever it takes, Mom. We'll do it in style."

Why were they doing it at all?

It had been Connor's idea. "Honey, if I'm going to move up in the force then I need to be married. I know you like your independence but you could still have it. We don't want kids. Neither of us want clinging vines for partners. But I do need a wife."

It wasn't fair not to agree, Molly had decided. Connor suited her very well. He was smart and funny. He was her partner when she needed a partner, he was attentive and solicitous and he knew instinctively to melt away when she needed personal space.

Molly had already made partner at her Boston law firm. Marriage wasn't a necessity for her. Years of spite and hurt between her parents—she'd buried her head under a pillow as a little girl to block out the sounds of hate—had put her off the institution for life. But Connor was insistent.

"Look, we can always get divorced afterwards," he'd said, and he hadn't been joking. "Molly, if I can't marry you…"

He'd left the sentence unfinished but she knew what he meant. He'd have to find someone else. And he did suit her.

Molly had spent a week thinking about it. She'd used Connor, as much as he'd used her. As a corporate lawyer on her way up, having a partner in her life made her seem reliable and respectable.

Already a senior detective, Connor truly believed marriage would help him advance even further. Maybe it wasn't a huge ask. And if he didn't mean what he said about maintaining her independence, well, yeah, a divorce was no drama. Her parents had surely shown her that.

And a little part of her had even thought maybe, just maybe, taking this next step might work. Despite her parents' example, other marriages didn't fail and she'd been lonely for so long…

So she'd agreed and then the ghastly Letitia had stepped in, decreeing they have their wedding in Connor's hometown of Dallas. And now she was surrounded by grapes.

"We have to wait a bit," Jean whispered as she smoothed the veil around her friend's shoulders. "The groom's not here yet."

"Connor's not here?" Molly almost fell over with shock. Under Letitia's direction this event had been choreographed to the last nanosecond. Right now Connor and his six groomsmen should be standing at the other end of the aisle, waiting for her grand entrance.

She was the requisite ten minutes late. For Connor not to be here…

"Maybe he's got cold feet," one of the other bridesmaids said, and gave a nervous titter.

"You want to drive round the block a couple of times and come back?" It was Sam, Molly's brother. He was standing on the far side of the car, looking doubtful. In truth Sam had looked doubtful since she'd told him she was getting married. He and Molly saw very little of each other—Sam was almost ten years older than she was and he was a free spirit, but they held each other in deep affection. He'd met Connor a few times before this and had been noncommittal, but last night…

"These friends of Connor… Moll, are you sure you know what you're getting into?"

"They're police officers. What could possibly be wrong?"

"They're not the sort of cops I know."

"What are you telling me?" It had been straight after the wedding rehearsal. She'd been preparing to go on to the formal prewedding dinner so there'd been little time to talk, but he'd been deeply uneasy.

"Molly, these guys…the groomsmen… Something's not right."

"Trouble," she said, and sighed. "You look for it everywhere. That's because you're a lawman yourself, these guys are in suits, they're all wearing hair oil and I'm your baby sister. Relax."

"They're nervous and I don't know why. Molly, I don't like it."

She didn't need this. She was nervous enough without it. "So Letitia's made this a bigger production than *Ben Hur*," she snapped. "I'm nervous, too. Sam, stop it." She'd taken a couple of deep breaths, calmed down and given him a hug. "I've been dating Connor for years. What could possibly be wrong?"

But now… She looked over at her brother and she saw the doubts of the night before cementing in his gaze.

Oh, for heaven's sake. If she got back into the car, Sam

would have her whisked to the nearest airport and somewhere far away. She'd decided to do this. Connor was late. So what?

"I'll wait on the porch," she said, and picked up the weight of the truly appalling gown Letitia had persuaded her to buy and headed up the path.

"You can't come in." Letitia was standing at the door to the chapel, barring the way. She had on the most extraordinary dress—floor-length, brilliant pink with burgundy sequins and exposing far too much bosom.

She looked like she was about to weep.

Despite her dislike of the woman Molly glanced sharply at her in concern. For this wedding to go awry...how could Letitia bear it?

But then Letitia was shoved aside, with such force that she almost fell. Connor's best man—Tommy Morrissey, a fellow cop—was pushing the door wide from behind her. He was barking orders into his cell phone and his other hand was on his hip.

"What's happening?" Molly demanded, but Tommy was looking past her.

Molly turned, expecting to see a car carrying her bridegroom. From where she stood on the steps she had a view back down the road, the way they'd come.

It wasn't Connor. There were three—no, four—squad cars getting closer. Police.

She turned back to Tommy, stunned. And what she saw stunned her further. The hand that had been on his hip was now holding a gun. It was small, blue-black and dreadful, held with deadly menace.

"Where's...where's Connor?" she whispered, appalled.

"He's done the dirty on us," Tommy snapped. "Hell...if he's told the cops... We have to get out of here."

He raised his gun hand.

She was hit hard from behind.

ONE MINUTE SHE was standing there, staring dumbly at Tommy. The next she was in the middle of the rosebushes in the side garden. She was pinned down by a deadweight. Dead? No. It moved.

Someone was lying on top of her!

"Shut up and keep still," a voice hissed into her ear as she tried frantically to push herself up.

"Are you kidding? Get off me!"

"Struggle and I'll hit you," the voice ordered. "Stay down."

"But…"

Her words were cut off as something zinged above their heads, so close she felt it in her hair. It smashed into the masonry wall, sending a spurt of dried mortar over them.

What the…

Gunshots?

This was crazy. What were people doing shooting…*at her wedding?*

Stupidly, instinctively, she shoved upward again. Two strong hands grabbed her shoulders and she was pushed firmer down into the roses.

They were carpet roses, she thought dumbly. No thorns. Thankfully or she'd be a pincushion by now. As it was there were twigs sticking into her all over.

She was a bride. On her wedding day. What was she doing lying in a rose bed?

With a man on top of her.

He wasn't even wearing a suit. That was a crazy thought, but it was the only one she could think of right now. It was a black leather jacket, fitted, smooth.

What was this creep doing wearing leather to *her* wedding?

"Get—get off me!" she stammered again. "Get off!"

The shots seemed to have ceased. The guy holding her down rolled over so they were side by side, allowing her to see him.

It was a leather jacket. Classy. He had the bluest of blue eyes she'd ever seen. His burned-red hair was cropped short. His face was tanned, weathered. He was thirtyish? Maybe a bit older? A bit life-worn.

What was she doing, making a list of his features? She was staring dumbly at him, but couldn't think where else to look.

"Are you okay?" he demanded, and she blinked and forced her fuddled mind to focus.

"Of—of course I'm okay. Except where you pushed…"

"Did they hit you? They were shooting."

"Who was shooting?"

"Just answer the question," he snapped. "You're not hurt?"

"No, but these…"

"I have to go," he said urgently. "I have to find the kids. Stay down until the cops give you permission to move." And for good measure he put his hand on the top of her head and shoved her farther down into the rosebushes.

THERE WERE COPS everywhere, spreading out. People running. Someone screaming.

But the kids were okay. They'd been standing well to the side of the porch when Tommy had burst out, brandishing his gun. It was only Letitia and the bride who'd been in the line of fire. They were both okay. The bride was in the rose garden, where he'd shoved her. Letitia was crumpled on the tasteful imitation grass, hyperventilating.

Joe didn't have time for Letitia.

The kids were terrified. Their grandmother was trying to

comfort Letitia, leaving the kids alone. Their grandfather hadn't appeared out of the chapel yet. Great. He strode quickly across the pavers to reach them, knelt down and gathered them all against him. The three kids hugged as close as they could get, white-faced and trembling.

He made a decision right there.

"Right," he said, "this is a mess, but it's a mess that's nothing to do with us. Let's go back to your grandparents' house, grab any clothes you need and go straight to the airport. Your grandmother's got your passports. We'll tell her what's going on and we're leaving."

"But Molly…" Charlie whispered. "What's happening to Molly?"

The bride. He glanced back at Molly, who was carefully extricating herself from roses. There were three cops surrounding her. One of her bridesmaids had made a weak effort to help her and then decided to go into hysterics instead. People were barking questions at Molly already.

She looked beautiful, he thought suddenly. Not as in bride beautiful. Her dress was a ghastly confection of too many hoops, too much lace. But underneath it…her glossy, chestnut curls had escaped the carefully coiffed knot and were liberally sprinkled with rose petals and the odd twig or six. Her veil was ripped and askew. The sleeve of her dress was torn almost from the wrist to the shoulder.

There was a trace of blood on her cheek. While he watched she swiped it away with impatience. It smeared further.

She looked stunned. Lost. Bewildered. Angry, too, he thought with approval.

And, yes. Beautiful.

Maybe if he hadn't had the kids, he would have gone to her. Maybe he would have even told her about Erica; told her that marriages with people like Vincent and Connor didn't work. That any sort of marriage didn't work, come to think of it. That whatever had happened to stop her marriage, it was for the best.

But he couldn't do what he wanted right now. The kids were hugging him tight.

Freckled, tousled-haired redheads, they all took after their mother. They looked like his baby sister, he thought as he hugged them back. Each one of them was a white-faced shadow of Erica.

They needed him.

"You're taking us away?" five-year-old Lily whispered, and he nodded.

"Yep. Right now." He glanced back one more time at Molly, and thought he'd remember her. He'd remember this day.

But there was nothing more he could do here. There was nothing he could do for Molly.

He had his own responsibilities. A villain for a bridegroom seemed minor in comparison.

Kids. Care. Christmas.

How could he cope?

"Where will we go?" Charlie asked, voice quavering.

"To Australia. Maybe to my place."

That wasn't going to work, he conceded, as he ushered the kids across the lawn to his hire car. His apartment in Sydney wouldn't fit them all. If he left now, he'd miss Ellie's wedding in Boston and he'd promised her he'd attend. But there was no time to think of anything but these needy kids. Ellie would understand.

"We could go to our holiday house in Queensland," Charlie said, without much hope.

"To your parents' house?" Joe knew the house. It was a

monument to wealth, a tropical oasis set on ten acres of secluded beachfront. Erica and Vincent used it maybe once or twice a year.

The house represented all Joe hated about Vincent. Vincent was involved in seedy deals up to his neck. The police were saying there were bullet holes in his crashed car. There'd been a chase. Erica was dead because…

It didn't matter why she was dead, he told himself harshly. The facts were she was dead, and Joe had two nieces and one nephew who wanted to spend Christmas with him.

Before they went into foster homes?

That didn't bear thinking of. He and Erica had gone down that route and…

And the alternative was responsibility. His responsibility. Christmas.

Maybe Charlie's thought about his parents' beach house was a good one. Erica had given him a key. "Use it all you want," she'd said, but he never had.

It didn't matter. The decision as to where to stay could be made on the flight home.

He stared at the cops surrounding them. There'd be massive media attention. An appeal to the Australian embassy would surely get a reaction now. He'd find someone who could expedite getting them through customs and immigration.

He'd do it somehow.

Next stop, Australia.

SOME WEDDING…

A shoot-out in the Southfork Texas Wedding Chapel. Every newsman in the country was headed their way. The cameramen hired for the wedding were already phoning media outlets negotiating deals.

Letitia had been shepherded away, close to collapse. Three

of the groomsmen had been led away in handcuffs. A couple more groomsmen had escaped. They were saying Tommy had been shooting at Jean—her very own maid of honor. Luckily he'd missed, but Molly had lost Sam and Jean in the chaos.

Some leather-jacketed piece of beefcake had tossed her into the rosebushes.

For twenty minutes it had been chaos.

Now it was over and fear had given way to confusion. Sam had just phoned in—via the police—to say he had Jean safe. That practically blew her away. The police were saying they thought Jean had been targeted. Some of these men were trying to kill her and no one knew why.

"But the police are working on it," Sam said. "Just accept that it's nasty and don't ask any more questions than you have to. And don't try to contact Connor."

Contacting Connor was the last thing she wanted to do right now. At least no one was dead.

The only death, she thought numbly, was her pride. It seemed Connor was a criminal. Big-league. One of the groomsmen had said enough to her as he'd been hauled away to make her feel sick.

She sank onto the portico steps, her lace hoops forcing her skirts to billow around her, and she let her shoulders slump in despair.

"I should never, ever have agreed to this," she muttered to the world in general. "I can't believe I was so stupid. But for Connor to maybe even be a murderer…"

She glanced out at the chaos surrounding her. A guy was ushering the ring bearer and flower girls into a car out in the parking lot, talking over his shoulder to Letitia's sister, the children's grandmother. He was the one who'd shoved her into the rosebushes. A big guy, with burned-red hair. He was hugging little Zoe before he put her in the car, and the sight of that small gesture of care made her feel even more forlorn.

Who was he? Maybe he'd saved her life, she thought numbly. She didn't even know his name.

It didn't matter. Nothing mattered.

"The cops are saying there's some diamond heist the boys are involved in." A plump-faced woman in turquoise—a distant cousin of Connor's—had her arm around Molly's shoulders and was clearly intent on comforting her. Molly wanted her gone, but then someone else would come and support the devastated bride. Sam was off somewhere saving Jean. Supporting Jean. But *she* needed support. It might as well be this woman as anyone, she conceded, and didn't pull away.

"The cops are saying there's millions at stake," the woman said, awed. "I heard one of them talking on his phone to some guy who took off with the maid of honor."

"That would be Sam," Molly said miserably. "My brother."

"Oh." The woman gave her a nervous glance as if she was expecting hysterics. But she wasn't going to pause in a good story for anything less. "The officer I heard was saying Connor framed some cop called Fitzpatrick for a murder. But he proved himself innocent, which leaves Connor and Tommy in the frame." She shivered with ghoulish gusto. "It's awful. Just awful."

"But…then why did he want to marry me?" Molly wailed, and the woman shrugged.

"I guess he loves you, honey."

"Like hell he does," Molly said through gritted teeth. "I have no idea what he's playing at but he's skipped out on our wedding. *Our wedding.* And we're supposed to be going to Australia for our honeymoon." That one fact suddenly stood

out like a beacon, emerging from the horror as a huge regret.
It was the one thought she'd held on to for these last frantic
weeks. As soon as this wedding was over she was headed for
a glorious month in the sun.

"I guess you still can," the woman said, searching desperately for something comforting to say.

"Oh, right. We're booked into the Paradise Island Honeymoon Resort on the Great Barrier Reef. Can you imagine me
going there now? Having a honeymoon all by myself? And
it's Christmas." She was trying hard not to indulge in a little
hysterics herself but she was about as close to hysterics as
she'd ever been in her life. Molly Broadbent, corporate lawyer, was way out of control.

"It's not Christmas for ten days," the woman said, like that
made it okay.

"I don't know what to do."

"You could still go to Australia." The woman took Molly's
hand and patted it. "Maybe…maybe it might even be sensible
to get away for a while."

"I'm not going to any honeymoon resort."

"I know a house you can use."

"Sorry?"

"It belongs to friends of the family," the woman said. "You
know Connor's cousin and his wife were killed in a car crash
six weeks ago? It was a terrible tragedy. It's left their little
family orphaned. They had this house in Australia."

"I know the kids. They were supposed to be my attendants. They've got nothing to do with this." This was getting
crazier and crazier. She should just pick up her hoops and
hightail it out of here—only one of the escaping groomsmen
had taken her Rolls-Royce. The bottom-feeding lowlife. *How
was she going to escape?*

"But the kids don't need the house," the woman said, warming to her theme. "They're staying with their grandma here in Dallas. The house was only a holiday home anyway and it's vacant. My son…" She looked doubtfully at a retreating cop car. "My son was intending to take a trip out there to check it was okay. He has instructions to put it on the market, so I have the key."

Molly's thoughts began to clear. Of course she knew the kids were in Dallas. They'd been staying with Letitia's sister since the accident. Having them in the bridal party was supposed to help cheer them up. Poor little things. "But your son…"

"He might have to stick around here for a while," the woman said uneasily. "Some of these men are his friends. But this house…it's beautiful. I went there once. It's surrounded by ten acres of tropical rain forest right on the beach. It has every luxury you might want. And more than that, it's completely isolated. You'll be doing us a favor checking that it's okay, and it's just the place for a bride to go and lick… For a woman to think about things. You could let things clear up here before you return."

Molly stared at her. "You think I should run away."

"That's exactly what I mean," the woman said bluntly. "If I was in your shoes, that's what I'd do."

Go to Australia?

Molly looked around her. Wedding guests had scattered everywhere. There were cars arriving with media logos emblazoned on the side. A couple of cameramen were heading her way.

If she didn't leave…

She thought about going calmly back into the Boston office on Monday. Facing Christmas alone. Coping with sympathy and voyeuristic gossip. Trying to figure out what the hell Connor was playing at.

"Where did you say this house is?" she asked.

"Just south of Cairns in Northern Australia," her supporter told her. "You don't have to tell anyone where you're going. You can just go."

"Then what am I waiting for?" Molly snapped and rose, her hoops rising with her. "Australia can hardly be worse than this."

IT WAS A LONG WAY to Australia. There was too much thinking time.

How the hell was he going to organize Christmas?

Joe stared out the plane window, trying to reassure himself for the thousandth time. Yes, he would go to the beach house. The house was over-the-top opulent but it was a place the kids knew. There was a beach and a swimming pool. Maybe they'd be self-sufficient. Maybe he could sit in the sun and read a book while they built sand castles.

They'd order in a tree and a Christmas ham and a bulk order of confectionary. That ought to cover it. How hard was it to look after three kids? People did it all the time.

"Uncle Joe, Zoe needs to go to the bathroom," Charlie said from the opposite seat.

"Right." Right? "Lily, can you go with her?"

"No," Lily said uncompromisingly. "I don't feel very well. Uncle Joe, I think I'm going to be sick."

People looked after three kids all the time?

Yeah, right.

CHAPTER TWO

IT TOOK THREE DAYS before investigators let her leave the country, and by the time they did Molly was feeling as bad as she'd ever felt in her life.

Her fiancé was on the take. More than that. The allegations were that Connor and a couple of fellow officers had discovered a plan to steal a consignment of diamonds from the mines in South Africa. It was a small pouch of uncut stones, bound for the best cutters in America. It was worth millions.

They'd let the heist go ahead. Then there'd been a shoot-out—the guy who'd stolen the stones was dead and his accomplice was missing with the goods.

Only now the cops were saying there'd been no accomplice. They were saying that Connor, his cousin Vincent, his workmate Tommy and a couple of others had cooked the scheme up between them. The setup was simple. As police attempting to thwart a robbery they'd killed the thief, pinned the missing diamonds onto a nonexistent accomplice and taken the stones for themselves.

Only their plan had started unraveling. Vincent was supposed to be in charge of the stones. Whether he was or he wasn't, all Molly knew was that Vincent and his wife, Erica, had been run off the road and killed six weeks ago. The homicide operation to find their killer had uncovered the plot within the police force. Tommy and Connor had swung blame onto another cop—a guy called Fitzpatrick—and that had deflected the search for a while. But too many people were in the know now. Fitzpatrick had been cleared, and the tight-knit gang of corruption was beginning to turn on each other.

On the night of the rehearsal Jean overheard threats being made against Vincent's children—seemingly the result of vindictive fury that Vincent had taken the stones. Jean hadn't told anyone at the time—she'd thought she must have been mistaken. Who could believe such things of her best friend's bridegroom? But Connor had noticed her listening. It must have been the catalyst for the drama the next day.

Humiliation was too mild a word for it. *Gutted* was a better description, but that didn't work, either. Now that both Connor and Tommy, his accomplice, were on the run, the authorities had decided the kids would be safe. Killing the kids at this point, when their own necks were at risk, would be crazy. Jean was in witness protection. Sam was with her.

Molly was on her own.

Christmas. Ha!

Four days after the wedding she sat on a plane heading for Australia and she felt smaller and smaller and smaller. Australia wasn't far enough away. Nowhere was far enough away.

"Are you okay, dear?" The woman sitting next to her had been watching her with concern for hours. "You seem… upset."

"Upset?" She summoned a weary smile. "Why should I be upset? I'm going to the holiday of a lifetime."

"That's nice, dear. Whereabouts?"

"It's a private house." That was a problem, too. The house had belonged to Vincent, and just the knowledge that Vincent was Connor's cousin had her unwilling to go anywhere near it. However, the weeks over Christmas were Australia's busiest period. Apart from the honeymoon resort, there was nowhere else to go.

Sun, solitude and peace to lick her wounds. That's all she cared about.

"It's on the beach in Queensland," she said, trying her hardest to sound perky. "It sounds fabulous. I'm going to have a ball."

"You do that, dear," the woman said. "If you don't mind me saying so, you look like you need it."

ALL I WANT FOR Christmas is help. All I want for Christmas is a smile.

These words became a mantra, said over and over in his head a hundred times a day.

These kids were traumatized. Six weeks ago their parents had been killed. Sure, Vincent and Erica hadn't exactly been hands-on parents. In fact, Joe suspected most of the time the kids were left with hired help. They clung together, they helped each other, they didn't look to an adult for comfort when things went wrong.

But their parents' deaths must have shocked them, and moving into their grandparents' sterile mansion had seemed to overwhelm them. The shoot-out at the wedding had rocked their foundations even more.

They now seemed like they didn't have any sense of security at all. They sat in a huddle on Erica's white-on-white settees and watched television hour after hour. They didn't want to do anything else. They looked totally miserable.

"Shall we set up a Christmas tree?" he asked, and they looked at him as if he'd spoken Swahili.

"If you like," Charlie said at last.

"Did you have a Christmas tree last year?"

"There's a big white one in a box in the attic," Lily ventured. "Back home."

"No, the white one was in the hotel in Vegas," Charlie said. "Don't you remember? Dad made room service take it away on Christmas night because the lights kept flashing and his head hurt. The one in the attic is purple and silver."

"Would you like a purple-and-silver one?"

"No," Zoe said. "I don't like purple."

They didn't like anything. They were polite, quiet and withdrawn.

Maybe he should have got trauma counseling for them before they came out here, he thought. Maybe they were damaged for life.

Hell, how would he know? He knew zip about kids. All he knew was that somehow he ought to make Christmas less than the ball of misery it promised.

He took them to the supermarket. They held hands as if the outside world was dangerous. They agreed to all of his suggestions as to what to put in the trolley.

"Isn't there anything you'd like for Christmas?" he said in desperation.

"We don't want to go back to Grandma's," Lily whispered, and he thought great, he could grant that wish, but he had to do better.

Patience. It was all he could think of. Time heals all wounds. It was a dumb platitude but when all else failed, what else was a guy to fall back on?

At least he was filling in time in style. The house was just plain fabulous. There was a staff but they were silent, ghostlike figures trained to arrive at dawn, do their work in stealth and then leave again. By the time he and the kids woke, the place felt totally isolated. The vast kitchen-living room opened right up to an enormous lagoon-style swimming pool. The water in the pool was raised to the brim, slopping over the edge. Backdrop to the pool was the sea, so gazing out the living-room windows they saw lagoon melting into the turquoise waters of the ocean beyond.

It was better than great. He watched the sea. Sailboards. Kayakers. Swimmers.

He took the kids there and they were miserable.

Home to the television. Reruns of the Road Runner.

He was going out of his mind.

He checked his watch for the tenth time since lunch. It was four o'clock. Another hour before he could reasonably be expected to cook up the macaroni and cheese that seemed to be the only thing the kids would eat. Another two hours before he could put them to bed and at least stop watching cartoons....

There was a resounding thump from the lower level. From the entrance hall.

"Scumbag suitcase. Bust for all I care. Stupid designer luggage. Take that!"

Another thump.

He looked at the kids. The kids looked at him.

"Is it a burglar?" Lily whispered, and Zoe crept closer to her sister.

"I don't think burglars bring designer suitcases," Joe said cautiously. "I'll check."

"Take a gun," Charlie advised, and he stared at his nephew in astonishment. It was a female voice swearing at a suitcase. What sort of background did these kids come from, where visitors were met with guns.

"We don't have many guns in Australia," he said in what

he hoped was a voice of authority. "They're against the law and I don't have one. But I'll check."

There was no need. Whoever it was was stumping up the stairs, swearing at each step.

"Dumb taxi drivers. Dumb luggage. Dumb stupid fiancés."

She reached the top of the step and stopped dead.

Molly.

HE WAS HERE. The guy who'd shoved her into the roses. She'd pick out that red hair anywhere. And those eyes. He was wearing faded jeans and an old T-shirt, but it was the same guy.

She glanced behind him. Sitting on the settee like stuffed toys were three kids.

"Charlie," she said faintly. "Lily. Zoe."

"Molly!" Zoe cried, and abandoned the settee and raced across the room. She grabbed Molly around the knees and held with such ferocity that Molly staggered backward and had to catch the balustrade or she would have toppled down the stairs.

"Hey." She stooped and hugged the little girl, her mind racing. What the…

These were Vincent's kids. Connor's cousin's kids.

Of course. This was Vincent's house.

"You're not supposed to be here," she managed to say. "They said your uncle was looking after you."

"He is," Zoe said, burying her face in Molly's shoulder. "Uncle Joe's here. He's trying to look after us."

Molly's gaze flew to Joe. He was staring at her like he was seeing a ghost.

"The bride," he said.

"Yep, this is my honeymoon," she ventured, trying to take it all in. She stood up again but Zoe clung to her legs and didn't let go. "What are you doing here?"

"This is the kids' house."

"I was told it'd be empty."

"It's not."

"Right." She couldn't think of where to go from here.

"Are you here for Christmas?" Zoe asked her, and she shook her head.

"Nope." Definitely not. Not now.

The faces of the three children drooped.

"It'd be good if you could stay for Christmas," Lily whispered, and Joe looked at her sharply.

"How do you know the kids?" he asked, and Molly glanced across the room at Charlie and Lily and her heart gave a sudden lurch. She'd spent only a little time with these children, but even in that time…she'd realized just how lost they were.

"They were supposed to be my ring bearer and flower girls," she said.

"Because they were Connor's relations. Not yours."

"What's his was supposed to be mine," she said, striving for lightness. "Connor and Vincent were friends, as well as cousins. Connor and I have been…together…for three years. So the kids and I have seen each other on family occasions."

"Connor and Molly had Christmas with us last year," Lily volunteered. "Molly didn't like our white Christmas tree, either. When the grownups started arguing, she took us for a walk and we looked in all the shop windows and decided what we'd buy if we had all the money in the world."

Molly swallowed. She'd hated it. They'd been at an opulent hotel in New York. "Let's abandon the family for Christmas," Connor had said, and even though Molly had known how hurt Letitia would be, she hadn't been able to resist. She had no family of her own apart from Sam, who was off doing his own thing as he always was. The thought of a Christmas in Manhattan with just the two of them sounded great. Only, of course, Vincent and Erica had been there with their kids. Connor hadn't told her they would be.

He hadn't told her lots of things. The relationship had been all surface, she thought. It had been a convenience. She'd never really bothered peering under the veneer.

Like last Christmas. She'd been surprised when she'd discovered Vincent and Erica were in the same hotel as they were. Her idea of an intimate Christmas dinner had turned into a much bigger occasion, a dozen or more people in the vast hotel dining room. The men had seemed…somehow grim. Talking in undertones. Arguing. Disappearing from the table.

The women were a type—accessory wives. They tittered and gossiped. At the end of the table a pale-faced nanny called Mandy had sat with the kids. Her job was to keep the children silent. Still in her teens, white-faced and lonely, she seemed almost to be one of the kids herself. She was surely just as miserable.

Finally Molly could bear it no longer. She'd excused herself, but the kids and Mandy had looked at her with such desperation as she left the table that she'd had little choice.

"We'll walk off some of our turkey," she'd said, but no one had listened. She'd taken the kids and Mandy away, and Erica hadn't so much as asked where they were going.

"We had fun," Lily remembered, in a tight little voice that said she hoped desperately it was true. "Only then Dad sacked Mandy and then…and then…"

Then their parents had died. "But this is still Christmas," Molly said gently. "You must be looking forward to it. Your cousin Betty had the key to this house and she told me it'd be empty. She said it'd be good if I could check up on it. But now you guys are here… I'll leave you to it."

"Where will you go?" Joe asked. He'd been watching her as if she were a genie who had suddenly appeared from a bottle and he didn't quite believe she was real.

"To a hotel," she said, and backed away from that look. The last thing she needed was a needy male.

"You can stay if you like."

"I don't like," she said flatly, and then winced at the look on three kids' faces. She regrouped. "Sorry, guys, but I'm feeling a bit sad at the moment. Because of what happened at my wedding."

"What happened to Connor?" Charlie asked.

"I don't know," Molly said. "The police are still looking for him. They think he might have done something bad." How to tell kids that not only was he suspected of stealing the diamonds, but he was also implicated in three murders—two of which were these kids' parents.

"He did a bad thing not marrying you," Lily said stoutly, and Zoe hugged Molly's legs tighter as if it was astounding that anyone could be so stupid.

Strangely it helped. She hadn't wept—not for the entire time since her abandoned wedding—but now she found herself suddenly blinking away tears.

"We're sad, too," Charlie said cautiously from the settee. "Maybe we can all be sad together."

"Welcome to my world." Joe's expression was cautiously hopeful. A man who'd seen a chink of light. "Endless reruns of the Road Runner."

"The Road Runner's good," she told him.

"In moderation."

"You have a beach."

"The kids don't like the beach."

"You don't like the beach?" She disentangled Zoe and

stepped back, gazing first at the kids and then out to where the Pacific Ocean lay in all its glory. "Why not?"

"It's scary," Lily whispered.

"But you have your uncle Joe to look after you."

Their glance at their uncle Joe said it all. They didn't know him. They'd been tossed into a terrifying environment where the rules weren't the same. They didn't know how to handle it.

"We always have a nanny," Zoe said. "The nanny tells us the rules."

"I suspect your uncle Joe knows some rules."

"He doesn't tell us."

"So why not?" Molly asked him, and Joe looked flummoxed.

"Hey. I told the kids to do what they like."

"Right. Kids need rules. Now if you'll excuse me…"

"You can't go," Joe said.

"Why not?" She gazed at him in astonishment.

"You…hell, you just can't."

"You throw me into a rose garden at my own wedding. You rip my gown—which, I might add, cost me a king's ransom—and now you tell me where I can and can't go?"

"I need you."

WHERE HAD THAT come from? He'd never said such a thing in his life.

He didn't need anyone.

But desperate times called for desperate measures. Sure it was a cliché, but someone had made it up for good reason. Now was as desperate as he was ever likely to get.

He had four days to go before Christmas. He was so far out of his depth with these kids he felt like drowning.

This woman knew them. She had some sort of link to their past. She'd spent last Christmas with them.

Zoe was back clutching her legs.

"No," Molly said.

"No?"

"It's my honeymoon."

"You can have your honeymoon with us," Lily said, but she sounded doubtful.

"We're nicer than Connor," Charlie said, and she looked across the room at him and she thought about it and she sniffed.

It was a pretty decisive sniff. Joe thought back to the last woman he dated. Elspeth would have given away her Manolo Blahnik shoes rather than sniff.

He didn't do emotion. He didn't do needy females.

That sniff sort of…touched him.

"You know, it's Christmas," he said gently. "Every hotel in Australia will have been booked out months ago."

"I still have my booking at the…" She stopped.

"Where?" he prodded.

"The Paradise Island Honeymoon Resort," she said on a little gasp, and he wasn't fast enough to repress a smile.

"Laugh and you're dead meat," she snapped.

"I'm not laughing." He schooled his expression into seriousness.

"I can still go there."

"You'd hate it." His voice became gentler. "Molly, we have a huge house. Five bedrooms. The kids and I are upstairs using two bedrooms between us. The whole bottom floor can be yours. There's even a little kitchenette down there."

"So Mom and Dad can eat up here and the nanny and us can eat downstairs," Lily said.

"That sounds real cozy," she said, before she caught herself.

"It's not great," Joe said. "Nothing for these kids has been great."

She fell silent. There was a long pause while Joe wisely decided not to say anything at all.

"I don't even know you," she said at last.

"I'm Joe Cartland. Erica's brother."

"I know that much at least," she snapped.

"Letitia knew we'd be here. I can't understand why she didn't tell…"

"If you think Letitia was capable of a coherent thought, you're so far off reality there's no help for you. Her son's wanted for…" She gasped and stopped and looked at the kids. She reformatted whatever it was she was about to say. "Her son's wanted for theft. Her husband's useless. Henry just nods and smiles like one of those bobble-head dogs you see in the back of cars."

"That's Great-Uncle Henry," Lily said wisely. "He nods all the time."

"He does look like one of those dogs," Charlie said, and giggled.

They all drew a breath. Joe looked across at Charlie. He'd giggled.

It was the best sound.

Charlie had taken on the weight of the world since his parents' deaths. His little sisters had clung to him and he'd reacted with a strength that belied his age. He'd asked for help from Joe because he didn't know what to do, but it wasn't working.

This woman had been in the house for five minutes and Charlie was giggling.

"You have to stay," he said, and he didn't even try to disguise the urgency in his voice.

"I don't want to."

"What else do you want to do?"

"I don't know," she wailed. "Set the clock back. Not get

engaged to Connor in the first place. Beam me up to some planet where none of this exists."

"Well, while you're waiting for your spaceship, why don't you go downstairs, get into a swimming costume and then join us in the pool."

"I wanted to escape."

"I guess we all want to do that," he said. Then, at the look on her face—a combination of anger, bewilderment and despair—he took a couple of strides across the room. He lifted Zoe away from her legs and popped her behind him.

"Let's give Molly some space," he said. "She needs to make her own decision."

"Right," she said. "As if I can. Blackmailing…"

"I'm not blackmailing."

"I don't know what else you could call this. It's a trap, ready-set."

"Not by me." He said it steadily, meeting her gaze with what he hoped was his most honest, reliable, nonconfrontational expression.

It didn't work. "Men," she said with loathing. "They're all the same."

"I'm not the same as Connor."

Her glare said she didn't believe him. "If I stay here, I stay completely separate."

"But you will have a swim with us?" Charlie said, sounding bewildered.

She cast a despairing glance across at him. "I might have known it. You're male, too."

"I'm just a boy," Charlie said.

"Me, too," Joe said virtuously, and she glared some more.

"Right."

"But you will stay."

There was another pause—even longer than the last one. He watched the warring emotions flitting across her face. She was right in thinking this was a trap, he thought. It was a trap for both of them. Three orphans for Christmas.

Three orphans and Molly. A battered bride.

It'd be interesting, he thought, and the gray fog that had surrounded him from the moment he'd heard of Erica's death lifted a little.

Just a little. There was no point in getting his hopes up yet. But his hopes were up. He forced himself to stay quiet, to school his face into impassivity, to try and make it seem like it was all her decision and he wasn't forcing things.

"You're a bottom feeder," she said into the silence, and he blinked.

"Um…why?"

"Because you're male and I hate the species."

"Except for me," Charlie said anxiously, and she sighed.

"Yes, Charlie, apart from you."

"Try and forget I'm male," Joe said hopefully.

"Yeah, right."

"But you will stay?" Lily asked, and Molly threw up her hands in surrender.

"Fine. I'll stay. Let's have Christmas. But if I'm staying, I refuse to watch the Road Runner. I want a real Christmas."

"Of course we'll have Christmas."

"No," she said decisively. "Not a white-plastic-Christmas-tree Christmas. A proper Christmas. I want a real tree and plum pudding and mistletoe. I want Santa Sacks and church at midnight and all the trimmings. I want ten miles of paper chains hung all round this crazy white house, and I want paper lanterns everywhere. It'll keep our minds off everything and that's the most important thing right now. Joe, pour me a drink. Zoe, Lily, come and help me unpack. Charlie, the handle came off my smallest case out by the driveway. Can you go collect my cosmetics, please? Not that I'll need them here. And, Joe Cartland, if you so much as think about being male, I'm hightailing it out of here so fast I'd leave the Road Runner for dead. Got it?"

"Yes, ma'am," he said faintly.

"Right," she said. "Let's do it. Let's get Christmas on the road."

CHAPTER THREE

WHAT HAD SHE agreed to do?

Molly stood in front of the big mirror in the downstairs bedroom and stared at her reflection in consternation. She was wearing her brand-new bikini. It was a slash of scarlet designed to make Connor's eyes water. It had cost a fortune.

She was wearing it for Joe and three kids.

There was no going back now. The kids had helped her unpack, she'd sent them upstairs to put their own bathing gear on and they were expecting her by the pool.

Joe was expecting her by the pool. He was up there making her a drink.

He was too good-looking by half. He'd hauled her into the rosebushes with such force that she still had bruises. But the cops had looked at the bullet holes in the chapel entry and had nothing but praise for the guy.

"Tommy was specifically aiming for your bridesmaid and his shots were wild," they'd said. "One of the other guys started shooting, as well. Everyone was in danger. We had no choice but to shoot back. If Letitia hadn't collapsed and this guy hadn't pushed you sideways, you'd probably both be dead."

"So you guys were shooting at me?" she asked, astounded.

"You don't understand, ma'am," they'd replied patiently.

"Tommy opened fire indiscriminately. He was firing on wedding guests, as well as us. We had no choice but to take him out."

"But you didn't," she'd snapped. "He got away."

It made her nervous. Connor was still out there somewhere. Who else was with him?

They'd made threats against these kids. She thought about it now and wondered whether Joe was aware of it. Maybe that's why he'd brought them here, she thought. Australia was about as far as you could get from Dallas and Connor and his thugs. And evil.

She shivered, feeling sick as she did every time she thought about it. How close had she come to marrying the guy?

Why had Connor wanted to be married to her? But she knew the answer to that. She was a high-profile lawyer. Her firm represented Boston's old money. She had it figured now. Connor was a crooked cop. He needed respectability and she could give it to him.

That was why the sudden pressure to marry. Apparently rumors had been spreading in the force and he wanted them squashed.

So much for wanting to impress Connor with her bikini. She stared into the mirror and winced. Had he even wanted her? Had he seen anything other than the respectable, boring, legal side of her?

She shivered, feeling lonely, sick and sad.

Maybe it was just as well she'd committed to spending Christmas with three kids, she thought. Otherwise…well…

"Otherwise" didn't bear thinking about.

But the package included Joe.

There was something not to think about. Joe with the kindly eyes, but the look that said he saw deeper. He was disturbing. Too big. Too male.

He was waiting with a drink.

She was committed. She had to go. But she picked up her sarong and tied it round her waist; then rethought and tied it higher.

Respectable Molly.

SHE WALKED THROUGH the glass doors leading to the pool and he almost dropped his beer.

This was the third time he'd seen her. The first time she'd looked like a rumpled piece of overly ornate candy floss. Then, when she'd arrived today, she'd been wearing a business-type skirt and jacket. It had been red but it was conservative. She'd even been wearing nylons.

But now…

The sliver of a sarong was transparent enough for him to see the outline of a smashing bikini underneath. Nothing else. Her legs were bare. She'd hauled her hair out of the knot she'd had it in, and her curls were brushing loosely against her bare shoulders.

She looked young, he thought. He knew that she was a lawyer—a partner in one of Boston's bigger law firms. She had to be in her thirties.

She looked about nineteen.

"Hi," he said for want of anything better, and she cast him a scared glance, accentuating his impression of youth.

"Hi, yourself."

"Molly," the kids yelled. They were sitting on the edge of the shallow end of the pool, lined up like three little birds.

"Why aren't you in the water?" she called.

"We're waiting for you."

"Molly's come all the way from the U.S.," he told them, reprovingly. "She gets a drink before she swims. It's in the rules."

Rules. He saw how the word resonated.

This was how these kids had been brought up, he thought. Molly had twigged it. What he'd been doing for the last few days—giving them choices, leaving the rules up to them—must have seemed an extension of the chaos their lives had become since their parents had died. Molly had it right. He had it wrong.

He didn't do kids. He was dumb with kids. What was he doing even trying?

"I want you to test out the water," Molly was telling them. "I want you to try it out and see if it's suitable for me to come in. Charlie, look after Zoe."

Right. The three little figures almost visibly relaxed. They knew the rules now. They slid into the water.

"You're not allowed to go past the curvy bit," Charlie said firmly to Zoe, clearly taking the take-care-of-Zoe rule to heart. "It's too deep." He looked up at Joe. "We know how to float. You want to see us?"

"Yes, please," Joe said weakly. He hadn't been able to get these kids in the water. He was feeling about as useful as a gnat.

But at least he'd made Molly a drink. He crossed to the sumptuous poolside bar and fetched his concoction, bringing it back to her as he watched the floating.

She accepted it with care and eyed it in astonishment. "What the…"

"It's Sex on the Beach," he told her with a certain amount of pride.

Her jaw sort of sagged. She stared down at the drink like it might contain arsenic. "Um…what?"

"Sex on the Beach," he repeated and grinned. "Peach schnapps, rum, banana liqueur, coconut cream, orange juice and ice."

"It's what you give all the girls," she said faintly. "Instead of a nice cup of tea."

"I'm working my way through a recipe book. Erica and Vincent had every form of alcohol known to man stocked in this bar. Half the liqueurs are open. If they're not used they'll go off, and there's a book called *Seduction by the Glass*. It's a hundred cocktail recipes. I'm up to number four." He motioned to his beer. "One a day's my limit before I swap to this. You, however, are not in charge. You can have as many as you want."

Maybe it was the wrong thing to say. She rearranged her facial muscles from disapproving to downright judgmental. Black cap judgmental. "This is no seduction scene," she said flatly.

"Get real. With three kids?" He raised his glass in a gesture of toasting her. "I'm drinking light beer. And the cocktail I made me was a Virgin Grasshopper. Nonalcoholic."

"How very noble."

"I hoped you might think that."

MAYBE HE WASN'T too bad. Maybe she should relax a bit.

Sex on the Beach? Virgin Grasshoppers? She stared down into her salt-rimmed glass with the gay little parasol and even managed a smile. She put her nose into her cocktail glass and took a cautious sip. It was strong and sweet and…

And not that bad. It sent the odd bit of fire into her solar plexus. She hadn't been aware she needed a bit of fire down there but now that it had happened…

It was sort of comforting, she thought. Or was it the man watching her as she sipped.

"Awful?" he asked.

"Not bad."

"But not good?"

"I wouldn't want two." She smiled again. These were her first smiles since the wedding chaos and they felt strange. Almost a betrayal.

A betrayal of what? Connor?

Right.

"I might try what's next on the list," she said, hugely daring. "But later," she added hastily, as he reached for his book with obvious enthusiasm. "With a meal in between. The last thing you need is a tipsy bride."

"The last thing I need is any sort of bride," he said before he could help himself.

She thought about that. She sipped again. She turned to the pool, where splashing competitions were being held, and watched the kids for a while.

"So domesticity's not your scene?" she said at last, attempting lightness. This situation felt awkward and weird and she was out of her comfort zone. She wouldn't mind knowing a bit more about the man she'd just decided to spend Christmas with.

"No," he said flatly.

"Your sister was hardly a family woman, either," she said thoughtfully.

"Our parents were dysfunctional, to say the least," he confessed. "Dad disappeared when we were two. By five we were in the first of a series of foster homes, and we were split up for much of our childhood. We learned pretty early that attachment hurts."

"Yeah," she said.

"You, too?" He frowned.

"Same deal, only with rich parents," she said. "Like these kids, my brother and I were raised by nannies and with rules. We're ten years apart in age so we hardly knew each other, much less our parents. Love sucks."

"Says the bride."

"Says the ex-bride," she said bitterly. "I figured it out on the plane over here. Connor and I were good together because we didn't need each other. We were independent. Then we broke the rules by trying to get married."

"You're not blaming what happened on a decision to get married?" he demanded.

"No, but it was dumb." Her sarong came loose and she tossed it onto the sun lounge. Whatever Sex on the Beach had in it, her need for protection suddenly seemed a little less.

"Character assessments aren't your thing?" he queried.

"You know, I would have said they were." Her tone was bitter. "Do you know what Jean heard the night of the rehearsal?"

"I got the gist. Have you seen Jean since the wedding?"

"Briefly. What she heard is important so she's being taken care of by the police. She wasn't specific but I gather she heard enough to terrify her."

"I know that much, too," he said gently. "The cops rang me yesterday, just confirming the kids are safe. They told me about the threats, but they've decided while there's a nation-wide search out for Connor, the last thing he or any of his henchmen will want to do is stick round to kill the kids for further revenge against a dead Vincent. The cops think the kids will be safe here."

"If you didn't hear about the threats until yesterday…why did you come?"

"I came because the kids were miserable with their grand-parents, they know this place, the media attention meant I could get the authorities in the U.S. to cut red tape to get them here…and they need a Christmas."

"You know, I think you're a very nice man," she said suddenly, decisively, and put her now-empty glass down on the table with a determined clink. "A very nice man." And before he could figure what she intended—before she thought about it herself—she stepped forward, stood on her tiptoes and kissed him.

It was a feather touch of a kiss but it met his lips and it burned.

She stepped back, her eyes widening. Whoops. Where had that come from? He looked…stunned.

"That's what you get for feeding me Sex on the Beach when I'm jet-lagged," she said a trifle unsteadily. "I…thank you. I'm going in now."

"Into the water?"

"Where else would I be going. Don't give me any more of those cocktails."

"No, ma'am."

"And don't think I meant anything by that kiss," she said, a trifle desperately. "I have a feeling I shouldn't have done it but I needed to, though just for the moment I can't exactly figure out why."

"No, ma'am," he said again.

She couldn't think what else to say. There was nothing else to say.

She walked to the deep end of the pool, businesslike and efficient, and dived neatly in.

HE DIDN'T GET into the pool. Not because he didn't want to, but because he didn't know what to do if he did.

Molly had found a beach ball. She and Zoe were playing a version of water polo with Lily and Charlie. Molly's height made up for Zoe's lack of inches so the teams were evenly matched.

The change in the kids was extraordinary. It was like the

cork had popped out of a bottle of fizz. They whooped and giggled and shrieked and they forgot all about being the miserable waifs they'd been for the last few days.

Maybe it was a combination of things, he decided, trying not to believe it was just him being insensitive that had caused the kids' misery. He and Vincent hadn't got on; therefore he'd hardly seen the kids. Even when he was in the States he'd made excuses not to visit his sister, and every time he did visit… He thought back to those few occasions and remembered the kids in the background with a nanny as Vincent and Erica ushered him out of their magnificent home to eat at an equally magnificent restaurant. Vincent felt the need to show him how successful he was in life. All he'd succeeded in doing was make Joe feel uneasy in his presence.

At least the kids had felt they knew him enough to phone him and ask him to rescue them from their appalling grandparents. But that didn't qualify as close.

They knew Molly. Maybe they saw her as a link to the past.

"Why aren't you swimming?" Charlie called out to him, and he shook his head at his nephew and smiled down at the four of them wallowing in the shallows. How to say it felt too intimate? Too close? Too much fun for the likes of him?

"I need to get dinner going."

"It doesn't take long," Charlie said. "Three minutes each in the microwave."

Whoops. His secret was out.

"What takes three minutes in the microwave?" Molly asked.

"Macaroni and cheese," Lily said, grabbing the ball while Molly's attention was diverted. "We went to the supermarket yesterday and bought twenty boxes of macaroni and cheese. That's five suppers for us."

"Yeah, but we had it for lunch today, too," Charlie said.

"So that means we have to go back to the supermarket the day after tomorrow."

"Is that all you eat?" Molly asked.

"Yes," they said as one.

"Wow."

Joe winced. Ouch. And he hadn't been going to cook macaroni tonight. Not now that Molly was here. He'd been planning on opening the refrigerator and finding inspiration in its depths.

Okay, maybe that wasn't going to happen. "Any suggestions?" he said, trying not to sound hopeful.

"I like macaroni and cheese," she said cautiously.

"Then you're in luck. I can have it on the table in three minutes times five boxes."

"But it's not my first choice. What are you intending to do for Christmas dinner?"

"You did say…"

"That we needed the trimmings," she said, fielding the ball and tossing it to Zoe. Zoe missed, the ball went long, and Charlie and Lily whooped after it. "I did. It's what I want but that doesn't mean you guys have to eat what I do. If you're hung up on your macaroni thing… Maybe I can get a frozen Christmas dinner for one."

"That's silly," Zoe said, grabbing fruitlessly for the ball.

"Why?" The older kids paused to take part in the conversation. Taking advantage of the distraction Molly did a neat, seal-like dive under the water, came back up and seized the beach ball and raised it high, out of reach of any of them. "Why is it silly?"

"You can't eat Christmas dinner on your own," Lily told her, staring at the dripping Molly as if a mermaid had appeared from the depths.

"I'm not eating macaroni for Christmas dinner. You guys didn't eat macaroni last Christmas."

"We didn't like the stuff at the hotel much," Lily said.

"So what do you like?"

"Strawberries," Zoe said.

"Hot dogs," Charlie said.

"Meringues," Lily added.

Molly nodded, serious. But still holding the ball out of reach. "Okay, we have a start. Are you really, really committed to macaroni?"

"What's committed?" asked Zoe.

"If you don't have macaroni, will you cry?"

"Not if I can have strawberries," Zoe said, her baby eyes filled with hope.

"Good girl," she said while Joe looked on with astonishment. "Okay, how's this for a plan? Let's see how many yummy things we can eat between now and the day after Christmas. If we get out of the pool now, we could probably go to the supermarket and get the makings of hot dogs and strawberries and meringues for tonight."

"How do you make meringues?" Lily asked, awed.

"I don't know," Molly confessed. "But if your uncle Joe can make Sex on the Beach cocktails I'm willing to bet he can whip up a meringue or two. Do we have the Internet?"

"Yes," Joe said, flummoxed.

"There you go then," she said smugly. "If you're not swimming, then in you go and surf the Net until you find a recipe for meringues. Zoe and I will beat the pants off these two at water polo and then we'll get dressed and all go supermarket shopping for ingredients. Oh, and we'll find a Christmas tree while we're at it. How's that for a plan?"

"Macaroni and cheese sounds easier," Joe said.

"Macaroni and cheese is so last night's news," she said in such a drawly, over-the-top voice that the kids giggled. "Tonight the menu consists of hot dogs, strawberries and meringues." Then, when he kept staring at her, she put her hands on her hips and fixed him with a don't-mess-with-me look. "Don't just stand there with your mouth open, buster. Hop to it."

WHEN HE'D FIRST BROUGHT the kids to Australia, Joe had reluctantly left his sweet little Alfa Romeo in the airport garage and rented a family wagon for the duration. He surely needed it. They drove into town, he and Molly in the front, the kids in the back.

"We're just like a family," Lily said from the backseat.

"Yeah," Joe said dryly, and glanced across at Molly. He was expecting to see her smiling. For an abandoned bride she'd been really upbeat. Apart from her initial shock, she'd launched herself into these plans with enthusiasm.

But she wasn't smiling now. Her smile had slipped, replaced by something he didn't understand.

Bleakness? Desperation?

She'd been jilted less than a week ago, he reminded himself. She'd be raw.

"He's not worth looking like that," he said gently, and she flinched and looked away, out the passenger window at the rain forest they were traveling through.

"Of course he isn't."

"You'll meet someone else."

"Sure."

"Molly…"

"Leave it," she said roughly.

So she'd loved the scumbag. That made it a whole lot worse.

But why had he thought she wouldn't? Why was the thought of anyone loving Connor O'Bannion inconceivable?

No. Why was the thought of Molly loving O'Bannion inconceivable?

"I'm sorry," he said gently, and she cast him a look that was almost scared.

"Let's have some music," he said, and flicked on the radio. Cricket. Cricket! He cheered up. Christmas in Australia was all about cricket. Men in white, leather on willow, yells of "howz that?" as cricketers appealed for umpires to rule the batsmen out.

"Australia is four for twenty-seven against the West Indies," the announcer said, and Joe groaned.

"Is that bad?" Molly asked, surfacing again.

"Awful."

"Four for twenty-seven what?"

"Four wickets for twenty-seven runs. A good inning is a hundred runs. Four for four hundred would be great. Four for twenty-seven is almost take-your-bat-and-go-home territory. Do you kids know about cricket?"

There was deathly silence from the backseat.

"Well," he said. "Well." He cast a surreptitious glance at Molly and thought she was doing her best to forget her pain by throwing herself into Christmas. He could do worse than to help her. "Here's my plan."

"What?" Charlie asked.

"Supermarket followed by sports store," he said. "We need a bat and ball, a wicket and a set of pads for the keeper. You guys are having an Australian Christmas. That means cricket in the backyard."

"I don't think I like cricket," Zoe announced.

"Like doesn't come into it," he said in solemn tones. "It's your heritage. Your mother was Australian, therefore you're bred to play cricket."

"What about me?" Molly asked.

"You're a jilted bride," he told her. "You need distraction."

"From what I've ever seen of cricket, it's the sport least likely to distract in the known world."

"That's where you're wrong," he said expansively. "You're all so wrong. Molly. You're in charge of Christmas eating. I'm in charge of Christmas education."

CHAPTER FOUR

IT WAS AN ENORMOUS, comprehensive shop. The supermarket manager must have thought all his Christmas shoppers had come at once, for Molly was in a buying mood. The deep sadness Joe had glimpsed in the car had been put aside with a vengeance.

"Of course you can have chocolate ice cream," she told Zoe. "But I like strawberry. We'll have both. You like caramel, Charlie? Of course we can have that, too."

They gave up on the one trolley. She gave the kids a trolley each and let them do what they wished with it.

For the first few minutes the kids were as hornswoggled as Joe. An empty trolley each. "But it's too much?" Lily whispered.

"Nonsense," Molly said firmly. "Nothing's too much at Christmas. If you think you'd like to eat it, let's buy it. That's the rule."

These kids' lives had been carefully controlled. They'd never shopped. Joe watched in awe as realization hit each of them that the rule here was no rule.

Zoe headed to the confectionary aisle. He groaned inwardly, imagining a trolley loaded to the brim with candy. But he needn't have worried.

"Zoe, there's little baby sausages in the fridge," Lily told her sister excitedly, as Zoe loaded her fifth box of chocolates into the trolley. "And there's grapes. And watermelon. And cherries. And there's party hats over in the last aisle. And party poppers."

Zoe looked at her older sister in astonishment. She looked at her chocolate boxes, wrinkled her small brow, put two of the boxes back on the shelves and headed for the other aisles.

"We'll have far too much," Joe said to Molly, who was piling mangoes into her trolley.

"Are you kidding? There are three refrigerators in that mausoleum of a holiday house. This is fun."

"It'll cost a fortune."

She stopped, a mango in each hand, and eyed him cautiously.

"So it will. Why didn't I think of that? But you know, I'm a lawyer. I have a few contacts. When the police were convincing me of Connor's guilt, they showed me a pile of cross-matched bank statements, including Vincent's. These children stand to inherit a fortune, and the police are saying it's almost all profits from illegal activities. Because Vincent's dead he can't be charged and the money is likely to remain theirs. The lady on the plane this morning told me this little town is struggling. There was a cyclone came through here last summer. The tourists have been staying away and the locals are doing it tough. We spend some of Vincent's ill-gotten gains, we spread Christmas fortune further than ourselves and we risk Zoe getting a tummy ache. So what? You want to stop us now?"

"You've thought it through."

"What else have I had to do but think? I spent twenty-four hours getting here and days before that being interviewed, interviewed, interviewed. Oh, and humiliated into the bargain. Of course I thunk. I gather you have access to those funds as you're caring for the children?"

"I…yes."

"And Erica told me once that her brother was loaded. She said you get paid an obscene amount of money for deciding why airplanes crash. But I'll pay if I have to," she said, and tossed her mangoes a couple of inches into the air and caught them again. She raised her brows and tossed them again. Tossing her mangoes as if they were hand grenades. "If I have to. If you really are too tight-fisted…"

"I'll pay," he said weakly.

"Very wise." She smiled and tossed her mangoes a final time. "And for my trolley, too?"

"I…yes."

"Excellent. I don't think Zoe has enough chocolate. My trolley needs some, as well. And we need a mass of candy canes for the tree. What's Christmas without candy canes, is what I want to know."

THEY FINISHED SHOPPING. They loaded the wagon—with difficulty. They went to the sports store and purchased cricket paraphernalia.

The store had run out of Christmas trees. There'd be no more until tomorrow.

"Excellent. That means we need to shop again tomorrow," Molly said, and Joe thought *what the heck.*

The kids were happy, and he sure as hell wasn't bored anymore. Things were looking up.

They returned to the house, exhausted, but Molly insisted the kids unpack their own bags, then help make hot dogs. Joe had put the makings in his trolley.

The hot dogs were excellent. They ate them while they dangled their legs in the swimming pool. Then, using Joe's Internet recipe, they made meringues. They ate strawberries while they cooked.

And they played cricket out by the pool.

It was dumb but it was great, Joe decided. Sure he still felt trapped. The house was chaotic and the fridges would hardly shut and he felt he had even less control, but Charlie was standing behind the wicket, Lily was holding the bat with fierce determination and Molly was bowling.

She bowled. Lily hit with ferocity, straight into his stomach. He grabbed the ball involuntarily and managed to hold on.

"Howzat?" Zoe yelled like a true Australian cricketer, and he grinned and looked at the three-year-old, who'd hardly had her thumb out of her mouth for the entire time she'd been here. She was coated with meringue ingredients and ketchup and unspecific dirt.

She looked happy.

He glanced at Molly. She was grinning, too. She was back in her bikini and sarong. She had a smear of meringue on her nose.

For one crazy moment he had an urgent desire to kiss her.

How to destroy the Christmas spirit right then and there.

"We're all out," Molly said in satisfaction, showing to a nicety she was catching on fast to cricketing language. "But not without a fight. We'll be champions in no time."

Right. He put away the plan to kiss her as ridiculous.

The concept stayed, however. As a concept it had definite appeal.

Cricket over, they trooped inside to inspect the meringues. They were cooked to perfection. Fantastic. Eaten warm, they tasted even more fantastic than they looked. Zoe, who'd eaten hardly anything for days, ate five.

"Showers and then bed," Joe decreed as the last meringue disappeared, but Molly shook her head.

"Showers are too much trouble and it's hot. Strip down to your undies and I'll hose you all down on the patio."

The kids gazed at her as if she was a sandwich short of a picnic, but she was serious.

"It's the rules," she said, and grinned.

Without a word they stripped to their knickers. They stood in a line out on the patio, and squealed and giggled while Molly hosed them off.

"Three towels, Uncle Joe," she commanded, and he jumped to. Once the kids were towelled dry, he shepherded them through the laundry, where Molly had set out their nightclothes.

Fifteen minutes later they were snuggled into bed. They'd elected to sleep together in one of the massive guest rooms— one king-sized bed fitted the three of them with room to spare.

Joe started their traditional bedtime story, but five minutes in their eyes were closed.

He stared down at them, feeling absurdly touched, absurdly thankful. Absurdly…he didn't know what.

He returned to the kitchen. Molly had her sarong wrapped round her middle and was tackling the chaos. Five inexperienced cooks meant wall-to-wall mess.

"Mop," she said, and he jumped to again.

"Are you always this bossy?" he asked as he mopped and she washed down the benches.

"Always."

"This isn't just diversion therapy for you."

"Of course it is. If I'm not diverted, I'll go nuts."

"He really hurt you?" It was a dumb question to ask. Of course Connor had hurt her. But Molly seemed to give it serious consideration.

"What do you think?" she said softly at last, and set her dishcloth down and turned and faced him. "I've had a lovely, controlled, planned life. I'm a partner in a hugely prestigious law firm in Boston. I've fought tooth and nail to get myself there. I've put everything into my career. I met Connor four years ago. He's almost as high up in the Boston force as he can get but he wants to get higher. He's as ambitious as I am. He's smart, he's witty, he makes my friends laugh. I got partnership on the strength of my relationship with Connor. Then he decides we need to get married and the whole thing blows up in my face. Again."

"Again?" he said cautiously, and her face closed. Once more he saw that flash of pain.

"Don't go there."

He held up his hands. "I won't. But you…" He frowned. "You had no idea what he was playing at?"

"Of course I had no idea. What do you take me for?"

"I don't take you for anything," he said wearily. "It's just a mess. The cops are saying Vincent and Erica's deaths were definitely murder."

Her expression softened. "Erica. Your sister. I *am* sorry."

"I hardly knew her," he said. "But that she was murdered… Do you know if they're definite?"

"How much do you know?"

"I got the kids out of the country the night of the wedding. The kids were traumatized. I had a brief conversation with some detective from Boston, simply about who I was and what my links to Vincent were. As soon as they found out I couldn't stomach the b—my brother-in-law…and hardly saw him, I was allowed to leave. In fact, I was encouraged to leave—they cut through all sorts of red tape for me."

She nodded. He was still mopping, getting closer to her. She hitched herself up on the bench so he could mop where she'd been standing.

He mopped under her feet. She was still wearing her sarong. Once again he had that strange feeling of vulnerability that had nothing to do with her age or her career or who she really must be.

"I'm sorry I threw you into the roses," he told her.

"They're saying it's likely you saved my life."

"Yeah, but I'm still sorry. You were a gorgeous bride."

"No, I wasn't."

"The hoops were a bit over-the-top," he said cautiously.

"They were. I might go down to my room and read a book."

"You brought books?"

"Of course I brought books."

"I thought you'd packed for your honeymoon."

"So why wouldn't I have packed books?"

"No reason," he said, and decided to opt for discretion and mop a bit harder.

"You're suggesting we weren't planning a real romantic honeymoon?"

"Hey, I'm not suggesting anything."

"Well, we weren't," she admitted, and swung herself off the bench. "Connor would likely have gone jet surfing while I caught up on legal briefs."

"Romance comes in all shapes and forms," he said blandly.

"It does."

"It was a very romantic wedding," he said cautiously.

"It was horrible."

"I meant, before it went wrong."

"It was still horrible."

He paused with his mop. She'd said she was going to read a book. She was standing in the middle of the kitchen looking like she didn't know what to do.

"How about we hit Vincent's book again and make one more cocktail before bed?" he said.

"From *Seduction by the Glass.*"

"They're not all about seduction."

"I don't want…"

"Neither do I," he said hastily, though if she kept standing there looking like she was looking… Seduction had a certain appeal.

Right. When he had three kids in the next bedroom.

"We have three chaperones," he said dryly, and she cheered up.

"So we have."

"So you'd like a cocktail?"

"Out by the pool?"

"You can even bring your legal briefs if you want."

"I've given up legal briefs," she said sourly. "I've decided I make an appalling lawyer. How can I tell right or wrong when I agreed to marry a murderer?"

"He might not be a murderer"

"And I might not be a half-wit. There's hope for everyone." She sighed. "Innocent until proven guilty. How would I know? Meanwhile bring on your *Seduction by the Glass*. I suspect it'll help me sleep and I feel like sleeping for a very long time."

SHE DIDN'T SLEEP.

She lay on an almost obscenely comfortable chaise out by the pool. She read *Seduction by the Glass* with legal thoroughness. She chose Caribbean Mama and then watched in disquiet as Joe made it for her and then made something called Parson's Choice for himself.

"It's nonalcoholic," she objected.

"One of us has to stay sober." He handed her the Caribbean Mama and sank down on the neighboring chaise with his Parson's Choice.

All of a sudden he felt too close. The situation felt too familiar.

It felt dangerous.

She was still in her sarong. He was fully clothed in his chinos and long-sleeved shirt…and boots, even. Yeah, his shirt had the first three buttons open, and yeah, his sleeves were rolled up, but he was drinking a nonalcoholic cocktail and she…wasn't.

"Zoe's having nightmares," he explained. "I can't afford to sleep deeply, which is what I do if I have more than a couple of drinks in the day."

"So sobriety is the name of the night."

"Not for you. You're a jilted bride," he told her. "Jilted brides don't have to do sobriety."

"I'll have this one then," she conceded, and took a sip and thought about it. "Or maybe one and a half."

He laughed.

She relaxed, lying back on the cushions and staring up at the stars glimmering through the canopy of palm trees.

This was a really romantic setting, she thought. Probably more romantic even than Paradise Island Honeymoon Resort.

"Where do you reckon Connor might be right now?" Joe asked, and she flinched. For almost a minute she'd forgotten about Connor.

"Cuba?" she said cautiously.

"How much money does he have?"

"Enough."

"He's rich?"

"There's family money."

"It'd take a lot," he said. "To stay on the run in Cuba, or anywhere else. We're assuming he doesn't have the diamonds."

"He probably does have the diamonds." She closed her eyes. "Let's not talk about Connor."

"Let's not," he said easily, and closed his eyes, as well.

The situation here wasn't all that bad, she decided.

Not bad at all.

She hadn't slept too well the past few nights. She was also jet-lagged. Her body clock had her somewhere around eleven o'clock in the morning.

She should be in bed now, but the combination of fatigue, alcohol, the warm sea air, the absolute comfort of the chaise…and the presence of Joe was producing a reaction that was almost euphoric. She felt safe. It was a weird word. She hadn't been aware that she'd felt threatened. But maybe she had.

The shock that Connor could be capable of killing his cousin had her feeling sick and shattered. She hadn't been able to come to terms with it. But here, on this night, with this man, she felt as if Connor was nothing more than a vague shadow to be dismissed like Zoe's nightmares.

"Tell me about yourself?" she said, and she knew it was simply the soothing pleasure of having him talk to her that she wanted. But when he answered, she found she was interested.

"I play with airplanes."

"Erica told me that. Tell me how."

"I wait 'til they crash and then I find out why they crashed."

"You're an investigator."

"You might call me that."

"So you travel," she said, and she was aware of a tiny stab of disappointment. That was weird, too. What was there in what he said to produce disappointment?

"Not so much as you might think," he told her. "We work with the Australian Aviation authorities and we have a pretty clean record. Yes, there are crashes, and when there are, I usually go on site for a bit. But there's mostly not a lot I can do on site. What I do is a preliminary, thorough examination, order a thousand pictures from every angle and then organize as many bits of the plane as we can retrieve to be brought back to a hangar in Sydney. Then we spend anywhere up to six months figuring out what went wrong."

"Like the pilot had been drinking Caribbean Mamas."

He grinned. She liked it when he grinned, she thought. It was a gentle smile that started in his eyes and sort of lit up his face. He had lines at the corner of his eyes that said he smiled a lot.

These kids could have done worse in the uncle stakes. She wouldn't mind him for an uncle herself.

Or something else…

What? She gave herself a fast mental swipe. She'd stick to one Caribbean Mama. One and only one.

"Pilot error's not my bag," he told her. "Once we establish pilot error I'm pretty much out of there. It's plane failure I'm interested in. Metal fatigue. Failure of backup systems to come into play."

"Technical stuff."

"I guess."

"So you're clever," she said, and listened to her words and decided she was slurring them. She was tired. She should put her drink down. But it was really nice. The night was really nice.

Joe was really nice.

"Maybe," he said cautiously.

"Where did you go to school?" she asked.

"Sydney."

"University?"

"Sydney, too. And then the States."

"But you were a foster kid."

"I had a pretty amazing foster mother," he said. "Ruby. She got her hands on me when I was twelve, and once she realized what I was capable of and what I wanted she moved heaven and earth to get me there."

"She sounds lovely. Why didn't she care for Erica?"

"She wasn't allowed to. We went into a comparatively wealthy foster home when I was six and Erica was eight. They liked Erica but they didn't like me. I got moved on. Erica stayed put until she met Vincent."

"I guess that really hurt," she whispered.

"Yeah." He said it flatly, without inflection, and she winced. She'd stepped on a nerve, then.

"So where's Ruby now?" she asked. "Will she help take on these kids?"

"I'd never ask it of her."

"She's too old?"

"She's too kind."

"That's a bit dumb."

"Maybe, but that's the way it is."

"So what will you do with them?"

"I don't know," he said heavily.

"Get a nanny?"

"No! Yes." He raked his hair. "Hell, kids have survived with nannies before."

"You're looking at one," she said, striving to keep her voice light.

He stared across at her in the moonlight. As if he was trying to see deeper than was possible. She stirred, uncomfortably. He unsettled her, this man. She wasn't sure why. He was just so…different.

"What about you?" he demanded suddenly, sounding angry.

"What about me?"

"You say you were brought up with nannies."

"Yes."

"But you're normal."

"I think I am."

"But you're marrying Connor."

"I'm not marrying Connor," she said, with all the dignity she could muster.

"But you would have."

"Thankfully, I didn't."

"You were planning a nice normal marriage? With kids?"

"No kids." She said it before she realized she intended to say it. It just came out, bang, a straight, flat rejection of the whole thing.

"Normal marriages have kids," he said, and she knew he wasn't about to let her off his carefully prepared hook.

"Not mine."

"So you were brought up with a nanny, nannies are okay, but you never want kids."

"This has nothing to do with nannies," she said.

"So why don't you want a family? You're good with kids. You're great."

"I had a daughter," she whispered. "Once. I'm never going there again."

CHAPTER FIVE

W<small>HY HAD SHE TOLD HIM THAT</small>?

She set her glass carefully down on the glass table beside the chaise and she felt absurdly proud of herself that she managed it without tipping it over.

She'd never told anybody. No one. Not her parents. Not Connor.

Not even Abby's father.

She felt as if her heart had just been ripped open, exposed for all the world to see.

"I—I'm sorry," she stammered. She somehow got herself to her feet. "I didn't mean… I've never said…"

He was standing up, too. In one graceful movement he set his own glass aside and was holding her. His big hands held her shoulders in a grip she remembered from the wedding. Strength. Warmth.

Security.

It was an illusion, she told herself harshly. Caring was an illusion.

"If you really don't want to talk about it," he said gently, "then I'm sorry I asked. But if you want to tell me…"

It was too much. The night. This man. The cumulative shock of the past few days—hurt, humiliation, fear. She'd spent years working on her defenses and they crumbled in a nanosecond…in the time it took to register the warmth of his hold and the sincerity of his words.

"I had a baby," she whispered.

"When?"

"When I was at university. I was eighteen." She shoved herself back, away from his hold, and crossed her arms over her breasts. It was an age-old gesture of defense. She felt exposed, alone, but she knew she was going to continue.

"What did you call her?" he asked, and she thought of all the things he could have asked and she hadn't expected that one.

"Abigail. For my nicest nanny."

"Abby for short?"

"Yeah." She hugged herself even harder, remembering those hours spent holding her tiny daughter. The beauty, the perfection. The vulnerability. The appalling devastation when they'd told her…

"How long did you have her?"

"Just…three weeks."

"You didn't have her adopted." It was a statement. He already knew the answer.

"She died. She had a problem with her heart. They operated. One of those pieces of miracle surgery you read about in the papers. Only there's a reason they report it as a miracle. Most times the surgery doesn't work. Abby died on the table."

"I'm so sorry."

"It's a long time ago."

"I can't imagine," he said softly, "ever losing that sort of pain. So you and Connor decided you wouldn't have kids because of it?"

"Connor didn't know."

"He didn't know you had a daughter?"

"No."

He frowned. "So what sort of support did you have? The father?"

"The father was a professor of family law at my university," she said. "He invited me to his rooms for a private tutorial. He spiked my drink. I was too young and too stupid to go to the police."

"But…"

"So I did it alone. My parents wouldn't want to know. The only person who did… Sam found me right at the end. My brother. He and I had never been close—too big an age difference, raised by too many different nannies. But he dropped in to see me unexpectedly the night after Abby died. I didn't want to tell him, either, but he guessed. If it hadn't been for Sam…"

"Sam's a lawman, isn't he?"

"Yeah."

"I can imagine him taking the guy's heart out."

It was a flat statement of intent, so cold, so hard that she blinked. Joe would do it for her, she thought. The anger on her behalf was implacable.

"Maybe he would but I didn't tell him. I just said it was another kid, a student as young and frightened as me. Even then he pushed for a name but I wouldn't tell him. What was the point? Abby was dead."

"Hell."

"It's a long time ago," she said wearily, and then regrouped. Sort of. "I'm sorry. I have no idea why I dumped that on you. I never have before. I need to go to bed."

"I think we need to put up a Christmas tree," he said, and the transition was so sudden that she didn't understand.

"Pardon?"

"Do we need a pine tree?" he demanded, seemingly off on another track and running. "Why can't we use palm fronds?"

"For a Christmas tree."

"Wouldn't it be great if the kids woke up tomorrow morning to Christmas?"

"I guess." She tried to focus. "But I'm tired."

"If you go to bed now," he asked, his voice gentling again, "will you sleep or will you cry?"

There was a loaded silence. Her arms were still crossed over her breasts. It might look like a gesture of defense and maybe it was. The memory of the warmth of Abby's little body in her arms was as real this night as it had been all those years ago.

"I thought so," he said, without waiting for an answer. "Okay, then. Christmas tree it is."

"Do we have any decorations?"

"There are bound to be. There's a vast storeroom out the back and I know Erica and Vincent spent at least two Christmases here."

"Did you come?"

"I don't do Christmas."

"But you're doing it now."

"If you'll help."

She thought about it. She uncrossed her arms. It hurt to do so. Like she was letting go.

But this man had needs, too, as did the three kids sleeping above them. She could do this.

"Okay," she said cautiously.

"Good girl."

"Don't patronize me."

"I never would," he said, throwing his hands up in surrender. "I'd get knocked down in flames. So no patronizing. No sympathy. What we need is 'Jingle Bells' on the sound system. Let's get Christmas underway."

THE STOREROOM WAS HUGE. It took them half an hour to hunt through it and in the end they found three Christmas trees.

All of them were appalling.

They were all fake—magnificent-fake, but fake for all that. They'd been purchased already decorated. They were color-coordinated. One was a huge confection covered with crimson and gold, the next a purple-and-silver fantasy and the third, Molly's personal favorite, was a black-and-gray Goth-looking monstrosity.

"Ugh."

"It's revolting." Joe was lining them up in a row, gazing at them in distaste. "How Erica and I ever came from the same parents… But there's stuff here we can use."

"Is there?"

"I remember helping Ruby decorate our tree," he said. "We'd haul in a branch of whatever we could find and stick on whatever we could make. She had a bunch of assorted decorations she'd collected over the years—a real mishmash. Our tree always looked like a dog's breakfast but a magnificent dog's breakfast."

"You want a dog's breakfast?" she said faintly.

"Yep. So we butcher these. Figure out what's the most kid-friendly decorations and strip 'em off. We'll put 'em together and see what we come up with."

So they attacked the three designer wonders. Molly hauled off the most garish of the flashing lights. "I do like a bit of bling," she admitted.

Joe grinned and said, "I knew that as soon as I saw your bridesmaids."

He was hit on the nose by a golden angel.

"Ow!"

"Maybe we need two sides of the tree," she said serenely, slicing off an angel. "Yours and mine."

"Five sides," Joe said. "Yours and mine and Charlie's and Lily's and Zoe's."

"Is that the way you and Ruby did it?"

"She had seven full-time foster sons plus the occasional ring-ins like me."

"No girls?"

"One." His face softened. "Ellie. Just for a while. Ellie and I still keep in touch. I was supposed to be going to her wedding until I had to step in and take care of the kids. I should ring her." He shook himself, moving on. "No matter. She'll be on her honeymoon I guess, and she won't have missed me at the wedding. Anyway, mostly Ruby just cared for boys. At Christmas she divided the tree into however many kids she had at the time. She took overall operation control with lights and the angel and we did the rest."

"She does sound great."

"She is."

"Why don't you spend Christmas with her? Or with Ellie?"

"Ellie's in the States now. We're not that close. And Ruby wasn't my full-time foster mother. The times Social Services tried to arrange for me to be with Erica saw to that. And besides, she's put up with me for long enough," he said lightly but she knew the statement wasn't light at all.

"It sounds as if she loves you."

"Yeah," he said uncomfortably, and she backed off. There'd been enough emotion for one night. She'd forced him to listen to her sad little tale. She had no intention of pushing personal boundaries further.

They worked, in silence. She was so exhausted she should be unconscious, but she'd gone past tired. What she was doing was so far out of her normal framework that it almost felt as if she had gone to sleep and this was some crazy dream.

They stripped the horrible trees of everything they thought was cool. Then they went out to the patio and Joe fetched a ladder and hacked off a couple of dozen palm fronds. They found a bucket, Joe made a swift trip to the beach to fill it with sand, they tied the fronds into a tight woven stem at the base and then wedged them into the wet sand.

The fronds fell over. Joe immediately purloined a curtain rod to use as a spine. Pity about the curtains. "But who's looking in?" Joe demanded. "And this place will go on the market soon anyway. Creased curtains might knock it down from oh, say seven million to six million, nine hundred thousand, nine hundred and two dollars and three cents."

Molly giggled. She'd hung candy canes everywhere she could reach and she was now threading ornaments so she could tie them onto the palm fronds. It felt ridiculous. She felt ridiculous. She felt light-headed and weird and strangely free.

They worked on, side by side, in a silence that was strangely easy. Eating the odd candy cane on the side. Something about crying on someone, telling them all your life secrets, was strangely liberating, Molly decided. Joe had seen her at her worst. After squashing her in the rosebushes she could hardly be seen as cool, calm and capable. Her corporate self was a long way away.

Playing with a Christmas tree. A fantastic Christmas tree. It looked… Wobbly. Garish. Weird.

Wonderful.

With all the ornaments on Joe flicked the light switch. Red, purple, green and gold lights flickered all over the place.

"Awesome," Molly breathed, but it was as if a switch had been flicked somewhere else.

There was a wail from the bedroom, high-pitched and terrified. Before Molly could register what was happening, Joe was gone, striding swiftly into the bedroom and flicking on the light.

"Hey, Zoe. Hey." By the time Molly reached the door he had the little girl in his arms, cradling her against him. But she wasn't to be cradled. She fought against him, screaming, still in the grip of terror.

"No. I want Mandy. I want to go home. No, no, no, no, no."

Charlie and Lily were stirring now, roused from sleep by the light and the screaming. Lily lurched sideways as if she'd done this a hundred times before, grabbing for her little sister's hand.

"It's okay, Zoe. We're here. We're here at Uncle Joe's."

It was too much. Molly stood in the doorway and she looked at Zoe, fighting Joe, then glanced at Lily and Charlie, who looked almost as frightened as Zoe was, and she thought her heart would break. How was Joe to handle this?

"Who's Mandy?" she asked Charlie, and Charlie cast her a look of desperation.

"Dad sacked her 'cos he said she had a big mouth."

"Oh, no." To lose their nanny, as well as their parents... Vincent's timing had been appalling. "That's right. I remember her from last Christmas. And now you're stuck with us this year," she said softly. And then, since Zoe kept screaming, she added in a louder voice, "Hey, Zoe, wake up! Come and see what Uncle Joe and I have been doing."

It took a couple of tries before her words got through and even then Zoe was dazed with the remnants of whatever terrors had got to her in her sleep. But Joe carried her out to the living room. Molly followed, holding hands with a child on either side of her.

They'd turned off the overhead lights to see the effect of

the Christmas tree lights. For the sleepy children it must have seemed a true transformation. When they'd gone to bed this living room was designer chic. Now…it was messy and non-designer and Christmas.

It really was the weirdest Christmas tree, Molly thought as she looked at their strange artistic creation and waited for the kids' reaction. These kids were accustomed to designer magic. What were she and Joe doing, hoping to impress them?

But…

"It's made with palm trees," Lily whispered, awed. "Palm trees."

"There were lots of palm trees at the first Christmas," Molly said, and if she sounded defensive she couldn't help herself.

She didn't need to be defensive. Lily was walking forward, her face a mixture of incredulity and delight.

"Here's my angel," she whispered.

Molly and Joe exchanged cautious glances of hope. At the bottom of each of the designer trees, tied in the centre so they could hardly be seen, they'd found kids' stuff. Every year when Molly was a kid, school activities had included make-your-own Christmas-tree decorations. Paper lanterns. Angels made with macaroni. Baubles made from Ping-Pong balls covered with sequins.

It had obviously been the same for these kids. Erica must have reluctantly put the kids' homemade decorations on the trees, but kept them well-hidden.

Joe and Molly had given them pride of place.

"There's the paper chain we made the year before last," Charlie said to Lily, awed, and he touched the chain. "Do you remember?"

"I think so," Lily whispered.

"We could make another one tomorrow," Charlie said. "To go on the other side."

"But Uncle Joe and Molly decorated the tree," Lily said, reproving. "It's finished."

"See, that's where you're wrong," Joe said, swinging Zoe down and setting her on her feet so she could join Charlie at the tree. "It's quite nice so far, but it's a work in progress. Charlie's right. It definitely needs another chain on the other side."

"You mean, we can put stuff on it?" Lily whispered in quiet amazement.

"I mean, you have to put stuff on it," Joe said. "It's our very own Christmas tree. Molly and I have started but you guys need to fill all the blank bits. If we run out of spaces, all we need to do is tie on another palm frond."

"Cool," Charlie breathed. And then he looked embarrassed, like he'd remembered he was eight years old and maybe too old for this sort of thing.

But Joe was grinning. He picked him up and hugged him, and Charlie let himself be hugged.

"It's definitely cool," he said. "I think Christmas is here, starting tonight. It started the minute Molly walked in the door. I think Molly is our Christmas angel."

"That's silly," Molly said, but there was a little bit of her that thought it wasn't silly at all. She'd never been anyone's idea of a Christmas angel. She wiggled her shoulder blades tentatively.

"My wings are under here somewhere," she said, and the kids giggled.

Great. It felt great. She was grinning like a fool and Joe was grinning with her. She felt...

Like something was opening up within her that had closed the night her baby died. She gasped and stepped back.

"What's wrong?" Joe asked, his expression changing to concern, but she shook her head.

"Nothing. I need to go to bed. It's way, way late."

"It is," Joe said, and he set Charlie down. "Christmas tree in the morning. I want you three back in bed straight away. You can go to sleep, planning what else we need to put on the tree. And what else we need to decorate the house. We only have four days 'til Christmas. We have to get moving."

The kids were already moving, scuttling back to bed as if getting there fast would bring the morning sooner.

"You want to help tuck them in?" Joe asked, but Molly was backing toward the door. All of a sudden it seemed too intense. Too personal. Too emotional by far.

"I'll go to bed myself," she whispered. "And I'll do my own tucking in."

SHE DIDN'T QUITE. She was in bed, but she was fighting with the too-stiff sheets when there was a light knock on the door.

She froze. "What?"

"I wanted to say good-night."

"Good night," she said breathlessly, and then gasped as the door opened a crack, allowing a faint chink of light in. Joe was behind the chink of light.

Joe took her breath away.

"Good night," she said again, and he chuckled and opened the door wider and came on in.

"I thought you'd be in bed. You want me to pull those sheets out?"

"No. I mean…"

"Whoever made up the beds has hospital corners down to a fine art. I found that out the first night and I knew your bed would be the same. You lie under the sheets like a corpse—

they don't move with you an inch. And they're tucked under so far it takes Superman to pull 'em out."

"So you came down to pull them out for me. Like Superman."

"That's me," he said. "You want to hop up and I'll pull?"

"No. I…"

"You can't sleep with them like that, you know. I tried the first night. I was so tired I slept, but when I woke up, I was wider and flatter."

"I don't mind…."

"Wider and flatter? I bet you do. Hop up."

"No."

"I'm not going to jump you," he said, exasperated. "I meant to do it before you came to bed but I sort of forgot."

"You've had lots on your mind." This was dumb. She was lying rigid in the straitjacket sheets, staring at him.

"One minute," he said gently. "Hop up. That is, unless you're naked under there."

He said it with a glimmer of hope and she gasped her indignation and shoved the sheets back. Only of course they wouldn't budge.

He grabbed the edge of the sheet and wrenched.

It still didn't move. She had sort of slithered under them from the top, too tired and too confused to care. But they really were impossible.

"No sweat, ma'am," he said, and grinned, and before she knew what he was about to do he'd simply picked up the corner of the mattress at the end of the bed and tugged it up a couple of feet. She lurched sideways and he was able to haul the sheet out.

He dropped the mattress. She lurched back onto her pillows.

"I don't need…" She gasped.

"You do need. Now you're free you can hop up while I do the other side."

He was clearly deranged. There was no sense arguing. She rolled out of the loose side too fast. Where there'd been rigid resistance there was now nothing.

She ended up on the floor.

"Hey!" He stooped in concern. "Are you okay?"

There was three inches of shag pile carpet. Why wouldn't she be okay? "Just haul the other side out, wonderboy," she snapped. "And then leave me alone."

"You don't sound very appreciative." He was still smiling, but obligingly he moved around to the other side of the bed and wrenched the covers free. Then, as she got to her feet, he smoothed down the covers and laid them back, ready for her to hop in again. Loosely.

"There," he said soothingly. "All done. Does madam require anything else before she goes to sleep?"

"No." Then, accepting the fact that she'd been less than gracious, she managed a half smile. "Thank you."

"That's better," he said approvingly. "Always be nice to the staff. You never know when we might come in useful again."

"Joe…"

"I know. You need to go to sleep." He smiled at her in the half light cast from the hallway. "That's a gorgeous nightgown."

It was. It was her wedding nightgown. Swiss cotton with exquisite embroidery.

She'd bought it thinking…well, she ought to have something special for her wedding night. She'd bought it for Connor.

That this man was seeing it instead of Connor… Strangely enough that didn't feel wrong.

But it ought to feel wrong. Her life was upside down. Her world was upside down. She was on the other side of the world but not where she was supposed to be.

"Thank you," she said again, awkwardly.

"My pleasure," he said softly, and then before she could guess what he intended, he took a couple of steps toward her and placed his hands on her shoulders. Lightly. Not holding her so she couldn't move away. Just…holding her.

"Hey, Molly, I'm sorry," he said.

"I… Don't be. Connor…"

"I'm not just sorry about Connor," he said. "I'm sorry for everything life's thrown at you. I'm sorry that schmuck made you pregnant. I'm sorry as hell you lost your baby daughter. And I'm really, really sorry that you're going to bed alone in a strange place when it should be your honeymoon and life should be giving you everything you deserve. The kids think you're special and I can see why."

And then, as she gazed up at him speechless, his grip tightened.

"Do you mind if I kiss you?" he asked.

What sort of question was that? The guy had come into her bedroom unasked. This was scream-and-run territory. Only just as she was gathering her scream-and-run reflexes, he went and asked a question like that.

Do you mind if I kiss you?

Her confused mind tried to work out a response. No? No, that was wrong. That'd mean she didn't mind. Yes? But that'd mean she wanted him to kiss her. No. Yes.

It was all just too hard. The feel of his hands on her shoulders was doing strange things to her. The night was doing strange things to her.

This man…

He was looking down into her eyes with a strange expression. There was compassion there, but something else. There were questions she had no hope of answering. Questions she had no intention of even thinking about.

But the biggie remained the question asked.

Do you mind if I kiss you?

Of course she minded. Of course she did. She just couldn't get her mind and lips to coordinate to frame the response. It was too late. She was too tired.

He was too near and he was too…Joe.

Too Joe to refuse? That shouldn't make sense but it did. She made a tiny noncommittal sound, just so he didn't get the idea she was enthusiastic. And then, just in case he got the idea she was unenthusiastic, she lifted her hands and ran her fingers through that crop of burned-red hair and tugged his head down to her.

He kissed her. Of course he kissed her. It was what she wanted—wasn't it?

Actually it was. If she was going to have an out-of-body experience—if she was going to feel like her world was upside down—it needed to be like this. Strong arms crushing her against his hard, muscled chest. Lovely hands caressing her face. His mouth taking hers against his, kissing her deeply, strongly, but with a strange tenderness that was her undoing.

For she hadn't expected tenderness. Connor's kisses were possessive, harsh, always a prelude. Not Joe's. This was a gentle exploration that said she could stop whenever she wanted; she could pull away whenever she wanted. But why would she? How could she?

For it was magic. She felt her whole body respond in a languor of delicious desire. Somewhere in that tiny murmur of assent she'd thrown away her reservations. She'd thrown away the control she'd nurtured carefully for all these years.

He was kissing her with tenderness, but her hands were pulling him into her with a fierceness that left her astonished.

She wanted him. Ever fiber of her being wanted him. The

shock of the last few days had left her limp and numb and suddenly here was life again. Here was warmth and comfort and more. Here was desire. Here was life itself.

She tugged him closer, closer. His hands wrapped round her waist, hauling her in so her breasts were flattened against his chest. He was lifting her so her feet barely touched the floor. Their lips were locked, and it was her tongue that started the delicious exploration that left her thankful he was holding her upright for her knees would surely give way.

Joe. Joe. It was like a mantra in her head. The horror had disappeared and there was only Joe.

How far she would have gone she didn't know—she'd never know. Or maybe she did, for the terms of her surrender had been ripped and shredded and she was as exposed as she'd ever been.

And maybe he knew that. For just as she felt the night disappear into a haze of white-hot heat she felt him put her away, break the contact of their lips, hold her at arm's length.

"Molly, do you want this?"

What sort of question was that? Yes. Yes and yes and yes.

But it wasn't a light question. His voice was husky with passion but his face was suddenly grave. His gaze locked to hers.

"It's less than a week since your wedding," he said softly. "We need to spend Christmas together. Will you wake up in the morning hating yourself—hating me—if we go further?"

It woke her up. The delicious, wondrous fantasy she'd dissolved into dissipated just like that. She stared at him, speechless, not knowing where to go to from here.

Lost. Empty.

"Dammit, I shouldn't have come in," he said ruefully, and the dream went even further.

"I…I'm so…"

"Hush." He put his finger on her lips. "Don't say it. Don't

even think it, for I'm sure as hell not. As kisses go, that packed quite a punch." His voice was unsteady but he was trying hard to keep his words light. "I didn't think…" He shook his head. "No. Maybe neither of us thought. But we need to keep this Christmas together for the kids. We need to keep this light."

Right. Of course.

"And you need to go to sleep," he said, and smiled at her with that sexy, crooked smile that was her undoing. "You know you do. I've done what I came to."

"Kiss me, you mean?"

"I've loosened your sheets."

He could loosen her sheets some more. A voice was screaming at the back of her head to say it out loud. Yell it out loud.

But he'd given her space and in that space she'd caught a fleeting glimpse of the woman she once was. The woman she needed to be again. Molly Broadbent. Corporate lawyer. Woman in charge of her world.

"Thank you," she managed to say, and even succeeded in summoning a quavering smile. "The kiss was a bonus. I'm jet-lagged," she added, and she knew she sounded vulnerable but she couldn't help herself.

"You're not yourself," he said ruefully. "Of course not. So into bed you hop and we'll see you sometime tomorrow. Lunchtime or after." And then, when she didn't move, as she stood feeling foolish and dumb and worried, he simply swept her up in his arms and set her down onto the bed. He tugged the covers up and over her, kissed her lightly—a feather kiss—on the forehead and then backed away quickly to the door.

She didn't want him to go. She didn't want to stay in this big bed alone.

But he was smiling at her from the doorway, and then he was stepping back and closing the door.

"Good night, Molly," he said gently. "Let's hope you're yourself in the morning. For both our sakes."

HE CLOSED THE DOOR and then he stood leaning heavily against it, as if to bar the way back in.

What had he done?

Put simply, the most beautiful woman he'd ever set eyes on had offered herself to him and he'd refused.

Why?

Because she was beautiful, he acknowledged wryly. Only it was more than that.

He'd never met anyone like her in his life.

He remembered her anger back in the rose garden at the wedding chapel. Angry, she'd been beautiful.

Cajoling the kids, bossy and bouncy in the supermarket this afternoon, she'd been beautiful.

Intent on decorating the Christmas tree, she'd been gorgeous.

Telling him about her daughter, she'd been…stunning.

He felt winded. He felt…

Like Ruby had told him he'd feel one day.

Ruby, his sometime foster mother. He'd stayed with her all one summer when he was a kid, and then the social workers had found a place he and Erica could stay together so he'd been moved on. When that placement had fallen through, all the places at Ruby's had been taken.

But Ruby had kept in touch. He'd spent a couple of Christmases with her, and she'd kept on saying, "One day you'll fall in love."

It was happening to Ruby's boys. Two of her permanent foster sons had fallen in love. He'd been invited to Pierce's wedding.

"It'll happen to you, too," Ruby had said warmly to him

then, and he'd grinned down at the dumpy little ball of energy who was the only person in the world he'd walk on fire for.

"Only if you want to take me on," he'd said, and she'd smiled her delight and tucked her arm possessively into his.

"That's lovely but I've had the love of my life," she'd said. Ruby's husband had died young—there were photographs all over her house and she talked of him all the time. "Yours is still waiting," she'd told him. "Let me know when it happens."

And now it had. Just like Ruby had said it would. He'd looked down into Molly's confused eyes and he'd felt his world shift.

So when she'd offered herself to him tonight, he hadn't accepted. For he didn't want her on the terms she was offering. No one-night stand this.

But what was it? What sort of relationship could this ever be? An Australian stuck with three kids. An independent career lawyer who lived in the States; a woman with more baggage than he had.

Where the hell did he start?

Not by taking advantage of her. That was all he'd been able to figure so far.

She'd need time. How long to get over a jilting bridegroom? And she wasn't close to being over the death of her tiny daughter.

Where to start? He didn't have a clue. All he knew was that he'd started.

Maybe it was just the cocktails, he thought hopelessly.

Nope. He'd had the virgins. Plus light beer.

It was definitely Molly.

So what did he have here? He leaned against the door and he stared incredulously into his future. Three kids. Molly. Three kids. Molly.

Impossible. How to ask Molly to take on not only him, but also three kids?

She never would.

"But it won't be for want of asking," he said, and then he realized he was talking aloud and Molly could hear and she probably already thought he had a kangaroo loose in the top paddock.

He summoned a smile. Sort of a smile.

He touched the door with the flat of his hand—a dumb gesture of a blessing to the woman inside.

And then he went upstairs to bed.

Alone.

AND ON THE OTHER side of the door?

Maybe Molly should be examining the kiss in just as much detail, but events of the last few days had caught up with her. Joe had laid her on her pillows, he'd tucked her covers around her and he'd kissed her good-night.

It was enough.

She slept. Smiling.

CHAPTER SIX

SHE SLEPT ROUND the clock and then some. She woke and looked at her watch. It was 1:00 p.m. and she almost yelped.

She'd hardly slept since the wedding. She needed the sleep. But this morning she'd intended to be up and chirpy, stepping into Christmas organization and in charge of her world.

The events of the night before had altered things.

There were sounds from outside. Splashing. Kids' laughter. They were in the pool. Joe's deep voice, offering watermelon. Whooping and more splashing.

She smiled.

But then her smile faded. She lay and stared blindly up at the ceiling and thought about the kiss. About how it had made her feel.

The first cold shards of fear flickered through her.

Last night she'd been too exhausted to feel them. She'd simply let herself get sucked into the sweetness of the moment and it had turned into something else with frightening speed. That it hadn't gone further was thanks to Joe.

Not her.

The realization hit her with shattering force.

She started shaking. Not a faint tremble but a full-blown, teeth-chattering tremor that came of terror.

She was a mature woman, a lawyer, and she was shaking because of one kiss?

It wasn't that. She'd let her guard down. Once she'd let it down and she'd ended up with her daughter, with tragedy, with a loss that could never leave her. Twice she'd let it down and she'd ended up jilted at a schmaltzy wedding where her friends and business partners had been left staring at her with a mixture of sympathy and incredulity.

And last night? She hardly knew Joe and she'd just thrown herself at him. Had she learned nothing?

Nothing.

That's what it had to be. She felt cold and sick and exhausted. Somehow she got her dumb, shaking body out of bed and into the shower. She turned the water on hot and stood under it until the heat seeped into her and the shaking stopped. And she had herself together. Almost.

She dressed with care, in a sundress that had tiny capped sleeves, the most demure item of her honeymoon wardrobe. She'd buy a couple of plain shirts and long pants in town today. That'd make things better.

She dried her hair and tied it carefully into her corporate style. Smooth. Controlled.

She'd told the kids she'd spend Christmas with them. She couldn't go back on that. Okay, she would, but she sure as hell wasn't having any more of Joe's martinis. And she was staying her side of control.

IT WAS LIKE A SWITCH had been flicked.

With the kids she was laughing, happy, bossy, steering them into a full-blown Christmas with an energy that left him stunned.

With him she was cool, polite, even friendly. But she was on one side of a line and he was on the other, and if he so much as put a toe over he knew it.

They made plum pudding. The kids stirred the pudding

while Molly held the bowl. He went to have his turn and she placed the pudding bowl on the bench and stepped back.

They hung paper chains from the ceiling. She was sticking chains up and she overbalanced on the ladder. He caught her as she fell, but she whisked herself out of his arms so fast he barely had time to register the feel of her. And then she glared.

"Hey, you could at least say thank you," he protested.

"Thank you," she said stiffly, and moved on.

He knew why she was doing it. She'd let enough of herself out in those first few hours for him to realize how terrified relationships must make her feel. A one-night stand might be okay, but the way he felt… This was no one-night stand. He knew by the fear in her eyes that she felt the same.

That was a good sign—wasn't it? That she was fearful must mean she felt something like he did?

But how to break down the barriers?

He couldn't push. He knew it. He'd stepped back last night out of instinctive knowledge that here was something infinitely precious that could be smashed.

But to see it and let it go…

"How long are you staying?" Zoe asked her as they organized stockings and she set them to making name tags to specify ownership.

"The day after Christmas," she said. "I've changed my plane flight back to the States."

The kids' faces fell.

Joe's face fell.

"We'd like you to stay longer," he said gently, and she flashed him a look that said get on your side of the line again.

"I'm sorry, Joe," she said softly. "It's your life. Not mine."

And that was that.

At least the kids were having a wonderful time. They loved

Molly to bits. She'd rescued Christmas. She bossed them into activities all the way to Christmas Eve. She even bossed him, sending him out with a shopping list a mile long including things she'd figured the kids would love in their stockings.

She took the kids on their own secret shopping trip. The house was full of secrets, full of Christmas anticipation.

It was also full of tension as he watched her and saw the loneliness in her dark eyes and wondered whether he could ever find a way to approach her.

Christmas Eve. Two more sleeps 'til she left again.

"One more sleep 'til Santa," the kids whooped, but the deadline until Molly left was an imperative one.

As dark fell they hung up their stockings and set out milk and cookies for Santa—and carrots for the reindeer—and then Molly bossed them all round the Christmas tree, set corny carols on the sound system and made them sing.

For Joe, who'd never done such a thing, it started off being almost embarrassing. But then…somewhere in the middle of "Silent Night," when Zoe's high little voice cracked and wobbled and she made up a couple of words of her own because she couldn't read the sheet, when Molly smiled down at her and hugged her and lifted her up so they could sing together, he felt salty tears sting at the back of his eyes.

This was magic. Somehow he had to find a way to keep this for all of them.

And then the glass of the back door blasted open and the peace of Christmas Eve was shattered.

IT WAS A GUNSHOT.

They were upstairs. The main entrance was downstairs. The door was plate glass, reinforced, and it broke but it wouldn't have disintegrated. The door was dead-bolted.

Fear had a wonderful way of focusing the mind. Joe could have stood motionless, waiting to see what would happen, but the shooting spree at the wedding was too recent, the sight of Tommy's gun too fresh in his mind.

And the knowledge of the words Jean had overheard...

The kids... Despite the cops' reassurance they'd come for the kids.

This was no burglary. Thieves didn't blast their way into a house. Whoever was downstairs didn't care that their presence had been announced.

Whoever was downstairs had deadly intent.

"Out," he snapped, and before they could respond he'd lifted Lily, shoved Molly and Zoe toward the main bedroom and grabbed Charlie's hand, tugging him along. By the time the second gunshot sounded downstairs they were in the master bedroom and he was hauling open the French doors.

The doors led to a balcony at the back of the house.

There was a massive palm tree hard against the window, with bougainvillea, a fabulous flowering vine, thick around its trunk. Was it strong enough to hold on to? It had to be. There was no choice.

"We need to run away," he said harshly to the bewildered kids, and he lifted Charlie and held him out until he clung to the vine. "Charlie, climb down, fast, don't wait for us but run until you get to the back of the pavilion behind the swimming pool. That's the rule. Go!"

There was no time for reassurance. He was already lifting Lily.

But these kids had been trained to obey rules and it stood them in good stead now. They didn't argue. Charlie was halfway down the vine before Lily had a grip. Joe grabbed Zoe out of Molly's arms and Molly didn't protest, either. She simply swung herself over the rail and down she went, acknowledging she couldn't climb herself with Zoe.

"Go, Lily," she said harshly to the little girl beneath her. "I'm right behind you."

She trusted him, Joe thought. It was a flash of knowledge, a fleeting impression, but it steadied him. Molly trusted him. She depended on him.

They all depended on him.

He hauled the French doors shut, hoping it might give them precious moments while the gunman—or gunmen?— had to figure where they'd gone. Then he swung himself over the rail.

"Hold on round my neck," he ordered Zoe, swinging her around to his back. When she didn't respond, he reached for her arms, linked them about his neck and said, "You're a baby monkey. Hold on to me or you'll fall off."

Heaven knew what she thought. To push a child so far…

But her arms tightened. Her hands linked around his neck and she clung.

He reached for the vine and swung out, away from the balcony.

The vine gave, not able to take their combined weight. He fell, but he grabbed more vine as he went. That snapped, too, but it was a series of lurches rather than a freefall and he landed on his feet, Zoe still blessedly attached.

Lily and Charlie and Molly were already three shadows flying around the side of the swimming pool pavillion. He ran, hauling Zoe to his front as he went so he could hold her in his arms, and shoving his way along a path that was overgrown from disuse.

A harsh male voice came from above.

"There they are…"

The blast of a gun.

He felt Zoe jerk in his arms but he couldn't stop. He ran, and he ran. Round the side of the pavilion.

Where…

They were there, flattened against the wall. Molly had the kids by each hand.

"The beach," he said. "Straight down the path and then to the left and into the trees. Go!"

It took less than a minute to reach the beach. The kids were flying, faster than he could ever have expected them to run, and Zoe was still clinging to him. Every moment he anticipated more blasts from behind. But he'd destroyed the vine. Maybe they'd had to go back downstairs and out and around. Whatever, Molly and he and the kids seemed to have been granted a few moments' grace.

The beach opened out before them, calm and clear in the moonlight, but this was no safe haven. Out here they were exposed.

"We go into the rain forest," he said, making it up as he went. "Molly, just push through. Shove in as hard as you can, as fast as you can. Kids, follow her and I'm coming behind."

Zoe whimpered in his arms. He clung tighter but there was no time for reassurance.

"Go," he said, and they did.

The rain forest here was so thick it was almost impenetrable, but they were in no mood to be stopped. Molly was tearing vines apart, shoving her way into the forest with a desperation born of fear. Burdened with Zoe, Joe could hardly help her but she didn't need help. She pushed and pushed and pushed.

Then emerged into a clearing.

It was a clearing made by rocks—a slab of granite where

nothing could grow. Molly almost fell out onto it, and the kids and Joe followed.

How far had they gone? They'd been pushing for twenty minutes.

Zoe was cradled against his shoulder. His shoulder was wet. Warm…

Startled he put his fingers up to touch and then held them up. They were thick with blood.

"Zoe!" He hauled her back so he could see her. Zoe gazed back at him, big-eyed and fearful. A jagged scratch ran down her temple.

Molly had seen. She reached for the little girl and held her as Joe checked the wound, running his fingers lightly over the damaged skin, feeling rather than seeing.

It wasn't deep. This was no bullet hole. Maybe a bullet had grazed the side of her head above Joe's shoulder, that was all, or maybe it was simply a graze from a branch she'd hit. Whatever—she was okay.

His knees damn near gave way under him.

"Is she dead?" Charlie quavered, and Joe ordered his knees to stiffen.

He managed a smile. Somehow. "You're not dead, are you, Zoe?" he asked, and the little girl shook her head. He grabbed the shoulder of his shirt and ripped—the sleeve came off on the third tug and he tied it round Zoe's head with speed. The blood wasn't pumping. Pressure should stop it.

They'd been lucky.

"Where to?" Molly whispered, and he looked at her in the moonlight and thought hell, if anything happened to her…if anything happened to these kids…

"It's miles to the nearest house, and there's only one road in. I don't think it's safe to try and get to help tonight. We need to go a bit farther into the forest and find somewhere safe to see the night out. Only let's go a bit slower now and keep really, really quiet."

"You think they're following?"

He was sure they'd follow if they could. But the damaged vine had given them a head start. Had they made so much noise they could be followed?

"I haven't got my phone," Molly said, distressed. "I can't call for help."

"Mine's in my pocket but I've checked. There's no reception. So we're on our own. We'll walk as far as we can, but from now on let's slow down a little, and creep. No talking. Not even whispering. Let's try not to damage the bush so they can't see where we've gone. And then let's find somewhere we can sleep the night."

THEY CROSSED THREE rocky outcrops, and each time Joe had them change direction and bush-bash farther along. But they couldn't go on forever. Lily was stumbling now, whimpering. Finally they emerged to a fourth open space with a cliff at the rear. This had to be it, and blessedly it was. In a cleft in the rock Joe found enough space for the five of them to stay. There was thick moss over the base of the rocks. There were ferns in front—he could see between them, just, so he could detect anyone approaching—and, best of all, the cleft wound into the hills and opened up again fifty yards back. If they needed to they could back away before they were seen.

But it would take the point of a gun to make them move. The kids had gone past exhaustion. He ushered them into their makeshift camp. Molly sank to her knees and gathered them to her and he thought they were close to collapse.

He sank down with them. He felt helpless and sick at heart. All he could do was watch as the kids clung and clung.

But finally Charlie broke away. He turned and Joe saw his face was tearstained and terrified.

"Uncle Joe," he whispered, and Joe was suddenly included. There were five of them in a sandwich hug, looking to each other for comfort.

He should be keeping guard. He should be looking behind them, but just for that moment he gave himself up to the sweetness and the comfort of the warm bodies.

It was Molly who emerged first. She looked…a mess, he thought. The moon was full tonight—a disadvantage for the hunted, but if there hadn't been a moon, maybe their flight would have been more perilous. Molly had bush-bashed her way through the undergrowth. Her face was a mass of scratches. Her hair was a tangle of matted curls, littered with leaves and twigs. He glanced at her hands and winced.

But she wasn't concerned about herself.

"You do lookout duty," she said softly to him. "Kids, I know this is scary but Joe's here to look after us. He won't let anyone near. I need to look at Zoe's head. Can you help me? Lily, see that trickle of water running down the rock? Here." She delved under her T-shirt and a minute later a soft cotton bra was in Lily's hands. "Wet this for me and we'll use it to wash your head, Zoe. Charlie, can you tug a bit more of this moss down and lay it over here. Let's make a Christmas Eve hidey-hole for all of us."

SHE WAS FANTASTIC. She almost turned their situation into something normal. She was prosaic and comforting and the worst of the kids' fear dissipated in the face of her practicality.

"No, how can they find us? We've gone so far into the bush

I think we're almost back to America. In the morning your uncle Joe will fetch the police, the bad men will be arrested and we'll get on with Christmas. Meanwhile…let's play guess what's in the parcels under the Christmas tree. Lily, you saw the great big blue parcel with the purple bow and your name on it? What do you think it might be?"

Maybe if they hadn't been exhausted it mightn't have worked, but she lay down with them, hugged the kids against her and they guessed presents in whispers. She let them talk of nothing else and finally, finally they slept. They were like a litter of cubs in a warren, he thought as he watched them, taking comfort from each other as well as from Molly. The terrors had been too big to take in. Zoe's scratched face had faded in her mind—she had no knowledge how close she'd come to death and for her the terror was over.

But Molly's terror was still with her. As the last of the kids drifted off to sleep she gently disentangled herself and wriggled out to join him at the opening of the cleft.

"Nothing?"

"They won't come this far," he said. He was pretty sure. They'd have to be experienced bushmen to follow them this far in. "Whoever…"

"One of them's Connor."

He turned and stared at her. "You're sure?"

"His was the voice that yelled out." She swallowed. "He'll be…he'll be the one that shot Zoe."

A final betrayal. "Molly, I'm so sorry," he said, but her eyes flashed fire.

"Don't be," she muttered, and hauled herself forward so she was staring into the darkness with him. A tiny wallaby was nibbling grass on the other side of the clearing. He'd be their sentinel, Joe thought. The little creature had leaped away when they'd arrived, but now that all was quiet, the wallaby was grazing again.

"Don't be sorry?"

"Not for me," she said. "Not because I agreed to marry a lousy, bottom-feeding, murderous scumbag. I don't need sympathy. I may need psychiatric assessment but not sympathy."

There was even grim humor in her words. He smiled and unconsciously his arm went round her waist and held. She stiffened for a fraction of a second and then relaxed and melted into him.

"You really think we've lost them?"

"What does Connor know about the Australian bush?"

"Zip."

"There's your answer. It'd take an experienced tracker to find us, I reckon, and daylight, as well."

"Then why are we whispering?"

"Because if there's a chance in a million I'm wrong…"

"There's not."

"You're very definite."

"I am," she said. "And you know what? If Connor comes, now I have a plan."

"The plan would be to keep deathly quiet and hope he goes away."

"No."

"Then we'd run?"

"That's a bad idea, too," she said. "With the kids he could outrun us without raising a sweat."

It was what he'd been thinking, but he wasn't going to say it.

"Then what?"

"We attack," she said.

"Um…right."

"No, really," she said, and she tugged over a tennis-ball-sized chunk of granite. "There's lots of these. If there's two of them, I might need help, but if it's just Connor... I can sneak out behind the ferns to the other side of the clearing. Then I can come up behind and *thump*."

"*Thump?*"

"I could do it," she said. Her face tightened, all humor gone. "He shot Zoe. I could do it."

There was a moment's stunned silence. Then he said, "I love you, Molly."

Where had that come from? Wham, out of nowhere, it was a declaration that was as dumb as it was inappropriate. For Molly, who'd spent the night in shock, this must be just one more shock piled on the rest.

"You love me?" she whispered, and he opened his mouth to say sorry, it was a mistake, he hadn't meant to say it. But his words turned into something different.

"I didn't think I'd ever say it," he said. "I wasn't sure such a thing exists. But I think I fell in love with you the first time I saw you and it's getting worse, not better. And dammit, you sit there with your hair full of twigs threatening to hit thugs with rocks..."

"Yeah, beautiful," she said dryly.

"You are beautiful. You're the most beautiful woman I've ever met in my life." Then, at the look in her eyes—bewilderment and the beginnings of fear—he shook his head, damning himself for being every kind of fool. "I'm sorry. I shouldn't have said that."

"I don't do love," she whispered.

"No?"

"It leads to catastrophe."

"Maybe it does, but maybe it doesn't," he said, trying to

figure out the U-turn his own thinking had done. "Maybe true love's the answer to catastrophe."

"That sounds like something you read in a fortune cookie."

"Yeah, me, the great romantic," he said dryly. "My love is like a fortune cookie."

"Joe…"

"Okay, let's leave it." What the hell was he doing, waiting for gunmen, telling a woman he loved her? If she thought he was a fruitcake, she'd be right.

"I'm scared," she whispered.

"That makes two of us."

"I didn't mean about Connor."

"Neither did I," he said softly. "You're not alone in thinking this is a huge, scary leap of faith."

"I've tried it before."

"Have you?" He lifted his hand to her face and cupped her chin. "Have you really tried loving? Can you look at me and say you loved the father of your child? That you loved Connor? That you knew and loved them both?"

"No, I…"

"Maybe it's because you didn't truly love that it turned out a mess." He sighed, seeing confusion and doubt. "Sorry, Molly, look, what the hell would I know? I know nothing except what Ruby's hammered into me and I didn't believe a word of it until I met you. But let's leave it. Go back to the kids while I watch."

"You think I'd sleep while you're out here alone?"

"It'd be sensible."

"Yeah." Then she shook her head. "No. I'm staying. Joe…"

"Yeah?"

"Whether you're right or not, whatever this love thing is or isn't, I can't figure it out right now. All I know is that this is deeply scary and I'm staying out here and I want your arm around me. Please. We can sort everything else out…afterward. Is that okay?"

"It's fine by me," he said, and tugged her to him and held her close.

SHE SLEPT.

She didn't mean to, but Joe leaned back against the rock face, she rested on his shoulder, he held her close and she sort of slipped down so her head was on his knees.

He ran his fingers through her curls, gently disentangling twigs and then raking her curls over and over as if she were a child who needed comfort.

He was watching out over the clearing. The children were soundly asleep behind them. She figured she should be watching out over the clearing, too—she was!—but the feel of his fingers in her hair was doing strange things to her. Weird, lovely sensations that made her feel…made her feel…safe and cherished. Home.

Which was a really dumb sensation. She was as out of her comfort zone as she was ever likely to get. Somewhere out there in the night was Connor with a gun. She was as far away from her home as she was likely ever to be. But she felt herself melting into the sensations he was creating. She felt herself sliding.…

SHE WOKE, startled by a sudden rush of movement. Joe jerked sideways. Her eyes flew open, adrenaline surging back.

"It's okay," he whispered, and pointed outward.

Their sentinel had turned into eight sentinels. Eight wallabies. There was a veritable army between them and danger.

One was staring back into the cleft in what looked like indignation.

"He stuck his nose in here," Joe said. "I gave him a helluva fright. He jumped about two feet, and hit me with his tail as he did a one-eighty turn."

She smiled, fear dissipating. Safer and safer.

"What time is it?"

"Just after five. An hour 'til dawn."

She'd slept so long? "Joe, I'm so sorry. I should have stayed awake."

"It was all my pleasure," he said in that deep gravelly voice that said he spoke the absolute truth.

"You…you think…"

"I'm not thinking anything."

"Hey," she said, and wriggled in his arms so she could smile up at him. "Hey, it's Christmas. Merry Christmas."

"Merry Christmas yourself," he said, and kissed her lightly on the nose, then went back to looking out past the wallabies.

He'd been watching all night as she slept.

He was still holding her, lightly, not possessively. If she wanted to move away, he'd release her in a moment.

She thought back to the night she arrived. He'd wanted her. She knew that.

But he'd backed off. He hadn't pushed her.

He'd told her he loved her.

Until this moment the enormity of what he'd said hadn't sunk in. She was too caught up in present terror and past tragedy. But it hit her now, not as a flash of knowledge, something cerebral, but as a sweeping tide of warmth that started somewhere deep within and grew and grew until it threatened to overwhelm her.

It was Christmas morning and this man had given her his love. Just like that. If she didn't want it, he wouldn't push it further. He was asking for nothing.

He was simply giving her his love.

There were complications. The Molly who'd been trained to stay impersonal, who'd been independent forever, who'd lost her baby, was screaming at her now. What sort of love could this be? Joe lives in Australia. He has three kids. He's been a foster kid; he'll know more than you do how to keep himself to himself.

But he wasn't keeping himself to himself now. He was calmly watching the clearing, keeping himself in harm's way while he protected those he loved.

Including her. His love included her. It was like a song, insidious in its sweetness. That this man might be her family…

And the knowledge was suddenly overwhelming, shoving aside all doubts. This was a risk worth taking. It was a leap into the unknown, but what a leap…

He glanced down at her, vaguely questioning. Concerned. "Hey, don't look like that," he said. "It was only a kiss on the nose."

"So it was," she whispered. "It wasn't enough."

His face stilled. "It wasn't…"

"Enough. Do you realize you've given me your love for Christmas morning?"

"I'm not sure that you want it."

"I wasn't sure that I did, either," she said, lifting her hand and running her fingers across the stubble of his chin. "It was all pretty much a blur last night."

"Yeah. It was inappropriate…."

"See, I've just been thinking," she whispered. "Is it ever inappropriate to tell someone you love them?"

"I'm not sure. I don't know the rules."

"Neither do I," she said, and summoned a smile. It was time to be brave here. It was time to take her leap. "But I do know a couple of rules. And the biggie right here is that it's Christmas morning and you've given me a gift and I need to give you something back."

"I haven't…"

"You don't think your love is a gift?"

"Only if you want it," he said gravely, and her heart seemed to turn over. With the first tentative acceptance of self-knowledge. How could she have been so blind? How could she have spent these last days with this man and not realized that he was so far apart from her previous life that he was a different world. A new and wonderful world that she needed to be a part of.

"See, I've been lying here and thinking," she whispered, allowing herself the luxury of running her fingers down the harsh bone structure of his face. "I'm thinking I've been a bit of a coward."

"You're no coward."

"Oh, but I am," she said. "In the love department. But I'm thinking I need to be brave. So I've figured I'm starting now. On Christmas morning. I'm not exactly sure how to do it—how to go about this loving business—but if you could help me…"

"I'd love to try," he said cautiously.

"So what to do about it?"

"I could kiss you," he said. "Would that be a start?"

"That'd mean no one was watching the clearing."

"We have eight wallabies watching the clearing."

"That's true," she whispered, and smiled. "That's very true."

"So if I kissed you now?"

"Not on the nose."

"Not?" He frowned. "Is that in the rules?"

"I guess it's not," she murmured, and linked her arms around his neck, then tugged his head down until his mouth met hers. "I'm not sure that the rules I've been working on are required anymore."

"Sometimes rules are good. The kids need rules." He sounded like he barely believed what he was saying.

"Then we'd better get started," she murmured, but she was hardly audible for already his lips were brushing hers. "We'd better get a whole new rule book written before they wake up."

THE TENSION WAS still there, but things had changed. By the time the kids woke, Molly couldn't keep the great goofy smile off her face, and neither could Joe, and as they hugged the kids and wished them merry Christmas they had to fight to remind themselves to keep their voices to a whisper, to remember that there was still a threat.

"We've got strawberries and cream and mince pies back in our kitchen," Zoe said mournfully.

"We've got stockings," Charlie reminded her, and all three kids looked so sad that Joe and Molly felt guilty about smiling.

"Why are you so happy?" Lily asked suspiciously, and Joe thought about all the things he could say, but while he was trying to figure them out, Molly answered for him.

"'Cos I've decided to stay in Australia and help look after you lot."

"Really?" Charlie asked.

"Yes."

"For always?" Zoe asked, awed.

"Yes," she said before she could think about it, before any of those damned rules that had been getting in the way of her life for so long could raise their ugly heads and shout her down.

"You're kidding," Joe said, and she cast him a wounded look.

"Don't you want me?"

Dumb question. She had a sandwich squeeze from the four of them—which pretty much answered her question.

"But aren't you a lawyer?" Charlie asked when finally they emerged from their very satisfactory hug. In fact, Joe was hugging her still.

"I guess people need lawyers in Australia."

"Goody," Zoe said, moving on. "We need a big house. Can we get a puppy?"

It wasn't a bad way to start Christmas. And the thought of a potential pup—followed by decisions as to breed and name and collar color—kept them happy while Joe slipped away.

That was a hard call but it had to be made.

"I need to find somewhere I can get phone reception," he told Molly, and she knew that he did. She also knew that for them all to go would expose them needlessly.

So she hugged him goodbye, and then she kissed him and then she held her breath for almost two hours until he slid back into the cleft to join them.

"Done," he said. "No problems here?" He hugged her, holding her naturally as if she belonged right there against his heart. And that's what it felt like. As if she'd slipped into her natural place. Home was where Joe was, from this day forward.

"I've been worried sick about you," he said, and kissed her hair.

She held him tight against her. "And me about you. But you didn't have to worry. Our wallabies kept us safe. You found reception?"

"I just headed uphill until it worked. Amazingly there's what looks like a telecommunications tower on the next ridge. As soon as I got over the rise my cell phone kicked in fine. It's okay, love. The police are on their way."

"Can we trust…"

"We can trust," he said. "There's been all sorts of stuff going down." He shook his head, still trying to figure things out. "My foster sister, Ellie, is involved. Remember I told you she tried to be friends with Erica? It seems the cop that Connor framed—a guy called Fitzpatrick—tried to talk to her about the connection. That blew apart when Connor came after them. Hell, if she'd contacted me…"

"She didn't?"

"I don't do family—remember?"

"That's right," she whispered, and smiled. "I forgot."

He smiled, too, but his smile was a bit crooked as he hugged her tight. "There's also been drama with your maid of honor, Jean, and your brother, Sam. No, they're both safe, but they've been yelling at the authorities. Someone even said they were on their way here, but no one's certain. Anyway, the upshot is that there was a tip-off to the Australian police last night that Connor might be in the country. There's worry he's targeting the kids. My phone call was put straight through to divisional headquarters in Cairns. We'll have big guns out to keep us safe."

"Jean and Sam…" she whispered, trying to figure it out.

"And Ellie," he said. "And a guy called Fitzpatrick. It seems we have family worrying about us, my love. Family, whether we like it or not."

She could scarcely take it in. She couldn't. "So…so we can go back to the house?" she asked, deciding the big picture was too hard and concentrating on the here and now.

"Not yet," he said ruefully. "We don't know whether Connor's still in the forest. We're only about three hundred yards from the beach. When things are safe, someone's going to come along here with a megaphone and a password."

"You're kidding."

"Nope," he said, and grinned. "Not as high-tech as James Bond but it'll do. Are the kids hungry?"

The kids had been watching from the sidelines, not understanding but obviously appreciating the fact that Joe was hugging Molly. This, however, reminded them of something that had been occurring to all of them for a while. "Yes!"

"Then we have coconuts," he said. "I know it's not quite the same as roast turkey but let's give it a bash."

So CHRISTMAS MORNING was spent splitting coconuts on rocks, telling stories, trying to remember old jokes from Christmas Crackers past, waiting, waiting. The wallabies were resting in the shadows at the edges of the clearing. They were a real comfort, Molly thought as the day wore on. They'd sense strangers before she and Joe could.

The kids were fantastic. Amazing. Wonderful. But by midday their patience was growing thin. There was a limit to how much coconut they could eat. But then…

"Joe!"

Joe's head jerked up, his eyes widening in shock. It was a stern female voice, the voice of an older woman, booming through an amplifier from the direction of the sea and echoing against the rocks behind them.

What the…

"Joe, if you're in there, come on out. Joe? Joe, I'm sick of stomping up and down this beach. It's safe. The police are here. Come out now."

"Ruby!" To say Joe looked astounded was an understatement. "Ruby?"

"My ex-foster mother."

"Oh," Molly said. Faintly.

"Who the… How the hell did Ruby know I was here?"

"That might have been me," she admitted.

He shook his head, bewildered. "What—you sent smoke signals?"

"I may just have contacted her a couple of days back."

"You what?"

"I was worried about you. I knew I was leaving after Christmas. I knew you wouldn't tell her you were caring for the kids."

"But how…"

"All I did was call Foster Parents Australia," she said. "They're in the phone book. Ruby sounded like just the person you needed. The woman I spoke to wouldn't give out any information. I knew she wouldn't. But when I said I was looking for an ex-foster mother called Ruby, 'cos one of her ex-foster kids was in trouble, and I described you she seemed to know exactly who I meant. I gave her a message to pass on to Ruby. Where you were and what was happening."

"You didn't," he muttered, stunned. "You're planning on me being bossed forever?"

"I was," she admitted. "I thought someone should do it. But now I'm planning on doing it myself so there's no need."

"Joe!" the voice behind the megaphone boomed again and Joe sighed and kissed his bride-to-be and gathered his brood together to leave their hidey-hole.

"Family," he said, "it seems to be growing."

"Don't we need a password?" Molly asked.

"If there're any villains out there with guns and Ruby's on the case…heaven help the villains."

RUBY WAS THERE, but she wasn't alone. They walked out onto the beach, emerging from the cover of the palms with some trepidation to be met by the sight of half a dozen men in camouflage with serious-looking guns, one little old lady…and one young woman with black-and-silver spiked hair, tatty jeans and a skimpy top, and a really bewildered expression.

The kids took one look and yelled in stunned delight.

"Mandy! Mandy!"

"Hey," the girl yelled back, and started running up the beach toward them. They met in a muddle of hugs and tears, and Joe stared at them in bewilderment.

"Mandy?" he said faintly.

"She's the kids' nanny," Molly said serenely, tucking her hand in his. "I love it when a plan comes together."

"My head hurts."

She grinned. "It was supposed to be my Christmas gift to you all," she explained. "Before I realized I was staying. I met Mandy last year and I knew she loved the kids. When the kids told me she'd been sacked, I felt dreadful. She's little more than a kid herself, but she's lovely. So I phoned the kids' grandmother, got the address of the agency Erica used, tracked Mandy down and offered her return flights and a year's salary. She has no family of her own and has been missing the kids ever since Vincent sacked her. She said she'd try to get here as soon as she could."

It was too much. He gave up. He hugged her tight and they made their way down the beach to meet…their future.

IT TOOK TEN MINUTES to walk back along the beach to the house and the kids whooped all the way. Even the state of the house when they reached it couldn't dent their joy.

The place had been ransacked. But searching had obviously taken precedence over prudence, and in their desperation Connor and his allies hadn't kept a lookout. The police had arrived before they found whatever they were looking for.

Connor and his companions were now in custody, but the

kids no longer cared. Their stockings were intact. The refrigerator was still groaning. They had a snack the minute
they got back to the house, then they attacked their stockings. Ruby and Mandy cleaned and rebandaged Zoe's head
while Molly and Joe showered, and then all of them settled
down to Christmas dinner proper out by the pool. The
turkey could be served in the evening—no one was prepared
to wait for it to cook—but there was more than enough
without it.

Molly was back in her bikini and sarong, serving Christmas pudding, feeling the warmth inside her grow and grow.

For her, too, Connor had faded to insignificance. She didn't
ask what was happening to Connor. As long as he was no longer
a threat to the people she loved, she didn't care about him.

She was sitting inches from Joe. What more could life hold?

There were two detectives at the table, as well—two senior
detectives from Cairns who needed to interview the children. But
Ruby had put her foot down. Christmas first, interviews second.

"So how did you get here?" It had taken this long for Joe
finally to be able to ask. Ruby helped herself to the brandy
butter and beamed.

"Easy. I got Molly's message that you might need me. Yes,
I was supposed to be having Christmas at Dolphin Bay but it
sounded like you needed me more. Then Ellie contacted me
and said she was coming here for Christmas, so that settled it.
I rang Ellie just now, by the way. She'll be here soon. Anyway,
I left a note for the rest of my family, and I caught the last plane
from New South Wales to Cairns. I got into Cairns and got
lucky—I hired the last car in the hire car rank. I was just out
of town when I saw Mandy on the side of the road with her
thumb in the air. It seems there aren't any buses on Christmas
day so she'd decided to hitch. I couldn't let a young girl risk

hitchhiking so I picked her up and we talked and found we were coming to the same place. We got here and there were police everywhere. And those horrid men were being led away. I was so worried about you, but then the nice policemen said I could come with them on the beach with the megaphone."

"Thank you," Joe said to the detectives and the detectives, complacent at the end of a very satisfactory case and a surfeit of Christmas dinner, waved their glasses in acknowledgement.

"Our pleasure."

"So how did you know what was happening when I rang?" Joe asked the detectives. His mind was operating on two levels here. First, everybody he cared about was safe. Second, Molly was sitting beside him, smiling and smiling. His foot was touching hers under the table. When pudding was over they might just be able to slip away…

But he'd asked a question. It was only polite to concentrate on the answer.

"You know Jean heard O'Bannion making threats against the children on the night before the wedding?" The senior detective looked at the children but Charlie and Lily and Zoe were preoccupied pulling crackers and had no interest in adult conversation.

"Yes, but we thought…"

"That they were revenge-type threats," the detective finished for him. "It seems they weren't. Apparently the night Vincent died he told a nurse to tell his wife that his son knew where the stuff was. Only of course Erica was already dead. And because he'd just referred to it as 'stuff'—not diamonds—the nurse forgot about it. But it seems when Connor got desperate as to where the stones were, he went back and grilled the nursing staff. The girl remembered. So Connor decided then that he had to get the information out of Charlie. Somehow. As soon as our colleagues in the U.S. figured it out, they let the Australian Feds—that's us—know to watch out for the kids. They knew O'Bannion's threats were deadly."

They all looked at Charlie. He was adjusting a yellow paper hat on his head. He looked eight years old again, Molly thought. Until now he'd looked too old for his years. He'd sounded too old for his years. But now he looked like a kid without a care.

This could work, she thought mistily. Connor O'Bannion's vicious menace disappearing into the realm of nightmares past. A great big house somewhere. Maybe not here. Too many memories. But somewhere near the sea. Somewhere where she and Joe could do a lot of work from home.

A nanny flat for Mandy had to be included. Mandy was here to stay, she thought with pleasure, watching the girl giggle with the kids.

And a granny flat for Ruby? Maybe not. Ruby had the look of a lady who moved around according to need.

But… Maybe a nursery.

She felt Joe's foot apply pressure. She glanced at him and she saw her thoughts mirrored in his eyes. He smiled at her and she smiled back and…

"Why is everyone looking at me?" Charlie asked and then amended his statement. "Everyone except Molly and Uncle Joe. They're looking goofy."

Joe and Molly did their best not to look goofy. Joe turned to Charlie while Molly tried hard to get her blush to subside.

"Your dad might have hidden some diamonds here," Joe said, trying to sound like it was no big deal. "That's why those guys came last night."

"They were looking for diamonds?"

"Yes."

"I don't think Dad had any diamonds," Charlie said.

"Did he have a safe or a secret hiding place?" the detective asked.

"Only the spot where he put the insurance."

"Insurance," Joe said, and everyone—except Zoe and Lily who'd found strawberry ice cream—held their breath.

"Three steps forward, eight steps to the right from the big tree at the corner of the pavilion," Charlie intoned. He frowned. "I think. Is it important?"

"Maybe," the detectives said as one, and would have left the table straight away except Ruby brought them up sharply.

"Have some respect. Molly made this pudding herself. Pudding first, diamonds a very poor second."

SO THERE THEY WENT, straight after pudding. Three steps forward, eight steps away from the big tree. The younger detective dug gently down. The earth was soft, as if it had been dug not too long before, and a foot down was a plastic ice-cream container.

"That was strawberry, too," Zoe said in satisfaction, checking out the container.

Joe stooped and lifted it out of the ground. "It's yours to open," he told Charlie, and Charlie did.

Inside the carton—a small chamois pouch. Charlie lifted the pouch and emptied it into his palm.

They looked like pebbles lying in Charlie's small hand. Rough, uncut stones, straight out of the earth.

"They're not even sparkling," Charlie said in disappointment. "They're not special."

"No, they're not," Ruby said, and she hugged him in approval. She was already hugging Mandy. There were relationships being formed everywhere here, Joe thought. Any minute now Ruby would invite the detectives to join the family, as well.

Well, why not? It seemed there was family to spare. Joe tried to conjure up last Christmas in his bachelor pad in Sydney…and couldn't.

"All this tragedy," Molly whispered. "For this."

"For this," he said, and he tugged her close and held. "For this."

"It's not treasure," Lily said, puzzled.

"These stones aren't," Joe said, and he couldn't help himself; he swept Molly up into his arms and kissed her, right there in front of them all, a declaration as loud and as firm as any wedding vows. "Connor had it all wrong. He thought treasure was stones. But we've found it. You kids and me and Molly and Ruby and Mandy."

"What's treasure?" Lily asked.

"Strawberry ice cream," Joe said. "And Christmas pudding and the very tasteful orange spotted tie you gave me this morning. And messy kitchens and the possibility of puppies and the lovely Mandy, who's going to be nanny for us for as long as she wants to be. And weddings," he said then, with laughter in his eyes as he smiled down at Molly in his arms. "Brides with hoops and purple flower girls."

"No!" the two little girls yelled together, and Zoe said, "I want to be pink."

"Does this mean you and Molly are getting married?" Charlie demanded, and Joe nodded.

"Yes. Yes, it does."

"I don't think you've asked me," Molly said.

He set her on her feet. He sank onto one knee.

"Molly, my love, will you do me the honor of being my wife?"

"You want us to go away?" the detectives said, grinning.

"I want witnesses. Molly, will you marry me?"

"Yes," she said. What was the point of saying anything else? Not in front of witnesses.

"There you go then," Joe said, rising and tugging her against him. Kissing her hair. Smiling and smiling. "The perfect end to a perfect Christmas."

But there was more. There was a whoop from the house, people calling. "Joe. Joe, where are you? It's Ellie." And… "Molly, Molly, hell, are we too late?"

"Ellie," Joe said faintly. "My foster sister."

"Sam," Molly whispered. "My brother. And my maid of honor."

And there they were, two couples running over the lawn toward them, hand in hand. Jean and Sam. Ellie and a man Joe didn't recognize. Worry was disappearing from their faces as they approached, to be replaced almost instantly by the radiance Joe felt himself.

"You're safe. You're safe! Hell, we came as fast as we could," Sam said, moving to kiss his sister. Which was tricky as there was no way Joe was letting her go. "But there were no rental cars to be had for love nor money. In the end we met together at a rental agency in Townsville. We hired a bus! Behold, you're being rescued by four people in a bus."

"They're already rescued," Ruby said serenely, hugging Ellie.

"Everybody, this is Fitz," Ellie said, almost bursting with pride. "Any rumors you may have heard that I intended to marry anyone but Fitz have been greatly exaggerated. You guys think this is your adventure, but we started it. Fitz kidnapped me for Christmas."

"And then rescued you?" Ruby demanded.

"Yes," Ellie said, and beamed.

"Like Sam rescued me," Jean said mistily.

"This seems like it might take months to sort out," Joe said, thoroughly confused…but then he grinned. A man had to get his priorities right, and he knew exactly where his priorities lay right now. "It's great to see you guys, but I believe there's pudding left over," he said. "I'm sure you're hungry. Now we need to do a bit of organizing. Officers, I'm sure you need to do something with these stones. Kids, there're presents to play with. The rest of you… I bet you haven't had Christmas dinner. Mandy, Ruby, do you think you could feed these guys? Keep 'em occupied for a bit?"

"Why?" Ruby asked, but her eyes were twinkling.

"Because Molly and I need an afternoon nap," he said, sweeping her off her feet and into his arms again. "Or something."

"Definitely something." Molly chuckled. "Oh, Joe, they've only just arrived. How can we leave them?"

"By the look of them, I'm thinking they'll be understanding," Joe said, smiling back at the linked hands, the goofy smiles. "Very understanding indeed."

And then, to laughter and to applause, and very properly ignoring any further protests, her love strode back around the swimming pool, into the ransacked house…carrying his love into their future.

"Merry Christmas, my love," he whispered. "And happy new life."

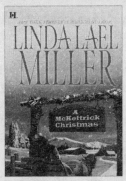

Silhouette®

SPECIAL EDITION™

FROM *NEW YORK TIMES* BESTSELLING AUTHOR

LINDA LAEL MILLER

A STONE CREEK CHRISTMAS

Veterinarian Olivia O'Ballivan finds the animals in Stone Creek playing Cupid between her and Tanner Quinn. Even Tanner's daughter, Sophie, is eager to play matchmaker. With everyone conspiring against them and the holiday season fast approaching, Tanner and Olivia may just get everything they want for Christmas after all!

*Available December 2008
wherever books are sold.*

[9]